G'Day L.A.

TONY MCFADDEN

Copyright © 2016 Tony McFadden

New Edition © 2024

All rights reserved.

ISBN: 978-1-7636425-9-1

DEDICATION

For Amy.

DISCLAIMER

There are references to television shows and movies that may feel dated, but this book was originally released almost a decade ago and I really can't be bothered to update them.

All characters in this book are fictitious. Any resemblance to real people is entirely coincidental.

Except for references to Tom Hanks, Colin Hanks and Kevin Pollak, which are done with love. They're real people, but the words coming from their mouths are, in their entirety, a product of my fevered imagination.

Don't let them tell you any different.

ACKNOWLEDGMENTS

You're reading this due to the support of many female beta-readers who have helped me capture Ellie's voice. Thank you Amy, Linda, Joyce, Kay and Reina. Any mistakes are entirely my own.

1

I watched Joel walk on stage. He grabbed the mic from the stand, looked into the bright lights and launched.

"Good evening every-fucking-BODY. My name is Sampson." He flexed a bicep. "Joel Sampson. Great to be back at the Improv. I hope you're all having a fantastic evening. And if you're not, what the hell are you doing here?" He peered through the glare. "Anybody here from Boise?"

I whooped—a support whoop. I'm from Australia. Before I met Joel, I'd never even heard of Boise. But you've got to help your friends, right? A few other half-drunk souls in the crowd whooped. I guessed there were roughly thirty people at the Improv. Light for a Thursday night.

"All right then. So, this pirate walks into a bar. He's got a ship's wheel attached to his crotch. The bartender looks at him and says, 'Hey buddy, you've got a ship's wheel attached to your crotch.' The pirate says, 'Yeah. And it's driving me crazy.'"

Crickets. Shit. I'd heard him rehearse this set continuously over the past few days. He screwed up the first joke. Seriously?

"Nuts!" I yelled.

Joel closed his eyes, a study in exasperated embarrassment. "Nuts." He shook his head and slipped back into the pirate's voice. "'Yeah, it's driving me nuts. The wheel. It's driving me nuts.' Well, hell, folks, I've gone and fucked up my first bit. Can only get better, right?"

I held my face in my hands and chuckled. No one would forget him, anyway. He continued with a bit about women Botoxing their faces but not their hands and the floppy-handed hilarity that would ensue if they did.

I used my finger to stir the ice cubes in my scotch and took a sip. The drink was getting weak, the melting ice diluting the cheap booze. Not a traditional woman's drink, but it gave me the required buzz and had zero carbs.

I was in L.A. almost a year now. Winter was coming up. The dry heat of summer was long gone, replaced by cooler, damper days and really bloody cold nights.

I flagged down a wandering waitress, an actress I had worked with before, both of us in small roles in a sitcom a few months earlier. "Hey, Char, can I get another scotch?"

"Is that you, Ellie? Are you working now? What are you doing here?"

I nodded at the stage. "Sampson is my roommate. Emotional and vocal support night."

She laughed as she took my empty glass. "He recovered nicely. Was that you who yelled 'Nuts'?"

"Guilty as charged." I pried a twenty from my jeans pocket. "Keep the change, okay? But make it a double."

"Sure thing Ellie. Thanks."

I looked back at the stage. Joel was winding his set down, closing strong on a potato/Keebler Elf bit. The crowd seemed to have forgiven him for his screwed-up opening.

Charlotte brought my drink back. "You got anything coming up?"

"A few auditions. Nothing big though. You?"

She shook her head. "It's been slow."

"Well you keep plugging. You're pretty good. If I see anything that needs sisters I'll let you know."

"Great. Thanks." She walked off to tend to a table of drunks.

Like I knew how to reach her if I did. This entire city was built on lies, and it was beginning to get to me.

"I take it you know that 'nuts' kid?"

A short, balding, vaguely familiar guy slid into the seat across from me. "That seat's taken."

"Really? 'Cause I've been watching you for the last thirty minutes and nobody was sitting here."

I pointed at the stage. "That guy. The 'nuts' guy. He's my roommate. You're in his seat."

"Oh, don't worry. He'll be backstage for a bit yet, watching the rest of the acts in this set. I thought you might know him. I'm interested in having a chat with him. Or his manager."

"Who are you?"

The guy smiled. "How refreshing. Where are you from? I've seen you in something. You're not from around here, I take it."

"I'm from Australia." The guy was really familiar in a I-know-that-face-from-somewhere-but-can't-really-place-it way. Too much drink, I think. "Sydney. But I've been here almost a year now. Why did you want to talk to Joel?"

The guy nodded and smiled. "Yeah, I recognize you now. Joel, he was funny. Made a good recovery. Not an easy task for anyone, and him so young."

"He's not that young. He turned 22 a couple of months ago." I took a breath. "His name is Joel Sampson. He doesn't have a manager, but his agent is Kyle Johnson. You know him?

The guy laughed. "Twenty-two is young. Trust me." He smiled, the quasi-familiar face driving me nuts. It was on the tip of my brain. "So, Joel Sampson. I'll have to remember that name." He nodded. "And I know Kyle. I'll give him a call. It was nice meeting you, Ellie. I'm sure we'll meet again. Loved you in *Beast of Bondi*. But you need to get bigger roles. And better ones, too. The writing on that picture was dreck, but sometimes you've got to take what you get, right?" He stood and tipped an imaginary hat, and left, heading backstage.

I was gob-smacked. He knew *Beast*? I didn't think it played outside of Australia. He was right, it was a pretty crap movie, but it was my first one. Not my first acting job, but my first feature-length movie. I spent three years on Australian TV before that. If you haven't seen "Beast", you're lucky. It's a slasher about a serial killer preying on skateboarders in skate parks around Sydney while living in a storm drain off Bondi beach. What a schlock concept. I had a supporting role in it. I got to live to almost the very end, and the reviews of my part were good, even if almost every review thought the 3D movie would have been improved if my breasts were the only parts in 3D.

And that was the problem. My breasts were getting me the roles more than my acting ability was. They weren't huge, but they were, apparently, the ideal setting of perkiness. I was the go-to girl for perky, counter-balancing the double-Ds in a movie. Usually a bad, straight-to-DVD movie. It paid the rent, but Christ, I was tired of getting them out.

I was watching the next comic, a woman doing a ventriloquist act with just her hand, no puppet, and getting a wild reception when Joel slid in across from me.

"Thanks for the 'nuts'. I can't believe I fucked that up." He carefully placed his drink on a coaster.

"Good recovery though, and the crowd seemed to forgive you." I pointed at his glass. "Not rum and coke I hope?"

He shook his head. "You know better than that. Just pop. No booze. Staying clean. Virgin."

I smiled. "We all were, once. You're welcome for the 'nuts'. All that practicing for nothing."

"I got better laughs off the recovery than I did from the original." He took a small notepad out of his back pocket and scribbled something. "I'm going to fuck it up intentionally next set."

"Whatever works. Hey, there was a guy here looking for you."

"Did you give him my number?"

I shook my head. "He chatted for a second, recognized me from "Beast", and then split. I gave him Kyle's name, so I'm pretty sure he'll be able to track you down."

"Did you get his name?"

"He didn't say. Something familiar about him, though." I looked over my shoulder. "That's him over there, leaving the club."

Joel looked in the direction I pointed and squinted. "No way."

"What? Who is it?"

"It looks like Kevin - no, couldn't be. That would be too awesome."

"Kevin? Kevin who? Do I know him?"

"I don't know. You're not much of a movie watcher, surprisingly. You might not." He closed his eyes and took a deep breath. "Never mind. If it happens, it happens."

"Oh, I got it. Kevin. The guy you try to emulate. The career you want to have. *That* Kevin." I took a swallow of my scotch. "It might have been him. He looked shorter in person." I tongued a piece of ice out of my glass and crunched down on it. "So, you're driving us back to the house, okay? This is my third. Double. I'm liable to fall off my feet."

Joel squeezed some lemon into his cola. "Sure. I probably won't kill us on the freeway. You drunk are still a better driver than me anytime."

"The cops don't seem to appreciate that though." I dropped the rest of my drink down my throat. "When are you ready to go? I've got two auditions tomorrow. I need my beauty sleep."

Joel looked up at the stage. The dummy-free ventriloquist had left, and a surfer-dude type was doing his Bill and Ted stoner shtick. He was cute. He was also bi and a some-time partner of my designated driver.

"You want to wait until Billy's finished and bring him back with you? I don't mind." I didn't mind. Billy and Joel together were hilarious. I just realized their names, together, made Billy Joel. "I think I've had enough to drink."

Joel took his eyes of the stage and shook his head. "Nope. Billy's got a girlfriend. Crystal, that female wrestler. Besides, celibate, remember?"

"Billy and Crystal?" I started giggling. Billy Crystal. This was too much. "You better take me home then. I'm losing it.

I waved at Charlotte, the waitress, who someday might be a good actress, as we left. I tossed the keys to Joel and then got in the driver's seat. I stared at the steering wheel in front of me for a full beat before it dawned on me what was wrong. "Oops."

"Yeah, it's a good thing I'm driving. You still think you're in Oz?" Joel waited for me to get out, then climbed behind the wheel. He held the key and looked at me as I slid in the passenger side. "Five bucks says it won't start this time."

"What kind of bet is that?"

"One I win, no matter what. If it doesn't start, I get money. If it does start, I get to go home without trying to navigate the public transit system in this damned city."

"Fair call. But no bet. She'll start." I patted the dash of the 1978 VW Beetle. She always ran. I put so many miles on her that I'd be in Miami if I drove her in a straight line, and that's just in the past six months.

Joel leaned forward, grinned and turned the key. The car wound over twice and caught. "Excellent." He sounded just like Mr. Burns.

"You ever try voice auditions, like I said?"

"What, for cartoons and stuff?" He shook his head. "I'm not famous enough."

I leaned back against the headrest and closed my eyes. "Do you know who Jodi Benson is?"

"Half of Benson and Hedges?"

"You don't, do you? Look her up on imdb.com. Almost every single one of her fifty credits has 'voice' beside it. Ariel from *The Little Mermaid*. Weebo from *Flubber*. Barbie in *Toy Story*. You wouldn't know her if you met her on the street. There's a lot of money in voices, Joel, and you've got a great voice."

He ground gears as he backed out of the parking lot. "Yeah, but I'm not quite there yet. I'll do standup for a few more years, I think. I need to get a better time slot at the Improv, then get Netflix special showcase my talent."

I was about to answer him when my phone rang. I looked at the caller ID, smiled and answered. "Hey, Melon-Head, what's up?" Ross Mellon was an Aussie legend in the L.A. radio scene. He had everybody who was anybody on his show.

"Just calling to remind you, pretty girl, that you're my primo guest Saturday night. Don't stand me up, okay? 8:30 sharp for a 9 o'clock start. I want you to expound on the trials and tribulations of an up-and-coming star."

I laughed. Loved hearing his voice. "Can I bring Joel?" I watched him vigorously shaking his head. "No, never mind. He doesn't want to come."

"I'll book him next time. Tell him I love his stuff. Don't be late, girl. I'm crap on my own. I need a guest to elevate my show to the level of witty repartee that wins awards."

"I'll be there, Ross. It's in my phone. I won't forget. See you tomorrow." I hung up and closed my eyes again.

"Who was that?"

"Ross Mellon. You know him. Does a radio show live on Saturday nights here, exclusively broadcasting it in Sydney on Sunday morning. Because of the time difference, right?"

"I get the concept."

"Then he rebroadcasts the taped version the next day for his Sunday afternoon L.A. audience. Every Aussie in the US has been on his show, I think. I'll get you on. He's a kingmaker. He's been here for almost twenty years."

"I'm not Aussie."

"Nobody's perfect. I'll talk to him." I yawned. This was late for me. It wasn't even 10:00 yet, and I was fading fast. "And I could hook you up with some movie auditions. You'd make a great comic sidekick. Every action movie needs one."

Joel pulled on to Melrose and headed east. "I don't think I could do movies. My act is driven by spontaneity. You saw tonight. The best part was the recovery."

We rode in silence until he pulled on to the 101 a couple of turns later. I opened an eye. "Stay on the 101 until Tampa. It's faster." I closed my eye again and listened to the traffic noise. I was really tired. I had an audition for a role in a soap early this morning. I screwed it up completely. And I wasn't sorry. It was a stupid show and the acting on it was terrible. I didn't know how it managed to stay on the air as long as it did or why my agent thought I'd like doing it. Anyway, that audition had me getting up at 6:00 this morning, and I had to get up at 6:00 again tomorrow. There were some days I wondered why I did this. The modeling I did in Australia was the same way. I did it for three years before I quit. The hours were terrible, I was treated like meat, like everyone else, and the money wasn't as good as I thought it was going to be.

But it got me the spot on "Home and Away", and I had to admit, that was fun.

I felt the car slow as Joel took the exit onto Tampa Avenue and headed north. We shared a guesthouse that sat behind the somewhat and sometimes great Bart Sweeney, director of *Beast of Bondi* and half a dozen other B-grade horror flicks. He was on the second tier of Hollyweird. Maybe the third tier. I aspired to that greatness. This place opened my eyes to the real world. It was a lot harder here than I expected it to be. At least I was making money, mainly because my height got me roles. And my tits. I couldn't forget my puppies.

I opened my eyes as Joel stopped in front of the house.

"We're home. Were you sleeping?"

"Resting. Thanks for driving. I shouldn't have had that much to drink. Tomorrow's going to hurt."

"You can always hop on my wagon and clean up."

"I thank you for that kind offer. Give me the keys now, kiddo." I closed the door and locked it. "I'll consider it."

"No, you won't. Although, it would be good to have company. It's not always easy."

"You're right, I won't. You know me too well. And you're doing great without me." I unlocked the door to the guesthouse and tossed the keys on the counter. "I've got an early start again tomorrow. Wish me luck. Some reality show, living in a house on an island. Apparently, even if they vote you out of the house, you're still there until they vote you off the island."

"Luck. I'm going to see who's on tonight. I'll use the headphones and keep my laughing to a dull roar."

"Thanks. I think I'm going to be out before I hit the pillow." I wandered into the bedroom, dropping items of clothing as I walked while Joel pulled the sofa out to his bed. It was a small guesthouse.

I slid under the covers, wondering who I'd have to kill to get a career in this business that would justify my being so far from home.

2

Joel moved his surfboard off the sofa and leaned it against the wall by the TV stand. He pulled the sofa into a bed, sat up, turned on the TV, and muted it. He retrieved his phone and turned on the recorder.

"Day 87. Had a pretty cool experience tonight at the Improv. Still getting the early time slots. Hopefully, I'll get moved a little bit later when the scouts come in. Anyway, an amazing experience tonight. I totally screwed up the opening bit. And spectacularly recovered better than if it had gone well to start with. Crowd loved it. I've got to thank Ellie for the recovery. She's my good luck charm. I so massively lucked out to get in this place with her. I doubt I'd be here, at this level of success without her as an example. Case in point, KP was checking me out today. Would swear on a stack of bibles that was his bald head leaving the club." Joel took a breath. "So that's day 87 without a drink, weed, meth, coke, smack, ice - wait, that's the same as meth, right? Anyway, clean and sober for almost three months now. Celibate, too, though God knows that's harder." He shook his head. "But I've got to put all of my energy into this career. This is what I want to do the rest of my life, and it's going to be nobody's fault but my own if I fail. And I'm not going to fail. Sampson out."

He thumbed off the recorder, looked at his laptop on the other side of the small room and tossed the phone on the bed. "I'll sync it later." He donned a pair of headphones and turned up the TV volume. Three late-night talk shows to catch, three sets of comedians to watch and learn from.

He fell asleep halfway through Jimmy Fallon's monologue.

The casting director looked at his watch. It was 11:45 and lunch still hadn't shown up. "Where in the hell are my sandwiches? We start in fifteen." Steve Bond had no patience for idiots. He wandered back to the casting area. "How many do we have out there?"

His assistant, a former paralegal from Tucson named Trudy, flipped through the pages. "Thirty-seven at last count."

"Anybody we know?"

"Half of them. It's going to be a long afternoon."

Bond held out his hand. "Let me see the list. I can cut some of them right now. I've got to be out of here at 2:30, 3:00 at the latest." He took the clipboard, ticked seventeen names and handed it back to Trudy. "Tell these ones to go home. They aren't what we're looking for. The tits on these ones are too small."

"I can't tell them that." Trudy was shocked.

"Why not? They should know the truth." He grabbed the list back from her. "I'll do it then. You might want to toughen up a bit."

He pushed the door open and looked at the sea of women facing him. "Ladies, time is tight, so I'm sending seventeen of you home now. The role I'm trying to fill is a recurring neighbor who shows up at the beach house with little or no warning. She'll be in a bikini for the vast majority of the shots, and she needs to have big tits. The following people can head to your next audition, the nearest frozen yogurt shop, or wherever." He read off a list of names, ending with, "…and Ellie Bourke. Thanks for coming by.

Better luck next time. Now the remaining twenty, I'll start seeing you in five minutes. My assistant will call your names in alphabetical order."

Sixteen of the seventeen dismissed actresses left. The seventeenth, a tall, boney blonde, approached him with a dissatisfied look on her face. He recognized the look from his first three wives. They all had it. "You can go, Miss…"

"My name is Ellie Bourke. You really want to cut me because my tits are too small? That's a first. Usually, you guys want me to take my top off. Now you're telling me you don't want to see them. I'm getting confused about you guys. Hell, I'm getting confused about this whole business."

Steve shrugged. "What can I say? The role has a specific body type requirement. The housekeeper had to be large, the neighbor had to be thin and buxom. I'm sure there'll be plenty of roles coming up for just your type."

"Do you know of any? Jobs coming up for 'just my type' I mean."

Steve sighed. There were days he hated his job. All he had to do was say the word, and he could buy into an extremely successful deli in Arlington. More days than not, he struggled to find a reason to stay in L.A. This young lady wasn't making it any easier. "I'm sure there will be. But here's a tip: Actually watch the TV show you're going to audition for. See what the sense is of the show. This sitcom is not much more than large breasts, poop jokes and the leading man's irascible self. You wouldn't fit in a million years. You seem smarter than most. You're absolutely wrong for the part. But thanks again for coming by. If you'll excuse me, I've got to listen to twenty slightly insipid actresses try to convince me they're the best bikini-wearing bimbos I've ever seen." Trudy escorted Ellie out of the waiting area.

Steve was tapping the clipboard, deep in thought when she returned. "Trudy, where do I know her from?"

"That tall blonde? Bourke? She the one who lives in Bart Sweeney's guesthouse."

"So that's her? Really?"

Trudy nodded and handed Steve the headshot for the first audition. "You tried her for a couple of small roles last summer. You took her for the pilot for that detective show that didn't go anywhere. You said you liked her."

"I did? Huh. Shame Sweeney's keeping her out in the Valley. She's going to miss half the auditions living out there. She should move. Get closer to the business and mingle in the proper circles." He took the headshot from Trudy and looked at the name on the back. "Desiray Abbot? Desiray? Really? I hate this city."

Trudy watched out the office window as Ellie leaned against her car, looked back at Steve, then back at Ellie. "She seems pissed."

"She? She who? Desiray? What are you talking about?"

"That Ellie girl. Sweeney's girl." Trudy sat at her desk and pushed the intercom button.

Steve sat back in his chair. "Sweeney's gay, isn't he? What's he see in her?"

Trudy shrugged and held up a finger. "Hold that thought." She leaned into the intercom mic. "Could Desiray Abbot come in, please?" She released the button. "I don't know if he's gay. I wouldn't care to speculate. It would just get me in trouble."

"That legal background is going to severely restrict any joy you might be able to extract from this city, Trude. The only fun I have these days is slandering people behind their backs. You keep holding it in, and it's going to build up until that inopportune time, at a producer's meeting or something, when it spews forth like a torrent of Tourette-fueled abuse. You've got to let it out a tiny bit at a time, so you can control it." He chuckled. "This is the shallowest place on planet Earth. Wallow in it. Or head back to Tucson and let someone who really appreciates the shallowness take your place." He looked at the door as a pneumatic, probably bleached blond entered on impossibly high heels. "You're Desiray?"

She popped a gum bubble and nodded. "I changed it. People kept calling me Desire, without the "ay" sound at the end. Some people can be so stupid, right? So I changed the spelling so they had to say it like I want them to."

Steve took a deep breath. "Right. How tall are you? The sheet says 5"7", but that's with those heels, I assume. I need to know your real height."

She cracked some more gum and chewed furiously. "I live in these heels so it's like they're a real extension to my body. You don't worry about hair extensions, do you? These are my leg extensions." She giggled, lowering Steve's estimation of her IQ by an additional 10 points.

Steve closed his eyes and imagined making a black forest ham and provolone on rye, extra mustard. "Take them off. And show me what you look like in your bikini."

"How can I do that?"

"How can you do what? Take off your shoes? You need help taking off your shoes?"

She popped another gum-bubble and giggled some more. "No, silly. How can I show you what I look like in a bikini when I don't have a bikini with me?"

"You read the casting call, didn't you? It explicitly said bikini."

Desiray started unbuttoning the front of her pants. "That's okay. We can pretend." She dropped her pants to the ground and exposed her frilly purple g-string. Her t-shirt was halfway over her head, breasts wobbling like the twin peaks of silicon jelly that they were when the door slammed open.

Ellie had returned.

"Listen, I object strenuously to being typecast as a tom-boy just because—" She stopped and watched Desiray's double-D dance. "Excuse me. I didn't realize the casting couch was real."

Trudy was up from her desk and running to shut the door. "You can't barge in here like that."

"I just did." Ellie couldn't take her eyes off Desiray, mesmerized by the sight.

Desiray, for her part, was still blinded by the t-shirt. She turned in ever-decreasing circles in an attempt to extricate herself, the t-shirt currently stuck on her chin, left ear, and the extensions on the back of her head. "Who just came in? I can't see. Can somebody help me with this?"

Steve nodded at Trudy. "My assistant will help you put the shirt back on. I don't want to see your breasts. Well, that's not entirely true. I've enjoyed seeing them, but it's not necessary. We need to see you in your bikini, not nude. Maybe for another day."

He looked at Ellie, shook his head, and sighed, imagining roast beef, lettuce, tomato, Swiss, and hot English mustard on a multigrain. "Career suicide? That's your next move? I can suggest better, more efficient ways, but barging into an audition nears the top of the list. What is your problem?"

"You. This whole business. The idea that only one specific person can play any given role. Any one of the girls out there, including the seventeen tit-less who you sent away, could do the three minutes a week on this show and it wouldn't make any difference. Nobody would care.

Viewers are going to forget the character as soon as she leaves the screen. She's a foil. A piece of eye candy distraction. The audition process for this should be the first person who shows up, gets it." She was breathing heavily now, full head of steam and going for the kill. "You just force this audition process," she air-quoted audition, "so you can parade a bevy of mostly unclad bimbos around for your sick sexual gratification." She paused. Steve opened his mouth to reply and she walked all over him. "Career suicide? I need a career first. I've been pushing boulders uphill since I got here. Sisyphus had nothing on me. I'm beginning to really hate this city. I came back here to force you to audition me, but fuck it. I'm heading back to Australia where at least people are real."

Steve had a half-smile on his face. "Sisyphus. Told you that you were too smart." He sighed. "So you're saying this is a disposable business?"

"Damn straight it is. Like plastic wine glasses. Fancy-assed from a distance, but cheap, disposable crap once you're up close."

"You'll do well here if you remember that. You're as good as what you've just done." He shrugged. "Sorry, but that's the way it is. When a thirty-foot wave comes at you, you can either try to swim against it, or ride it. You should ride it." He winked at her. "And you might want to reconsider your views on these small parts. Robin Williams played a small part on "Happy Days" that spun off to "Mork and Mindy" and launched his career. "Happy Days" also spun off "Laverne and Shirley" from a couple of small parts."

"And "Joanie Loves Chachi", so don't tell me they all work."

Steve shook his head. "You're missing the point. Laverne and Mork were small, 'three-minute parts,' as you call them. Joanie and Chachi were main characters who tried to have a life after their gravy train made its final stop."

"Oh. Like 'Joey'."

Steve put his left index finger on his nose and pointed at her with his right. "Perzactly. By jove, I think she's got it. Now get the fuck out of my audition and stop bothering me. I've got tits to judge." He smiled and pointed to the door. "Please."

He watched Ellie back out of the office, hoping she would show up at some other audition he held. "Trudy, send Miss Desiray on her way and call the next hapless bimbo."

Trudy watched out the office window as Ellie walked out to her car. The tall blond stopped at her car, an old Beetle, kicked the wheel one more time and fumbled with the lock before she got in. The car started and idled for a couple of seconds before it slowly pulled out of the parking lot.

"Trudy? You with me here? Who's up next?"

"Sorry. Just a second." She flipped the headshot over and read the name on the back. She pressed the intercom button. "Miss Heaven Dee. Please come in."

Steve winced. "Heaven Dee? Are these porn stars? Am I in the right office?"

"Sorry boss. That's what it says."

"Quit apologizing, will you? You sound Canadian."

"Sorry."

He took a deep breath, thinking of turkey breast, cheddar, sprouts and mayo, lots of ground pepper, on rye.

The door opened. "So, Miss Dee, did you bring your bikini with you or are you going to flash your tits at me?" Even peanut butter and banana on white sounded good right now.

3

I slapped my steering wheel. "I hate this city." I checked the time. Not enough of it left to get to the beach for a brain clearing before my next audition. My absolute favorite times were spent on a long board at Bondi, Narrabeen, Warriewood and other beaches along the coast just north of Sydney. I hadn't been on a board more than a handful of times since I got to Los Angeles, in part because I didn't have my board with me—it was still at my father's place in Sydney, if he hadn't sold it—but mostly because the water off the California coast always felt too cold. But I could plop my ass in the sand and let the roar of the surf wash over me, deadening my seemingly never-ending feelings of inadequacy.

"Ah, shit, I'm starting to feel sorry for myself. Again."

There was a sure-fire antidote for that. I was near Glendale and a visit with Sweeney never failed to cheer me up.

It was well into being one of those days. That last audition was bad enough, over before it even got started, and all because my tits weren't big enough. Asshole. And then there was the reality show audition this morning, where my accent was considered a liability. For God's sake, what in the hell did that have to do with anything? I told them I could do American. Not the point, they said. My real accent would come through when I was tired, or drinking, or some other time I can't really remember right now and besides, they already had an Australian. Some bogan asshole who tried to cop a feel any time I got near him.

It's probably a good thing I didn't get that one; I would have ripped that guy's nuts off in the first eight hours and voted myself out of the house *and* off the island.

I locked the car, although anyone who wanted to steal a thirty-five-year-old car with torn seat cushions and more surface area dented than not was welcome to her.

Sweeney was on the phone when I walked into the outer office. His secretary, or assistant or whatever she was, was away from her desk. He spied me through his open office door and waved me in, pointing at a seat. He held up two fingers, either telling me he was going to be a couple of minutes or 'Peace'.

It had been a few months since I'd last been in here, and nothing had changed. Pictures of vaguely familiar actors, most in some form of horror movie-related prosthetics, adorned the bookcase behind his desk. There were precious few books in that case. Sweeney wasn't a big reader. The desk itself was reserved for a single picture of him flanked by Rod Stewart and Al Pacino. I couldn't imagine the circumstances that would get the three of them together, and whenever I asked, he just smiled and shook his head. He had more hair and fewer wrinkles in that picture.

Bart dropped the phone in its cradle and smiled at me. "My favorite Aussie. What's up?"

One of the reasons I liked him was the fact he said "Aussie" the right way, with the "s" making a "z" sound and not the "s" sound the way most Americans said it.

I dropped into the chair across from his desk. "A shit day, Bart. Two wasted auditions and nothing from either of them but insults."

"What's an insult? Just someone else's opinion of you based on incorrect facts. Insults should slide off you like water off a duck's back or shit through a goose."

"The first guy said I was too Australian, and the second guy said my boobs were too small. My two core selling points slammed in the one day." I rubbed my right eye with the heel of my hand and sniffed. "And I think I'm coming down with a cold."

He picked up a pen and poised it above a pad of paper. "Who were they? Tell me their names. I'll have a word with them."

Christ. That's the last thing I needed. "No, Bart. No. I need to fight my own battles and work this out on my own, right?" I looked down at my chest and lifted my right breast, weighing it. "Should I get them done? Do you think that it would help?"

Bart pursed his lips. "I'm no expert, you know, but from a career point of view, larger breasts do get you more work. You can count the small-breasted woman with a solid career in this business on one hand. There's that girl from 'Easy A'."

"Emma Stone."

"Right, her. And who else, Calista, what's-her-name from that Ally show."

"Flockhart. McBeal."

"Exactly. That's it, right?"

"Kiera Knightly, Lara Flynn Boyle, Milla Jovovich, Paris Hilton, although I don't think she has a career, per se, Mena Suvari. There are a few."

"Still counting on one hand, though. You might want to consider it. I think you can claim it as a business expense."

"You're well into your second hand, Bart. And there's Debra Messing and Kate Moss. No, I'm not going to do that. I'd rather quit than go under the knife." I hated the thought of needing to augment my breasts just to get a job. That smacked of the ultimate in hypocrisy—baring your soul to the world through acting, with a fake body.

"Oh, I've heard it doesn't hurt much. You're completely under. There's a bit of tenderness for a few days after, but really, not that bad."

I shook my head and stood to leave. This was getting me nowhere. "No, that's not what I meant."

"You're a beautiful girl. If you want to keep them small you can still return to modeling. You've got perfect tits for modeling."

I laughed. "And crawl back into the herd? I had enough of that. The shallowest profession on the face of the earth. No way I'm going to do that again."

"Suit yourself. The money's good. So look, let me know if you want me to call those guys and have a word with them, okay?"

I shook my head again. "I won't. Catch you later, Bart."

"You heading home?"

"No. I think I'm going to blow off the next audition and head out to Zuma and watch the sunset. I need to cleanse. I miss Bronte."

"Who's Bronte?"

"The beach? We spent three weeks shooting *Beast* there because you couldn't swing the permits for Bondi."

"Yeah, yeah. I remember. Hey, I'll catch you later, okay? Say hi to Joel for me. Word is he's killing them on stage."

I thanked him and drove to the beach. The crowds were thinning by the time I got there. It was cooling off and only die-hard surfers were still in the water. A young couple with small kids was bundling them into their van when I got there. "Water cold?"

The mother looked up from the car seat. "A bit, and getting rough. I think there's some weather coming up." She spoke with a slight French accent.

I grabbed a sweater from the back seat. "It's a beautiful beach though. Hopefully, it stays clear long enough to see the sunset." I switched to French. "*Est-vous la France ou le Canada?*"

She smiled and replied, in English. "Originally from Quebec. We moved here a few years ago. We're keeping the English going for the kids. Not much call for French in this city. Where did you learn to speak? The accent is strange."

"I learned it in school as a kid. I love the language. You're right, though. Don't have much call for it around here."

The woman smiled. "You're Australian, aren't you? I've always wanted to go there."

"I am. And you should. You'd like it."

"What brings you to California?"

"Work. I followed a director. I'm your stereotypical struggling actor."

The woman cocked her head to one side and squinted like I was some out-of-focus connect-the-dots puzzle. "Do I know you from anything?"

"I wouldn't know. I did three years in 'Home and Away', but I don't think that airs in this country, and I had a supporting role in *Beast of Bondi*, a B-grade slasher flick made in Australia."

She shook her head. "No. Not those."

"I've had a few small one-off things, bit parts in TV shows. And supporting roles in a couple of failed pilots I know for fact you wouldn't have seen."

She shrugged. The city was filled with struggling actors, and my only claim to fame was that I was from the land down under and Paul Hogan. "Well, good luck with it. I'm sure you'll do well."

I thanked her, pulled my sleeves down over my hands and walked out to the southernmost lifeguard shack on the beach. The lifeguard was packing things up. "Mind if I sit up there and watch the sun go down?"

"Go for it. I'm closing down now, though." He pointed just north of us. "There's a strong rip out there. Stay out of the water unless you're a very experience swimmer, okay?"

"Don't worry. I'll be staying out, but because it's too damned cold. Thanks."

He grinned, hopped on his small all-terrain vehicle, and drove off. I sat on the ramp and watched as the sun slowly dropped to the horizon, turning the sky a brilliant orange. This was a rare occurrence for L.A. Most sunsets were pretty ordinary, nothing to write home about.

I seriously wondered what I was doing here. The money I was making wasn't anywhere near what I needed to make. My credit cards were getting close to maxed out and the jobs were getting thinner. I'd been to over a hundred auditions in the past year, and from that got less than fifteen paying jobs. A few paid well, thank God, or I would have been forced to something drastic to make ends meet. Like modeling.

I shivered. The wind was cold. I looked at my watch. It was 6:30, and the sun was almost at the water. Winter would be here soon and with it the bloody rain. But even in bad weather the ocean fed my soul. The smell of the sea and the sound of the surf calmed me to the core. I needed to do this more often.

I walked slowly back to my car, not looking forward to the forty-minute drive home. I vowed to do something fun this weekend. It was Friday night, and I had no plans, and my next audition wasn't until Tuesday, late afternoon. Maybe I could convince Joel to drive out to Palm Springs with me. Or Vegas, not that we had any money to gamble with.

I drove south on the Pacific Coast Highway and turned up Topanga Canyon. The drive up Topanga, from the beach to the Valley, was like sliding back in time to the sixties. My old Beetle felt like she was in her element. The area was as hippy as anything I'd ever seen. A gym near the bottom of the canyon advertised free membership to anyone who could beat the owner in a game of chess. Small farms lined the road, tended to by aging flower children and growing, I'm sure, not your conventional crops. The road wound through some switchbacks that would make the boys from Top Gear salivate. I made a mental note to see where they shot their American version. That would be a fun show to do.

My spirits were actually lifting. I was feeling the best I had in weeks. The ocean fed me, I got some fresh air, and Bart was showing a willingness to help wherever he could, even if it was misguided. Someone had my back. It was a good feeling.

That feeling was short-lived.

I turned the corner near the house and saw an ambulance in Bart's driveway, lights still flashing. Two police cars were parked in front of the house.

I pulled in behind one and jumped out of the car. "Is Bart okay?"

I went to run into the main house, but a cop stopped me. "Hold on a second. Do you live here?"

I pointed to the back. "In the guesthouse. What happened? Did Bart have a heart attack? Is he going to be okay?"

The cop looked over his shoulder at the guesthouse. "Wait here. Someone needs to talk to you."

"What happened?" I called after him but he ignored me. I started to the front door when an older cop stopped me.

"Evening miss. You say you live in the guesthouse?"

"Yeah. Why?"

"Do you know a—" he flipped back a few pages in his little cop-issued notepad, "—Joel Sampson?"

Joel? This was for Joel? Shit. I nodded. "He's my roommate. What happened?"

"Sorry. Can I get your name?"

"Ellie Bourke. B-o-u-r-k-e. Will you tell me what the fuck is going on here?"

"Were you close to Mr. Sampson?"

"Were? Past tense? Oh my God, what happened to him?"

"A few questions first. When were you last in the house?"

"What, the main house? A couple of weeks ago. The owner invited us over for dinner."

"I meant the guesthouse. When were you last in it?"

"This morning. I left at eight for an audition. Joel was asleep on his bed, headphones half on his head and the TV on." I had a horrible thought. "Oh God, no. He wasn't dead this morning, was he? Oh no. I walked right past him when I turned off the TV."

The cop flipped back a few pages. "No. It appears he died between three and five hours ago. Can you tell me where you were during that time?"

I looked at my watch. It was almost eight. "Five hours ago I was in Bart Sweeney's office in Glendale. Then I went to Zuma, watched the sun go down, then drove here. Tell me something. Anything. What happened to Joel? Did somebody kill him?

"Sorry, Miss Bourke, but it appears as if your boyfriend crawled into the tub and committed suicide. I know that must be difficult to hear."

I shook my head. "No, that's not right."

"Depression is the silent killer, they say."

"It might very well be, but Joel wasn't depressed."

"Hard to tell sometimes. Depression is a disease, not a weakness."

I shook my head in amazement. "You just get off some suicide sensitivity training course or something? Joel was not depressed. And if it's a suicide, why are you interrogating me?"

"Until the coroner ascertains a definitive cause of death and our investigators confirm absolutely that it was a suicide, we need to treat it as a potential homicide. Although, I have to say, based on my fourteen years experience on the force—"

I had to interrupt that. "Fourteen years, and you're still a Constable?"

"Be that as it may, my experience would indicate your boyfriend killed himself."

"He was my roommate, not a boyfriend. And I can't believe he killed himself."

"Male roommate and you weren't in a relationship?"

"He's gay. Was gay. Still is gay. Whatever." It was sinking in. Jesus. Joel was gone. There would be no more laugh-filled nights of me heckling him while he practiced his act. Shit. "I want to see him. How did he do it? You said in a tub. Did he cut his wrists?" I swallowed. "Is there a mess to clean up?"

"Relax. It was a drug overdose. Was he a habitual user?"

"Hell, no. Clean for almost three months. We were going to celebrate the three-month anniversary next week. I can't believe this. Who found him?"

The cop flipped through a few more pages. I felt like screaming at him to get a fucking PDA and join the rest of humanity. "I think the guy's name was Sweeney something."

"Bart Sweeney? He owns this place."

Constable, whatever his name was, nodded. "Yeah, that's it. Said he was going in to invite him in for a bite when he found him. Were they close?"

"What do you mean, like in a relationship close?" The cop actually blushed. He was older than I thought he was.

"Well, yeah. I guess that's what I mean."

I thought back over the last six months since Joel moved in. "Nothing overt, but it's possible, I guess. Nothing lately, though. Joel was obsessive about his career. He was clean and sober and celibate for almost three months. He said he needed to focus all of his energy on his work and didn't want to waste it on anything, or anyone, else."

The cop snapped the notebook closed. "Even more convincing that it was a suicide. Thanks for your help. If I need a statement, I'll contact you. If you think of anything, give me a call." He handed me a card.

I slid it into my back pocket and watched a gurney roll out of the house up to the back of the ambulance. A body, in a body bag, was lifted into the back and the doors closed. A tear rolled down my cheek. A perfect end to a terrifically perfect day.

The ambulance driver turned off the bubblegum lights and slowly drove away. There was no need to hurry.

4

Constable Larry Perkins watched the young lady—he flipped through his notepad, one Ellie Bourke—as she stood on the side of the road watching the ambulance drive away. Suicide was a sad and selfish thing he'd seen too much of in his career. He sighed and walked back into the guesthouse. The investigation would continue, as he said, until homicide was definitively ruled out, but the signs were unmistakable. His young partner was in the bathroom, instructing the photographer on what pictures needed to be taken and telling the forensic team which evidence needed to be collected.

"Hey, kiddo, let them do what they do. They know their jobs better than you do. Some of them have been doing it since before you needed to shave."

"Sure, pops. And when they forget to collect something, you can come back for it." Constable Dave Stanfield checked his watch. "Shouldn't the homicide boys be here by now?"

"I wouldn't hold your breath. It's gone in as a likely suicide. They've got real-life shootings, stabbings, people pushed under train tracks and spousal abuse-gone-too-far cases to worry about. Killing yourself isn't a crime, or there'd be a lot of dead people in jail."

Stanfield snorted. "That's funny. I'm going to use that."

"What, you a comic now? I think I've seen you crack a smile maybe five times since we've met." Perkins looked around the room. "So what have you got so far, smart-ass?"

Stanfield slowly turned in the small room. "He really went all out for this. Candles lit, show tunes playing when I came in. Lights were low. He really got into it." He indicated the metal spoon with traces of crystallized liquid and the syringe that had been stuck in his right arm, now in an evidence bag. "And drugs."

"Sound more like one of your dates."

Stanfield deadpanned. "One of my better ones, except the owner said the Sampson kid was by himself, and nobody else was here this afternoon as far as he knows. The roommate?"

"Yeah, I talked to her outside. She's still standing there, shocked. She was at auditions and the beach this afternoon." He flipped through the pages of his notepad. "Zuma."

"Pops, you ever think about retiring? Or would you need to have it written in your pad to remember to? You've got one of the crappiest memories I've ever seen."

"Don't need to remember what I've written down."

"Right. You just need to remember where you wrote it down."

Perkins ignored him. "Any next of kin?"

"There's a contact number in his wallet." He opened the billfold and showed his partner. "You want I should call him?"

Perkins wrote down the name and number. "Jacob Sampson? In Boise. What time is it in Boise?"

"Where is Boise? North Dakota?"

Perkins sighed. "I despair for this country. Idaho, you cretin. I'll call him." He strolled into the living area of the guesthouse and dialed the number on his mobile. After three rings a male voice answered with a grunt.

"Is this Jacob Sampson?"

"Who's calling?"

"This is Constable Larry Perkins, L.A.P.D., Valley Bureau, Devonshire Division, Badge number 14987. Are you related to one," he flipped the pages in his note book to find the name, "Joel Sampson?"

"Yeah, what about him? Is he in trouble?"

"I'm sorry to have to tell you this, but Joel Sampson was found dead of apparent suicide this afternoon at," flip, flip, flip, "5:45 p.m. You can contact the county morgue for collection. There will be a mandatory autopsy if there are any suspicions of foul play. The remains should be available early Monday."

"Dammit. I knew something was wrong. He's my twin. Constable, I'm also a cop, a detective in the Boise PD. Anything you can tell me will help. You're positive it was a suicide?"

"In the tub, by himself, a syringe with what I suspect will test out to heroin stuck in his arm. Cut and dried." Perkins listened to silence until he thought the call had dropped.

Jacob finally expelled a breath. "Yeah, that doesn't sound very good. It's a tough place out there, isn't it?"

"It can be, yes. Again, I'm truly sorry for your loss. Call me when you get into town, anytime, okay?" He gave the brother his mobile number and signed off. He looked around the small room. It was neat. "About what you'd expect with a girl and a gay in the house. Neat as a pin." He strolled back to the bathroom. "You finished in here, Stanfield? We've got to get going."

"What's going on?"

"You know. Extra patrols for the Presidential visit in two weeks. I'm hating the hours and loving the overtime. It's going to kill me. But I'll be rich."

"Leave your money to me when you die, okay?"

"Better than the ex- getting it. Both of them." Perkins tossed the keys to his younger partner. "You drive. Topanga Shopping Centre. Some kind of disturbance at the yogurt shop. I don't know what, and I don't care. It may not even be real, but I sure could use a frozen yogurt right about now. Let's go."

Stanfield caught the keys. "You just want to nap, right?"

"Piss off, kid."

"Shouldn't we talk to the owner of the place first?" Stanfield slid the keys into his pocket.

"You haven't? I thought you did already."

Stanfield shook his head. "Nothing but the first responder stuff. No details."

Perkins sighed. "Fine, don't get up. As you were. I'll go talk to the guy."

"I'll go with, pops."

Bart watched the two cops approaching his house. "Damn. Again? We already talked. I'm not ready." He looked around. A bag of pot sat on the coffee table beside a small handgun. He slid the bag behind one of the books on his bookshelf. He stood in the entryway with a drink in one hand and the gun in the other, looking for a quick place to hide it. He dropped it in the cutlery drawer and slid it shut just as the cops knocked on the back door.

He composed himself and pulled the door open, looking Valley casual, drink in his hand. "I was wondering when you were going to come and talk to me again. What can I tell you? How can I help you? Can I get you guys a coffee?" He held up his glass. "I'd offer you some of this, but hey, it's too expensive, and you're still on duty."

Perkins tapped his pen on his notepad. "I just need to get some more details, in your words. Easiest if we do it here, but if you're more comfortable doing this tomorrow we can do it downtown."

"Oh, no. Here and now is fine. Coffee?"

"No thanks. We're backed up a bit."

"Coffee is a good laxative."

Stanfield smiled. "Backed up with work. Tell us how you discovered Joel Sampson this afternoon. Provide as much detail as you can."

Sweeney pointed to the settee and sofa set. "Make yourselves comfortable. I'm a detail guy. This could take a little while."

Perkins looked at Stanfield and rolled his eyes. Movie people. They both smiled graciously and sat on the sofa, beside each other and across from Sweeney. A few minutes were spent adjusting their gun belts until they were comfortable, careful not to tear the leather.

"Ready?" asked Sweeney.

"Action." Perkins smiled.

"I was at the office this afternoon until 5. The usual things a person in my position needs to do in his day-to-day job. I'm pulling together a new project that has had me pretty busy. Joel and his roommate, Ellie Bourke, are struggling in this industry, and I would like to help where I can. They're both getting the guesthouse for rent, which should be a crime, it's so low. I wanted to have them over for dinner tonight. I knew Ellie would be a bit later because she told me she was heading out to Zuma to watch the sunset. It's an Australian thing, I think."

Perkins nodded. "She told us the same thing."

"That it's an Aussie thing? I thought so."

"That she went to the beach. I don't know if it's an Aussie thing; I enjoy doing it too, and I've never been out of California." He flipped the booklet back to a clear page. "Continue."

"Okay, where was I? Right. Dinner. I knew Ellie would be late, but I thought I'd get Joel to come over for a couple of beers and shoot the shit if you know what I mean. I knew he wouldn't be working on a Friday night because that's when the a-list get stage time in the stand-up business, and he's just scraping by on the c-list. He's got potential though." He realized what he said. "Had, I mean."

"So," Stanfield prompted, "you went over to invite Joel for a beer or two before dinner. Next?"

Bart took a sip of his scotch and composed his thoughts. "I went over to the guesthouse and knocked. I'm a good landlord. I won't just barge in. There was no answer. I never suspected he was dead. As old as I am—I'm going to be fifty this year—I've never been in the presence of a dead guy before."

"Why didn't you call him on the phone?"

"Personal touch. Phones are so impersonal, aren't they?" He took a sip of his drink and looked at his glass. Almost time to top it up. "Where was I?"

"Knocking on the door."

"Right. I knew he was in there."

"How did you know that?"

"Where else would he be? Like I said, he's not going to be working on a Friday night. He's not big enough yet." He stopped and shook his head again. "Never will be. I keep forgetting. Where was I?"

"By my records, you're still knocking on the door."

"Right. I knocked a couple of times and got no response. Since I knew he was in there, I was concerned for his safety. I've got a set of keys, obviously, as the landlord, so I let myself in. I want you to know, for the record, that I was very uncomfortable going in like that, without advance arrangements. I'm very particular about that. I try to give at least twelve hours notice before a visit."

Perkins looked at the drink in Sweeney's hand and wished harder than he had ever wished for anything that it was in his own hand and not the yammering asshole across from him. "So you went in. Concerns noted. What did you see? Did you touch anything?"

"Oh, God, no. I've watched CSI and NCIS and Bones and Law & Order. I know the drill. Touch nothing. Let the crime scene techs do their job."

"He was in the bathroom, right?" Perkins flipped back through his notepad.

"Yes, of course. I thought you knew that."

Perkins checked a couple of other notes. "The bathroom is in off the bedroom, which you can't get to until you go through the kitchen, correct?"

"Exactly." Bart sat forward. "Good notes. Good notes are extremely important. Go on."

"So how did you know not to touch anything and to leave it for the CSI guys if you didn't know he was dead until you travelled through the majority of the guesthouse."

Stanfield smiled. "Excellent question. Do you have an answer?"

"What's this about? It was a suicide, right?"

"Until we learn anything different. So, the question? Do you have an answer?"

"I meant I didn't touch anything in the bathroom once I saw him in the tub, obviously dead."

"How was it obvious?"

"He wasn't responding to me, he was cold to touch, his eyes were open, and there was a fucking needle stuck in his arm. Wouldn't that be obvious to you?"

"Perfectly obvious, sir. At that point, you called us and didn't touch anything after that?"

"I called 9-1-1 and exited as quickly as I could." He took another drink and looked at his empty glass, shaking his head. "It's just horrible. He had such great potential. It's always a terrible waste when someone that young loses their life. Even worse when they take it themselves. If only he had talked to me about his problems. I'm always available to lend an ear, to be a shoulder to lean on, to offer any support I could." He placed his glass on a coaster and stood. "It's always sad, isn't it? Is the guesthouse a crime scene?"

Stanfield stood. "Pretty sure we're all finished in there. I'll check with the techs, but if there's no tape up you can go in."

"Have you seen Ellie Bourke yet? I expected her back by now."

Perkins flipped through his book and checked his notes. "Yes. Talked to her before I went in. I left her standing by the side of the road. She looked upset. Will she be okay?"

Sweeney nodded. "She's strong. I've known her for about three years now. She's a tough one. From Australia. They make them strong there." He walked the constables to the door. "If you need anything else from me, by all means, feel free to drop by or give me a call." He gave them each cards. "Call me any time."

Stanfield pocketed the card and gave him one of his own. "If you ever need a technical advisor related to police procedures and techniques, please give me a call."

Sweeney laughed. "I love it. Initiative." He tapped the card. "I'll keep that in mind." He waved as they left.

Perkins clapped Stanfield on the shoulder. "You want to be one of the movie guys now, do you? Trying to achieve maximum douche-ness?" He hopped in the passenger seat of the squad car. "To the yogurt, boy."

He started at a knocking on the car window. He rolled it down, and a young blonde leaned her head in. "He didn't kill himself." She chewed her lip. "Did he?"

"Miss Bourke, it appears that he did. We'll let you know for certain on Monday. His brother is coming in from Boise."

"He has a brother?"

"I thought you knew him well. His brother Jacob will be coming."

She stood. "Can I go in there?"

"The guesthouse? Yes. We're finished. Sorry for your loss." He rolled up the window.

Stanfield pulled away from the curb. "Yogurt, partner?"

"Hell, yeah." They drove away, leaving Ellie standing alone at the curb.

5

I walked up to the door of the guesthouse. The last crime tech had just left. I looked over my shoulder at Sweeney on his back porch with a drink in one hand and his phone pressed to his head in the other. He raised his glass in some morbid salute and turned his back to me, talking in his usual over-animated way. What a perfect end to a perfect mother-sucking sock-fucking day.

I couldn't go in the place, not now. My best friend had died in there. I shivered. "Shit." I looked back at Sweeney. "Hey. Bart."

He held his hand up, ignoring me while he continued to talk. Fine, actually, since I didn't think I could sleep in his place either. And my car was too small. I took a deep breath and slid open the glass door to the guesthouse, but still, I couldn't take the step. I slid the door shut and turned, and leaned against the wall. "Shit, shit, double shit. I don't need this." I sniffed and scrolled through the contacts on my phone. Bernie. Maybe Bernie could help.

He answered out of breath. "Ellie. Long time. What's up?"

"Am I disturbing you?" I loved his throaty laugh. And that he was built like Adonis. But he was in a very long-term relationship with a girl I liked, and I didn't do that.

"No." He chuckled again. "We just finished."

I heard his girlfriend say, "this round" in the background.

"How is Cathy?"

"As good as she's ever been. What's up?"

I wasn't one who liked asking for help, but I didn't have much of a choice now. "I need somewhere to crash until I find a new place."

"Sweeney kick you out?" An older-brotherly concern edged his voice.

Tears. Why in the hell were there tears? "No." I sniffed. "You know Joel?"

"Yeah, the funny guy. What, he kicked you out? That doesn't seem right."

"No. He killed himself in the tub this afternoon, and I don't think I can go back in there, and I can't stay at Sweeney's, and my car is too small." The tears were flowing freely now and they almost pissed me off more than Joel's death.

"Oh, no, Ell. Were there any signs?"

I shook my head. "He seemed fine. It's weird, and I can't believe it, but I can't sleep in the same place he died. I don't think I can do that. Can I please sofa surf at your place until I find somewhere else to stay?"

"I'd love to, Ellie, but Cath and I are in Reno until Monday. I'm stage-managing a play she's in. Sunday night is the last show. That doesn't help you, does it? Really sorry. I usually leave a spare key, but not this time. Cath grabbed it the other week, and I haven't put it back in the rock."

"Thanks anyway Bernie. I'll sleep in my car tonight and find something tomorrow." I hung up. I didn't want to talk. I crawled into the back seat of my Beetle and cursed the genetics which made me almost six feet tall. I curled into the fetal position and tried to fall asleep.

I don't know if it was the sun shining through the side window of the car, or my full bladder that woke me, but I woke at 7:00 a.m., cold, sore and stiff. And a bit disoriented. I've slept in cars before, but usually after drinking copious amounts of alcohol.

And I really had to pee.

I knocked on Bart's door. If he didn't answer in the next five seconds, I'd go behind a bush in the back yard.

The door opened and a bleary and tousled Bart stood in front of me in his boxers and nothing else.

"Ellie? Are you okay?"

I pushed past him. "Need to pee. Thanks."

I rejoined him in the living room a couple of minutes later. He'd put on a robe, thank God, and had a pot of coffee ready.

"Help yourself to some java. Is the toilet in the guesthouse broken? I should call a plumber."

"I haven't been back in there since, you know. I can't. I slept in my car."

He had the gall to laugh. It slowed, and his face slid into a concerned fatherly look. "No, really?" Then he put his cup down and got all serious. "Why didn't you tell me? You could have slept in here. I have a guest room."

"No, I couldn't put you out. I'm afraid I'll have to give my notice and find somewhere else to live." I took a deep breath and said what I'd been thinking for the last twelve hours. "I'm actually thinking of heading back home. It's not going great here. And you know it. I've been bouncing around from bit part to tit parts for the last year. I expected more by now." I sniffed and drank some coffee. My stomach growled. Embarrassing.

Bart patted me on the leg. "I'll get some breakfast. And don't be so hard on yourself. It has only been a year. I worked for almost a decade before I saw any success. You've got the talent needed to succeed, but I question, sometimes, the confidence. Which is ridiculous on the face of it. You're tall, good looking, a good actress." He padded into the kitchen, scratching his ass. "Keep plugging. To the persistent go the spoils."

At least the old guy was trying to cheer me up. But really, a decade? Shit. And if this was what he calls success, I think I'll pass. "I'm not going to wait another nine years, Bart. Sorry." Not for a shit house in the Valley. He was rummaging through his refrigerator. I wasn't sure he heard me.

Then his head popped up. "Scrambled eggs okay? I think I still know how to cook those."

My stomach grumbled again. "Okay. Thanks." I could smell myself. A shower would be necessary too. I'd hit the gym after.

I wandered into the kitchen while Bart whisked eggs and milk in a bowl. The frying pan was warming on a flame. I never understood why a city with so many earthquakes insisted on piping flammable, explosive gases to each and every house. Some sort of Southern California death wish, I guess. "Want me to make toast?"

The asshole sniffed. "You need a shower, doll. Want to have one while I cook this stuff, or do you want to wait until after we eat, and we can have one together?"

What? "Mate, that is not on. I thought you said you were gay? I was sure you were gay. And besides, yech."

"Yech? What, am I that distasteful?"

"You're older than my father, for Christ's sake. I don't have any father issues. Yet." What an asshole. "I'm going to leave, Bart. I'm not that comfortable now. Especially after that. I'll shower at the gym. I could use a good workout. I need to punch something. Repeatedly."

And then he did something which surprised the hell out of me. He slid the pan off the flame, turned off the burner and took my hands in his. "I'm really sorry. Go to the gym and shower. Get yourself a good breakfast. Forget my advances, they're from a stupid old man. Come back this afternoon around 2:00. I'm having a barbecue for some colleagues. Leaders in the industry will be here. I'll make some introductions, and maybe we can kick-start things for you. Forget what I said about the shower." He looked at the pan with the egg mixture. "And it's probably a good idea you don't eat what I cook. I'm not that good at cooking. Rarely do it. That's what I attribute my longevity to—avoiding my own cooking." He smiled and gently squeezed my hands again. "I'll get a professional cleaning company in and do the guesthouse from one end to another. It'll be like a new place. I know a guy who can have it done by tonight. Reconsider heading back to Oz. You'll be throwing away potentially a great career."

"You're having a barbecue today? Less than twenty-four hours after Joel killed himself? That's heartless."

"No, no. You don't understand. I arranged this weeks ago. I can't change it. I'm trying to get something off the ground myself, and this is the only chance I've had to get all of the parties together. This afternoon. If I'm successful and I get the financing and the ducks in a row, then you've definitely got a part in it. The most pleasure I got out of *Beast of Bondi* was working with you. You were the one true talent on that set. I mean that."

How could I answer that? I was a bit wobbly. I needed a think. "If you see me, you see me. I need to think this out. I'll be back later, if only to pick up my stuff." I retrieved my hands from his sweaty grasp. "Thanks for the pep talk. Really."

The fork in the road. The fuck in the house. Decisions, decisions. The gym was a ten-minute drive. Less, the way I normally drove. I needed to run. I stopped running the streets in the Valley the day I was mugged, less than a month after I got here. Some ass-hat sped by on a moped and grabbed my purse. I wasn't actually jogging with my purse. I was walking down the sidewalk and this freak took it. That was also the day I stopped carrying a purse. Wallet and for those special days of the month that cursed half the population of the world, a small carry case. My phone and wallet stayed in my pocket. Purses were targets.

I hit the treadmill. Phil Collins, John Farnham and vintage Rolling Stones shuffled on my iPod. It felt good. The sleeping-in-the-car kinks worked themselves out within the first mile. I had to avoid sleeping in the car again, though. I'd end up a cripple. And Bart, the pervert, was right. Going back to Australia would certainly cut any career I had short. I'd get work, but I'd be looked at like a failure. I just wasn't sure if I cared what people thought. I'd be happy. Happier, anyway.

I wasn't quitter, but I was smart enough to know when to back away from certain failure. I didn't want to get in whatever state Joel ended up in, where the only solution he could find included a loaded syringe in the tub.

"No. Joel wasn't like that. I would have noticed something." I stopped the treadmill and took a drink of water. Others can drink while running, but the last time I tried, I fell off the treadmill and fractured my arm. I may be clumsy, but I'm not stupid. Didn't try that twice.

The rowing machines had a few vacancies so I strapped myself in and set the pace for a good 10-mile row. I thought back over the past couple of weeks. Joel was in fantastic spirits. He'd been moving up on the comic pecking order, out of the Comedy Store and into the Improv, and getting better time slots at the Improv. That Kevin guy at the club recognized him and thought he was a comer. It didn't make any sense. There had to be something going on in his life I didn't know about. Something shameful. But this was Hollyweird. Nothing was considered shameful here short of pedophilia. And it wasn't anything like that. He liked the studly surfer type. No, there was no inclination of that.

He came from the Midwest, though. I didn't know what those people thought. It was a strange set of puritanical guidelines that informed their lives. He was embarrassed when I caught him watching some gay porn one night. What the hell, no biggie. I only wished he'd had the chance to visit Sydney during Mardi Gras.

God, I missed him already. He showed up on my step six months ago, a puppy who Bart brought home needing a place to stay. And compared to then, he was doing well now. Was. He liked old movies, and I liked old movies. We both preferred beer to wine. At least until he went all dry on me. We both liked old Rolling Stones and shunned the newer stuff. We were a perfect fit, except for the fact he liked dick even more than I did.

And I know he would have told me if there was something bothering him that much.

A sweaty, overweight guy mounted the rowing machine to my left and gave me a smile. Now, I'm not one of those girls too hung up on body shape, but you've got to keep yourself at least somewhat presentable. This guy looked like he was homeless. I got a whiff of his armpits when he reached for the rowing handle and gagged. I had three miles to go. I'm no quitter. He smiled at me again as he started his workout. My eyes watered and I increased my tempo. These would need to be the fastest three miles I'd ever rowed.

I made it without retching and made my decision. For today, anyway. I'd go to the barbecue and see what Bart could pull out of his ass.

And besides, it was free food, and I hadn't had work for a couple of weeks.

I doubted I could stay in the guesthouse, though. That was a bit too freaky. I cranked the shower as hot as I could bear it and let the spray beat on my shoulders, draining the tightness and tension from my muscles. I didn't really want to go back to Australia. I just didn't know if I had any other choice.

I pulled my hair into a damp ponytail and examined the look in the change room mirror. Maybe I'd cut it short. Get some lesbian roles. Whatever it took, right?

The gym sold food, and I was starving, but Bart had free food in three hours, so I just bought an apple and a bottle of water. And I was feeling somewhat better mentally. Physically, I was gold. Maybe, just maybe, I'd pull through this.

6

"Boys, perfect timing." Bart followed the portable barbecue to his back yard. "Set it up under that tree there. Put the table and the chairs over by the guesthouse. And guys, set the bar up on the patio, okay? There's already a wet bar there. It's small, but you can use it as a base." He clapped his hands together. "This has to be perfect, guys. Help me make it perfect. Help me help you make it perfect."

He checked his phone for at least the fifth time in the last ten minutes. No messages, which could be good, or could be bad. Nerves. Always nerves. A white van pulled in to the drive, blocking in the "Valley Port-a-Cue" van. "Fantastic." He pointed at the guesthouse. "That place. Asshole to teakettle. I want it to look, feel and smell like it just came out of the wrapping. Brand new. Understand? Excellent."

Bart paced. Barbecue to wet bar to guesthouse. Back to the bar, where he poured himself a Jameson and ice. He looked at his watch and noted that it was 5 o'clock in Nova Scotia. Legally allowed to drink as long as it's 5 o'clock somewhere, and Nova Scotia was as good a place as any. Back to the barbecue. "It's ready to go, no? The caterers will be here any moment. Shit. You're going to have to move your van. Damn, the cleaners have to move first."

He ran to the guesthouse, nimbly avoiding any alcohol loss from his glass and intercepted one of the cleaners on their way out. "Hey Pedro. Luis. Whatever your name is. You've got to move your van to the street. The caterers are going to be here any minute. Thanks."

"The name's Dave. I'll get right on it."

"Gotta be now. Move the van onto the street."

"Relax, dude. I'm moving it."

Bart smiled shark teeth. "I'm relaxed. But I don't want you relaxed. I want this place cleaned zippy quick."

Dave fished the keys out of his pocket and walked to the van. "Chill, dude. This is a small place. We're going to be done in about thirty minutes, maybe an hour, max."

Bart beamed and walked backwards along side him. "Fantastic. Make it smell lemony fresh, boys." He slid a fifty into Dave's shirt pocket and tripped over to the barbecue. "This is looking great. And I need you out of the way for the caterers who will be here eminently."

"You mean imminently." The barbecue guy winked at him. "But I know what you meant. I'll be back later. Just sign this." He held out a clipboard.

Bart balanced the clipboard on the counter, held his drink in his left hand and scrawled a signature. "You guys can come back after 9 and pick this up, okay? Okay." He shook the main man's hand and clapped him on the back. "Looks absolutely fantastic. You guys are artists. Thanks a million."

Both vans vacated the driveway just in time for the caterers to arrive. He buttonholed the guy who looked in charge. "I've got producers and agents and other types of important people coming for a nice afternoon barbecue. Everything needs to be perfect, got it? Good."

He took a deep breath. Puzzle pieces dropping into place nicely. He had pre-loaded each of his guests with snippets of ideas for the movie he was writing. Had written, actually, first draft on paper. Sure, it would be re-written half a dozen times, and at one-fifty pages it was a bit too long, but the concept was there. It was killer. He had some ideas for actors, and that reminded him: he wondered if Ellie would show. He really liked her. It would be a shame if she left.

He looked at the guesthouse. Unfortunate. That was the best word he could think of to describe the Joel situation. Unfortunate. It didn't need to be that way. He was a good kid. "He had promise, the young man. Unfortunate that things turned out the way they did. Still, better him than me, I guess."

Bart's reverie was disturbed by the arrival of his first guest, a producer who had worked with him a number of times. He met the man and either his secretary, girlfriend, wife or some combination of the above as they got out of the car. "George, great you could come. I'm setting up out back. Looks like it's going to be a helluva day." He turned to the young lady with him. "And this is?"

George cocked an eyebrow. "My wife. Daphne. I introduced you two last week."

"Ah, Daphne. I must be getting old." He held up his glass. "Can I get you two something to drink?"

"A little early, isn't it Bart? We'll have soda water. Will Joel and Ellie be joining us this afternoon?" George nodded at the guesthouse. "They're great kids."

"You know them? I didn't know you knew them." He cleared his throat. He was forgetting too many things. He frowned in thought.

Hopefully he didn't forget anything important. He looked at his drink. Maybe he'd back off a bit.

"So?" George looked at Bart deep in thought, wondering if it was a good idea to be here.

"So? So what?"

"So, about Joel and Ellie. Are they a couple? I think they are, but my lovely here is convinced that Joel is gay. And are they going to be at this?"

Bart nodded. "She's right. He is. Was. The poor boy went and killed himself yesterday. Right in there. That's why there's a cleaning crew here."

"Ohmygod," Daphne ran the words together, her hand on her ample, not entirely natural chest. "It was messy? What are you doing having a barbecue today when there's blood all over the place in there? That's just terrible." She took her husband's hand. "I think we should leave, George."

"No, no. Wait a second. It wasn't messy. He had a drug overdose in the bathtub. I've got a cleaning crew in there because Ellie doesn't feel comfortable about the place right now, and I don't want her to leave. Hopefully, this will help." He attempted a disarming smile. "I seriously considered rescheduling this thing, but rescheduling would be a bitch, excuse the French. Everything was already in place. Seemed best to proceed with it, no?"

"I never would have thought Joel was one to kill himself. Drug overdose? Intentional or accidental, do you think?"

Bart was tired of this discussion. Other cars were arriving. "Hard to say. The needle was stuck in his arm, just hanging there. It could have been accidental, I guess. Yeah. That's a possibility." He shook his head. "Another one with great potential snuffed," he winced at that word "in his prime."

"He wasn't at his prime yet. I've seen him on stage. He was a piece of coal ready to be squeezed into a diamond. The potential was certainly there. Too bad," said George.

"Yes, too bad. You can ask that man over by the bar for your drinks. If you'll excuse me, I've got more guests coming." He pointed them in the direction of the bar.

Two more production type people, Steve Bond, the casting director and a writer arrived before Ellie did. He broke off from the conversations and went to meet her.

"Ellie. Fantastic you could make it. How are you feeling?"

"Dumb question, don't you think, Bart?"

"You look good. Great. Keep looking forward. The past is the past."

"The past is the past? Have you been to Tibet recently, gaining knowledge from some high astral plane? I don't look fantastic, Bart. I'm still in yesterday's clothes. I need to go in there and change. But I don't know if I can." She twirled her hair around her index finger and shook her head. "Can't go in there alone."

"There's a cleaning crew in there. Go do what you've got to do and come back out and eat. Everything always looks better after food." Bart slid his hand into hers and slipped her a small plastic envelope. "Or if you need a bump, these will perk you up and take the anxiety away for at least four hours. They work great. Everything will seem abso-fucking-lutely fantastic."

Ellie opened her hand and looked at the packet of pills. "You are a grade-A asshole, Bart. My best friend just died of a drug overdose, and you're pushing pills at me? Son of a bitch. Go fuck yourself." She threw the pills on the ground.

"Oh, hey, sorry. I didn't think. But, no. He died of a heroin overdose, I think. This is nothing like that. Some Xanax mixed with a bit of amphetamines. Nothing hard like smack. Sorry. Really. Forget I said anything." He retrieved the packet off the ground and clumsily stuffed it back into his pocket. "Really, forget it. I was stupid. Pretend the last five minutes didn't happen. Get your stuff and come out and have some good American food."

Ellie shook her head and slowly entered the guesthouse, hanging at the entrance.

Bart turned to welcome a leading B-list actor who had just arrived. He was pleased. The pieces were sliding into place.

Steve Bond walked up to him. "That was Ellie you were talking to, right? How's she doing? I turned her away from an audition yesterday. Told her that her tits were too small. She looks like she's taking it pretty hard." He shrugged. "But they are. Nothing I can do about that. She needs to thicken her skin if she wants to survive in this town. Maybe she should get some work done." He shook his head. "She's a good actress, though."

Bart winced. "Don't go talking about her that way, Steve. Her roommate killed himself yesterday. Drug overdose. She's probably forgotten all about you by now. She's pretty distraught. I'm trying to convince her to stay."

Steve winced. "Suicide's a selfish thing. Damn shame."

Bart nodded. "Yeah. She's talking about going home and leaving all this behind."

"Back to Australia?"

Bart nodded. "She wants to go back. I've invited her to this thing to try and lift her out of her funk. Be nice to her, okay? Don't promise anything, but help build her confidence."

Steve shrugged. "Yeah, I can do that, I guess."

"Thanks."

Steve nodded at Bart and looked at the guesthouse. He liked Ellie. She was a good actress. A bit impatient, maybe, but definitely on the top half of the pile. It would be L.A.'s loss and Australia's gain if she went back home. He took a deep breath and slowly exhaled. Of course it would be L.A.'s loss and Arlington's gain if he headed back to the deli. He looked at the set-up Bart had laid out and shook his head. He didn't want to be here, schmoozing. He only accepted the invitation because of the promise of free food and drink, and he heard a producer he wanted to work with would be attending. He wandered back to the bar to freshen his drink.

Bart jogged back to the assembled crowd. He hoped for a successful pitch, maybe after a couple of drinks. He had to figure out how to get George into a bottle. Maybe he'd enhance his soda with some pharmaceuticals. All's fair in love, war and the movie business. The lure of money and success and the respect that both bought was strong.

He gathered the guests under the trees. "Gentlemen. And lady. Thanks for coming by this afternoon. Take your time with the food and drinks. Some other guests will be joining a little bit later. I want you all to have an afternoon where you can relax. You all work extremely hard. I know. I'm the same way. We all need to take time to sharpen the saw. To pause and refresh and smell the flowers. This is your opportunity." He pointed to the barbecue stand. "Mario here will cook anything you want in any way you want. We have red meat. We have frozen yogurt—he won't be barbecuing that, heh, heh, heh—we have fruit, salad, fruit salad, high-speed wireless and relative solitude."

The group he invited, all of them currently half a step or more above Bart on the food chain, put up with him because he had been around forever.

None of them would outright call him a friend, but they were friendly. They knew quite well, with the exception of a small percentage of personalities in Hollywood permanently stationed in the top echelon, positions in the food chain were fluid. The man you looked down on today might be the one green-lighting your project tomorrow. It didn't pay to antagonize people, especially one who had been collecting skeletons for over three decades.

"Bart, great party. Love this place. I'll have to have you out for golf one day."

Bart nodded and smiled, temporarily forgetting the man's name. He had other things on his mind. He ran through the pitch in his head one more time, top to bottom and left to right. He could see no flaws. Now, all he had to do was make sure he didn't stuff up the timing or forget a crucial plot point.

He took one more look at the guesthouse. He'd deal with Ellie and her problems later.

7

I was never one for nerves. I was always the one as a kid who led others into trouble. I was not so much fearless as an adrenaline junky. But a year in this city could really beat that out of you. Criticism of everything about me in one audition after another really took its toll. I hated the thought of quitting, but I seriously contemplated abandoning everything I owned and calling my father to set an extra place for dinner. I was a heartbeat or two away from going straight to the airport and putting this damned place behind me.

Except I had kept driving north to Bart's place and not south to the airport. At the very least I had to get some clean clothes on me.

I parked half a block away. It was as close as I could get. The street was filled with high-end leased cars. Bart was really going through with the barbecue. I was amazed as many people showed as did. The guy had more influence than I thought he had. He started chatting with me when I got there—doesn't the guy understand when to shut up—and then tried to slip me a couple of pills to make me feel "abso-fucking-lutely fantastic". What a douche.

I stood at the threshold of the guesthouse for a couple of minutes. A very efficient cleaning crew was going over the place like a pack of OCD parasites. Nothing was missed. A thin, wiry guy approached with a smile.

"Hi. I'm Dave. We'll be finished here in about twenty. If you need to come in, don't worry about us. We can work around you."

"Well, Dave, I need to change my clothes. You're not going to be able to work around that."

He smiled. "Damn. I was hoping I could. No matter. We've finished in the bedroom. Just finishing up out here."

That was nice of him. "Thanks for the compliment, Dave. I needed that." I closed the door and sat on the edge of my bed. I could see into the bathroom. Twenty-four hours ago, Joel was here, alive. I shook my head. Not my first experience with suicide. My mother, years ago. I was a lot younger then. Still, it's not something I wanted to get used to. And I'd be damned if I'd let this city get me to the same place Joel got to. I still couldn't understand how somebody so seemingly happy and on top of his life could take that route. And with a drug overdose. He was clean. I knew he was clean.

I walked into the bathroom, facing what I'd been avoiding. My father had drummed into my head since I was a little girl that fear is just a defense mechanism against the unknown, and once the unknown became known the fear diminished drastically. He would have gotten through to me a lot faster if he just said, "face your fears".

So I faced them. And I don't think it was the unknown I didn't want to face; it was the sadness. Being in the room where Joel killed himself evoked a painful hurt in my chest. He was the closest thing to family in this country. He was gone, and I was meant to believe he selfishly took his life. All those nights, we talked about what hurt us, who helped us, the difficulty with putting ourselves out there, baring your soul every time we stepped out on stage or showed up to an audition, the dreams we had, fantastic dreams that might never be realized, but still dreams to aspire to. I would have thought he would have talked to me about whatever drove him to this. I was angry, and I was sad. Sad I wouldn't see him. Sad he wouldn't get to go on Conan, or Pollak's chat show. Angry he felt this was the only solution.

And sad he felt that way.

My father was right. Again.

My stomach growled. I might as well take Bart's free food.

I splashed water on my face and dried off. I looked at myself in the mirror. Normally I'd approach the gathering of people outside with a case of nerves, but this time, I didn't give a fuck. I'd eat Bart's food, and later I'd pack and book a flight back to Sydney. This place killed my best friend. I wasn't going to let it kill me.

I changed into a pair of jeans and a button-down shirt and walked out to the gathering. Bart was neck deep up some bigwig's ass, gesticulating like a Frenchman. I spied the casting director who cut me yesterday and decided right then and there, I'd make as many people here as uncomfortable as I could. There were half a dozen bridges right here in front of me, waiting to burn.

I snagged a beer from the bar, waving away the mug and drinking from the bottle. "Hey, remember me? Tits-too-small?"

The guy turned, saw who I was and smiled. "Ellie. Great to see you. No hard feelings, right?"

"Right. You told me my tits were too small. No hard feelings at all. I'm sure you're hung like a horse, right?"

He laughed. "Look, I know you've been to at least a hundred auditions in your career, here and in Australia, right?"

I shrugged. "At least."

"And we - casting directors - are given a clear-cut description of who we have to get for the job. It's the least fair thing in this country. Can you imagine if an accounting company placed an ad for someone that said only 5'-8", large-chested blondes need apply? The lawsuits would be never-ending. But in my job, that's what I have to do. We needed a bimbo to play alongside the star. He's only 5'-10". You're almost 6 foot, I'd guess. There's no way he'd allow a girl to be taller than him on set. And the generally accepted trope is that IQ decreases as bust size increases. You should be flattered I thought you weren't bimbo material. Plus, your agent or manager shouldn't have been stupid enough to send you on that call." He took a mouthful of his drink. "It's Hanson, right? Dave Hanson? He knew what I was looking for. You should find someone else. He's getting lazy."

"Huh. I didn't think about it that way. Maybe you should explain it that way when you cut people."

He shook his head. "Too much talking, not enough time. Plus, I'd be telling all the girls who I kept I thought they were bimbo material, and the last thing I want is a bunch of low self-esteem basketcases on my hands. It's hard enough dealing with them when their egos are over-inflated. Really, dump Hanson and find someone else. You're missing out on some good roles."

"It doesn't matter now. I'm heading back to Sydney. It's not fun any more."

He stopped his glass halfway to his mouth. "Bart said you were planning that. Thought he was stretching the truth. Don't do it. You've got the potential to be huge here. If you give up now, you'll wonder what could have been for the rest of your life."

"At least I'll have a life. Joel had fantastic potential too. He's dead. I don't want the same thing to happen to me. I'd rather be a waitress at Bronte, surfing on my time off, than getting chewed up by this place. Thanks for the kind words, though. Did you find your bimbo?"

He looked at me for a moment and ignored my question. "I heard about your roommate. Terrible thing. But he isn't you, and you aren't him. What happens to someone else in this town should have no impact on what you do. Terrible as this sounds, I think you give too much of a fuck. Be more selfish. And yes, I think I found my bimbo. Bringing her into a meeting with the director and the producer, who just happens to be over there. George. You know him?"

I nodded. And shook my head again at the surreal nature of the industry. Tossing lives out like yesterday's moo goo gai pan, and not appearing to give a shit. "Catch you later, Steve. Or not, actually."

Steve was a nice enough guy. I got what he was saying. I wouldn't audition for the part of a short Asian girl. They didn't need to be so assholey about it, though. We all had feelings. The George guy was looking at me and signaling me to come over. He was with a woman. I'd met her before, and I think she was his wife, but it was dangerous to assume around here. I smiled and walked over.

"George and Daphne. How are things?"

Daphne took me by the hand with both of hers. It looked like tears were welling up in her eyes. I swallowed. "Ellie, we heard about Joel. That's terrible. I can't imagine how you feel. There were no signs?"

George cleared his throat. "I know how you feel. A good friend of mine died when I was younger. It hurts now Ellie, but it does make you stronger. You'll come out the other side of your grief a better, stronger actress."

"I'm quitting. Packing up tonight. I should be able to get a flight back tomorrow."

Daphne shook her head. "Don't listen to my husband. There's a reason he doesn't work as a grief counsellor. He's got all the empathy of a picket fence." She sighed. At least now I knew she was his wife. Crisis averted. "Look, Ellie, I don't know how you feel. Go back home, get some perspective. Play on those beautiful beaches you've got, but don't quit. Take a breather. Come back when you're ready."

I shook my head. "Don't think so. Joel was on top of the world. He was making strides, getting the gigs he should be getting. His career was unfolding like he thought it should. And still something got to him, and he figured the only way out was death." I smiled at her. "I appreciate the kind words, even the clumsy kind words, but I'm going to use Joel's death as a warning." I pulled on my beer. "Where's the food? I'm going to eat my last month's rent worth of Bart's food."

Daphne had the decency to laugh, but I was serious. I was starving.

Bart held court, talking about some movie idea he had. Half a dozen attentive faces were listening to his pitch. Best of luck to him. I caught the attention of the dude on the barbie. "What do you have?"

"Anything and everything. What do you want?"

"Can you do up a kangaroo steak, medium rare with some mango chutney and a nice garlic mash?"

He deadpanned me for about five seconds. "Kangaroo? Are you shitting me? Kangaroo? You eat that stuff?"

"Abso-friggin'-lutely. It's very healthy, too. Almost no cholesterol, and as long as it's not over-cooked, very tasty."

He shook his head. "No. No kangaroo."

"So if no 'roo I'll have a t-bone, medium and some of that salad."

"Medium? Pink line down the middle okay?"

"It is. You fry up any onions?"

He shook his head. "You're from Australia, right?"

I nodded and opened another beer. "Why?"

"So this must be old hat for you. Barbecue, I mean. Kinda rare here, compared to your home."

"Yeah, this is the first one I've been to since I got here. Forgot how much I missed it." I took the plate of food and saluted him with my bottle. "Remember, try the kangaroo. It's not that expensive and very healthy. This mob will be all over it like a terrier on a rat."

The barbecue guy laughed. "I'll remember that. Thanks. Enjoy the food. There's plenty here, so come back if you want more."

I picked a seat at the table facing the crowd assembled around a more than usually animated Bart. He had them gripped. I recognized most of them, all at the same or slightly higher strata influence-wise as Bart. All of them willing to do anything to claw themselves to the top of the commercial success heap. This city was like a sausage factory. The end product was loved by the world. Usually. But if they knew the backstabbing and bullshit that went into the production they'd lose their lunch. I chewed on the steak. Not bad. Actually pretty good. I wiped the corners of my mouth with the napkin, and the crowd burst out laughing. Self-conscious me thought, for an instant, they were laughing at something I missed on my face and took another swipe. George poked Bart in the chest and said something that got them all laughing again. Self-conscious me then realized they didn't even know I was still there. I was. And was prepared to eat Bart out of his house. At least my appetite had returned.

Steve Bond pulled himself away from the crowd and beckoned me over. I held up a finger and waggled it. I was too busy eating, and whatever it was they were talking about didn't interest me anymore. I had quit.

And the steak wasn't half bad at all.

Out of the corner of my eye, I saw Steve approaching the table. "Ellie, Bart's got a pretty good thing going over there. You might want to pay attention. I think it's a winner. We all think it's got potential. And in my professional opinion as a casting director, I think there's a good part in it for you."

That little flutter in the heart and stomach region showed up. That feeling I always got before an audition or the first day of shooting. I stomped on it and smiled at him with a mouthful of salad. I shook my head while I chewed. "Thanks for the thought, Steve. You have been really supportive, and it's helped and all, but I said I quit. Q-U-I-T. Not coming back. Out for good. Off the call sheet. No longer on the market. Get it? This time tomorrow, I'll be cramped in the back of a Qantas jet heading back to Sydney. Frankly, I'm looking forward to putting this behind me."

"I can't talk you out of it?"

"I can't imagine anything that would make me stay. For certain something Bart's cooking up isn't going to do it for me."

He raised his eyebrows. "You might be surprised. This is pretty good."

"From the same guy who put *Beast of Bondi* together? I was in it. I know what kind of crap he puts together."

"Not this time. He's hit on something. Says he's got a draft screenplay, which, frankly, is more than he's ever had before for any of his other projects."

I rubbed my nose. "As promising as all that sounds, I'm outta this place tomorrow. Thanks for thinking of me. That was sweet of you."

He shook his head and gave me a strange look. "I'm handing this to you on a platter, Ellie, and you're turning it down? Maybe you should go home. You clearly aren't warped enough for this place."

I saluted him with my bottle of beer and returned to the attack on my steak.

8

Steve shook his head and walked back to the crowd. She befuddled him. This had the potential to be a blockbuster. Nothing was guaranteed, of course, but the starting material looked promising. Extremely so.

"So, Steve, what did she think?"

"Blew me off. Figuratively of course."

George elbowed him in the ribs. "Too bad, on both counts."

Bart frowned. "Ease up guys. Not cool. Not today anyway. So, you guys seem to like the concept."

George thought in terms of past successes. "Brilliant, Bart. "Twilight" meets "Avatar". So give us more story details."

"Okay, so we've got these otherworldly alien vampires living among us. They come from a planet just beyond the reach of current space-travel technology. This planet has an underground fuel source that would revolutionize space travel. Our planet is the closest civilized planet to them by a million light years so we are their only threat. The vampire-aliens have been here since the industrial revolution. Keeping an eye on us. Nobody really knows they're here. All of the usual vampire symbolisms are explained in Act One. The sunlight is deadly because the radiation is different from that on their planet. Any water burns their skin, not just holy water. Garlic isn't poison, but they have an incredible sense of smell. We work in some of the more obscure things. Need to do some research on that." Bart looked at the assembled. They were eating it up.

"How does Act One end?" George, always the practical one.

"I'll get to that in a minute. Some characters first. The earthling, Sam Stevens, nerdy guy works at JPL. His live-in girlfriend Susie, let's make her a yoga teacher and the love of his life. She dies, of course. The point man for the vamp-aliens is a tall, dark brooding guy. I'm actually thinking Colin Hanks after he loses some of that baby fat. Put him on a zero-carb, high aerobic regime and harden him. Do for him what *Speed* did for Keanu. Don't have a name for him yet. It's got to be something exotic and foreign. We'll research that too. Find a name the girls melt over. He's the anti-hero.

"Act one ends with our anti-hero in a nightclub. He overhears Stevens, the JPL nerd, tell his girl they are on the verge of a breakthrough. They've now got the technology to travel to this new planet they've discovered. All hush-hush. The planet has something—it'll be the MacGuffin, the unobtanium—that mankind will reap the benefits from forever. Stevens is excited because it's his work that has made interplanetary travel possible. It's a one-way trip and he's hinting that he wants her to go with him to help colonize the planet." He sipped his scotch. "You guys want to freshen your drinks? I'll tell you Act Two in a minute."

The assembled crowd drifted toward the bar. Bart buttonholed Steve. "What did she say?"

"She's leaving. I don't think I changed her mind."

"I've got her as the girlfriend. It's a killer role. She'd be a fool to turn it down."

Steve shrugged. "To her, it's just a role. She's heading back to the land down under. Tell me about the second act."

Bart nodded. "As soon as the rest get back with refreshed refreshments. You liking it so far?"

"Has potential. Certainly."

"I think if we all work together on this, it could be the thing that gets us the respect we all deserve."

Steve scratched his chin. He hadn't thought about sandwiches in hours. "It's possible."

The rest returned with their drinks, George and Daphne finally succumbing to the alcohol, each with a glass of wine.

"Shall I continue?" Bart looked at the assembled friends and colleagues. They seemed eager to him. He launched back into it.

"Act Two starts with parallel streams. Our as-yet unnamed anti-hero reports back to his home planet—some sort of faster-than-light speed communications. We can get an advisor from CalTech for this stuff—and informs them that the serenity they've been experiencing for the past however long it's been is about to be broken, that the threat they all assumed earth would posed is about to become a reality. There is obviously a time lag between the launch on Earth and the arrival of earthlings on the vamp-alien planet, but it is now inevitable, and the defenses better be ready. He tells his planet's leaders he'll try to sabotage the launch, but there are no guarantees.

"Parallel to this, our hero is working hard on the final stages of the project. His girlfriend has said yes and the plans are in the works for their wedding. There'll be the usual family background stuff: the girl's parents think she's crazy, the boy's parents think he's a hero."

George interrupted. "What's the shift in Act Two? The midpoint?"

Bart smiled. "I was just getting to that. Our anti-hero is shadowing Stevens, looking for an opportunity to at least talk him out of it and at worse, kill him. I'm actually leaning toward kill from the get-go. A civilization is at stake. He uses the girl to get to Stevens. At the mid-point simultaneous tectonic shifts happen: Stevens discovers there is a military backing to the project and the "seeding another planet for the benefit of mankind" story is just that, a story. But he doesn't care, demonstrating his true character, and looks forward to the opportunity. The girl realizes she's falling in love with the tall, dark and handsome stranger. She is now not keen on traveling to other planets and leaving Earth forever. She, obviously, doesn't know tall-and-dark is not actually from our planet. Like that twist? Tall and dark, meanwhile is aware of the interest from the earth girl, but isn't interested in her. He's trying very hard to keep from biting her neck and sucking her blood. Trips to farms to kill sheep and goats fill his spare time. His midpoint is the knowledge that he is going to have to kill Stevens to make him stop."

One of his guests raised his hand.

Bart looked at him and laughed. "It's not grade school, Bowens. What's up?"

"How techie is this going to be? So far everything you've talked about can be done on camera. No real special effects. If you want to get the teen boy audience, you've going to need something to counter the vampire angle. The girls will definitely come for the dark and brooding, but technical shit will get them coming in pairs."

"That's an excellent point. There are lots of opportunities for JPL interiors with advanced computer technology, as well as some pure CG alien planet shots. And it amps up in the second half." He took a drink. "Let's get some food and I'll tell you about the second half of Act Two, and then the climax in Act Three."

They nodded, agreed and made their way to the barbecue, where the waiter was patiently waiting. Ellie left the table and headed back to the guesthouse. Bart vacillated between intercepting her and trying to talk her out of leaving and just letting her go. Letting go won. There would be others. He made a mental note to call a real estate agency and get the place back on the market.

The table was filled. Waiters served wine and the guests tucked into their food. Halfway through the meal Bart tapped his glass with his knife. "Part two of Act Two, ready? You keep eating while I talk."

Nods around the table prompted him to continue.

"Okay. We've got our three main characters in complete disarray. Stevens is now backing a war effort. A secret war effort. He's conflicted but generally supports the idea. His girl is straying with the alien, but she doesn't know yet that he is an alien. The alien is starting to have feelings for the girl and knows he has to kill her boyfriend. They circle for the remainder of the second act. Stevens and alien have an all-out battle where the alien reveals where he's really from and what he's meant to do. Stevens escapes with life-threatening injuries and is rushed to the hospital by his girlfriend. The all is lost point at the end of act two has Stevens fighting for his life, the girlfriend finding out tall and dark is an alien, and the alien thinking he's actually succeeded in stopping Stevens, but lost the girl. This sets us up for the end."

George dropped his knife on his plate. "Not going to work. Who's the hero? Vamp-alien or the nerd?"

"Both."

"You need one. And it sounds now like ET is the hero and he's the one who needs to have the lull."

Bart squinted and after a beat smiled. "Valid point. Minor detail, though. You can help with the rewrite. Maybe an emotional low point—he's falling hard for the girl and knows his planet is planning a pre-emptive strike that will obliterate Earth. It's just a scene, after all, and it doesn't change the third act much."

"So tell us the third act," someone yelled out. "And speak up. I missed a bit of that last part."

Bart lubricated his vocals with a slug of scotch. "Stevens gets primo medical care by the best doctors the Pentagon and NASA have access to. He's fast-tracked through recovery and is well on his way to succeeding with the launch. He now becomes the anti-hero." He raised his glass in acknowledgment to Bowens. "Our tall-and-dark tracks down the girl and confronts her. He tells her he has feelings for her but is afraid it will never work. She now knows he's an alien, remember, and tells him they can make it work even if they are from different planets. He tells her about the military angle of the launch and that her ex-boyfriend is the linchpin to the entire mission." He paused and looked at each of his audience one at a time, directly in their eyes. "The climax—the alien enlists the help of the girlfriend to stop Stevens. The scientist's incapacitation will put the program back decades. He doesn't necessarily want to kill him, but he does need to stop him somehow. She joins forces, there's an interspecies love scene in there somewhere. Together, they storm the labs in a battle to end the project. She gets killed in the crossfire; Stevens realizes the enormity of what he's doing, takes out the critical components and destroys them, disabling the space project. He takes off with the help of tall and dark, both of them mourning the death of the girl. Issues are resolved, anti-heroes become heroes, and we're set up for a sequel." He sat back and waited for the criticisms. If everybody said they liked it, they would be lying. If they really liked it, they'd be pointing out areas that needed a bit of work.

The audience was quiet, digesting the story. The elements were familiar—there were no new stories in the world—but this had a unique slant.

"Aren't you afraid that you're going to be catching the end of both vampire and sci-fi trends? Could be the last man standing. Never good to be the closer of a fad."

Bart smiled. This was promising. "No, I'm not. Twilight clones are coming out for a few more years. Cameron has the Avatar sequels going on. If anything, if we move fast," he went for the close, "we could be hitting screens at the peak of the frenzy. The best time to open would be halfway between the Avatar sequels."

Nods around the table. He had thought this through, and that answer might prompt some early signers.

"Have you figured out the budget yet?"

Bart looked at his audience. No one around the table, as far as he knew, worked on anything larger than $40 million and in most cases their budget was less than $20 million. "Just back of the envelope. Top end, about 250. If we trim back some of the exteriors on the alien planet, I think we can get it down below 200. I say we look for 250 and expect two."

George choked on his drink. "Two. Hundred. Million. Are you fucking nuts?"

"No, I'm fucking my secretary. Think big, people. We need to get some artists in and do a detailed storyboard. An electronic one we can animate and put on a DVD. We'll take it to the studios and see who'll green light this project. Act like you belong, right? If we go in with hat in hand like they owe us a favor, they'll kick us out on our butt. We go in like we're doing them the favor. Who represents Hanks? We'll do even better if we can get him attached. With Hanks attached, a good storyboard and a rough animated version, I think it'll be a cakewalk."

The plates were cleared away, and a dessert menu offered. Low carb alternatives were selected by all but George who had long ago given up. A fat cat had to be fat, right? Sherbet and white wine ended the meal. Bart watched his guests talk among themselves. The seed was well and truly planted. The hard work started now, keeping everybody on task. "So, who is this with me? Who wants to make the next blockbuster and show this town how it's supposed to be done?"

George nodded and raised his glass. "I'm in. I can help with the financing. Not personally, of course, but I know a guy with money who wants to do a movie."

"Excellent. Thanks, George. Anyone else?"

Steve cleared his throat. "Bart, baby, I'm your guy, but I want points. If I work on this, I'm going to have to drop the rest of what I'm doing, and I get paid by the job. I've got kids in school, Bart, and none of them are smart or talented in sports, so scholarships are out of the question."

Bart pretended to consider. "Points are risky, Steve. Points mean you get nothing if the picture flops."

"Base plus points, Bart. I'm not a complete idiot."

"We'll talk. I'm not averse to the idea. Our managers can sort it out. Anyone else? Come on, people. This is the opportunity of your lifetimes. Bowens, are you in?"

He nodded. "Yeah, I think so. It's a unique idea. I like it. Get the right girl and it will draw the teen boy crowd like ants to sugar. Casting is going to be the key. You know that, right Steve? Any ideas for the girl?"

Steve shook his head. "I had planned on Ellie Bourke. She fits the profile of an athletic character and carries herself well. Very spunky girl."

He shook his head. "She's pretty definite about moving back to Australia, though, so I'll be running a cattle call for that role."

George leaned forward. "So change her mind. She'll be opposite Colin Hanks, for God's sake. Potentially."

"She's in the guesthouse packing right now. Her roommate committed suicide yesterday and she's pretty down on the industry. I've tried a couple of times and so has Bart. She's leaving."

There was a quiet around the table. Everyone there knew somebody who had killed themselves, or tried. It was a tough business. Tougher than most realized.

Bart clapped his hands and broke the spell. "Come on people, out of the funk. This is a historic meeting. We'll look back at this meal as the genesis of all of us hitting the big time. All of us who get into this opportunity, that is."

The guests chuckled. A few more committed themselves immediately, and the rest promised they'd get back after talking to their business managers. The bar was opened again, and Bart grabbed his Blackberry and sent an email to his manager. Contracts would be drawn up for those who committed and sent to their respective managers. He sent a second message to send contracts to all of his guests' managers, whether they had already committed or not. Maybe the paper in front of them would push them the final step. He smiled with some satisfaction. They were out of the gates.

He was headed for the big times.

9

I left when they approached the table. I didn't want to talk to any of them. They seemed too happy and too pretty and so too drunk. I had to pack. It was unfortunate that I'd miss Joel's brother, but seeing him would just make it hurt more.

Joel's things were stacked neatly around the house, as usual. I picked up his iPhone. It was dead. I absently plugged it into his laptop and turned it on. His home screen was a picture of the two of us at the beach. It was taken nearly three months ago when I tried to teach him how to surf. That was a miserable, hilarious failure. I smiled. There were good memories. I wanted to remember him with good memories and not the thought of him slumped in the tub, beaten by the business.

I scrolled through his photos. There were more of me than the both of us, naturally, but there were a few of us both. I forwarded the good ones to my phone. Someone else could sort out the bill.

His guitar stood in the corner with a pile of sheet music. He had tried doing the singing comedian thing, kind of like the Flight of the Conchords, but dropped the idea after the first night. He bombed horribly. Things were actually thrown at him on stage. We sat up and killed a bottle of wine after that, laughing our asses off.

I was smiling more. That had to be good.

I myself didn't have much of value. My few clothes, my laptop, my iPhone. Amazing how little crap I accumulated over the past year. Maybe not so amazing if you saw my paycheck. I packed all but a change of clothes and my laptop and phone. Two suitcases and a backpack. That took all of fifteen minutes. My life in L.A. reduced to one checked and two carry-on. Pretty sad, when you think about it. I tried not to think about it.

I got on my laptop and booked a flight back to Australia. It would take the rest of my savings, but I could stay with my dad in Sydney. I would start over. No biggie, really. I was young still and I'd be leaving this mess behind me.

I couldn't avoid what I had to do next.

Joel's things had to be packed. I wouldn't be here to meet Jacob, but the least I could do was get his brother's stuff together. He didn't have much more than me. I put his clothes in a pile, laid his guitar on the sofa and put his laptop in its case beside it. His surfboard stayed leaning against the wall in the living room. I did another circuit around the small guesthouse. Nothing was missed. I couldn't do much more than that.

I couldn't stay surrounded by the shadow of my best friend. I had to see the beach one more time before I left. It was a clear day, the sunset would be beautiful. I grabbed Joel's phone to take with me. I would scroll through the memories while the sun went down. It would be our last time on the beach together.

I don't remember the drive to Zuma. Autopilot kicked in. With any luck, I didn't hit anybody on the way. The last year meandered through my head, random memories of the successes and failures that would mark my year here. It seemed hollow, a glancing attack on the city. It was a shame to leave it here, but enough was enough. Too many good people were swallowed whole in this city. I had no desire to be included in that list.

The last heat of the day was still trapped in the sand. I sat on a dune and watched the surfers. The water was too calm to surf, but these guys didn't seem to care. They were catching the two and three foot waves and riding them for a bit before stacking. Looked like fun. I was looking forward to getting back on my board back home. I had put off having my dad ship it to me, almost like I knew I wouldn't be staying here in California very long.

The sun dipped lower, touching the waterline. My last sunset in California. I opened the photos on Joel's phone and slowly scrolled through them. Too many good memories. I hadn't realized how many pictures he took of me. Smiling, laughing, more than a few of me grinning at him and giving him the finger. Fuck, I was going to miss him. Why in the hell didn't he talk to me? I scrolled to the next picture and the alarm went off on my phone in my pocket, scaring the crap out of me.

"Shit. What is it now?" I dug the phone out of my pocket and swore. Again. Melon-Head. Oh, sweet Jesus. I was supposed to be in his studio in an hour. I forgot all about it. Better cancel. No point in showing up now. I called his mobile.

"Ellie honey, tell me you're sitting downstairs in the coffee shop anxiously waiting to come on air with the Melon-Head."

"I'm at Zuma, watching the sun go down. For the last time."

"What in the hell are you talking about?" The folksy, laid-back Ross was gone. There was genuine concern in his voice.

"Oh, God, no, Ross. I'm not planning on packing it in. I'm flying back home tomorrow, for good."

"What on earth for? I thought things were going well for you."

"Joel killed himself yesterday. It all seems pointless now." I sniffed. "I'm going to bag your show, Ross. I've got to get some rest."

The silence on the other end was long enough I thought the call had dropped. "Ross?"

"Ellie, this is not the time for you to be alone. Seriously. Come in. We'll chat. Just the two of us. You can tell our audience about Joel. And about the days leading up to his suicide. Maybe we'll reach out to someone else who is feeling the same way and prevent a senseless death."

I shook my head and exhaled a long breath.

"I know you're still there. I can hear the heavy breathing. Do this for Joel."

"Asshole." I sniffed again. "Okay. I'll be there. My swan song. I hope you're on a seven-second delay. I'm not feeling very politically correct." I stood and brushed the sand off my ass. "I'll be there in an hour."

"Don't run any lights."

"Why not? I'll be gone. They're not going to chase me all the way to Bronte for a moving violation."

"Just be careful. I'll see you when you get here."

I pocketed my phone and took a last look at the sun sinking on Zuma. I hopped in my trusty Beetle and tossed Joel's phone on the passenger seat. It was a half-hour's drive to the studios in Century City if I took it easy. I had plenty of time. Ross's concern worried me. I wasn't prone to do something stupid, was I? I didn't think so, but the brain is a strange thing. I liked the idea of eulogizing Joel on national radio here and in Australia. He deserved nothing less.

I passed through Malibu and headed east on the Pacific Coast Highway to Century City. Traffic was light. I zoned out and went with the flow. I'd have time to grab that coffee Ross was talking about if traffic stayed this way.

My daydreams were interrupted by a phone ring. It wasn't mine. The ringtone was a Lady Gaga song, certainly nothing I would use. I reached over, grabbed it, and put it on speaker. "Joel Sampson's phone."

"Is this Ellie? Put Joel on, would you? I've been trying to reach him all day long."

"Kyle Johnson, is that you?"

"Yeah. Joel, please. This is urgent."

I sighed. What a city. "Doesn't matter how urgent it is, Kyle. Joel's not coming to the phone. You'd think an agent would be on top of things like that."

"Like what? Where is he? He was supposed to get back to me this afternoon. I've guys crawling all over me to book him."

"I can't believe this. You guys are snakes. You don't know that your client killed himself yesterday? Drug overdose. Son of a bitch. I'm glad I'm splitting. Unconscionable."

"Hang on a second. He did what?"

"He O.D'd on a syringe full of heroin. In the tub."

"When? Exactly." Kyle grilled me like a cheese sandwich.

"I don't know. The cops think it was mid-afternoon, 3 or 4 o'clock. What difference does it make?"

"It explains why I haven't been able to reach him. He was supposed to call me back last night at 6. I've been trying to reach him ever since."

"Dead men tell no tales, Kyle. Sorry." I hung up and dropped the phone back on the seat. It rang less than a minute later, Joel's agent calling back. I put it back on speaker. "You weren't finished?"

"I wasn't finished. When's the funeral?"

"I don't know. I'm flying back to Australia tomorrow. Could give a rat's ass, if the truth be told. I'm angry with him for not talking to me about whatever was bothering him. His brother is coming out in the next day or so. I'll make sure he's got Joel's phone. You can call him and ask him. What was all the urgency about reaching him?"

"It's not that important now. I lined up a gig for him that could have launched his career. I needed him to confirm that he'd do it."

"Since when did you wait for his confirmation? He went wherever you booked him, and without complaining."

"This wasn't a standup gig. It would have been a ninety-minute sit-down interview, talking about his career so far, how he got to where he was, and what his influences and aspirations were. That sort of thing."

I snorted. "Right. They don't do True Hollywood Story stories until you're at the far end of your career. His was just starting to take off."

"Exactly. Kevin Pollak caught him at the Improv on Thursday and was impressed with what he saw. He's starting up a new show. Rising stars."

"So that was Pollak? I thought he looked familiar."

"Yeah, *Usual Suspects*. Short bald guy. One of the lawyers in *A Few Good Men*."

I was getting impatient with Kyle and this conversation. "Yeah, yeah. But you're losing me, Kyle. So what?"

"He does a live webcast every Sunday afternoon. Sits down with comics, directors, actors and shoots the shit for an hour and a half. He's expanding his guest list to include up and coming comics and actors one show a month. Newbies. When he's impressed with what he sees he wants to give them a platform. He saw Joel and was impressed. He was planning on launching his new artist shtick with Joel. Was going to announce it on tomorrow's broadcast. I needed a confirmation from Joel to feed back to his camp. I guess it's a no then."

"So Joel knew about this?"

"Hell yeah."

"When did you tell him?"

"Yesterday morning, around 10:30. He said he'd try and rearrange things and would let me know if he could do it."

I turned into Century City. "Look, I don't know this show. Is it a big deal?"

"It is. Pollak's getting a lot of positive press, and his guest list keeps getting better. Colin Hanks. Tom Hanks. Rob Corddry. Kevin Smith. Not small names. This is a very high profile thing in the industry. Adding a segment for new talent was designed to give their careers a kick in the ass."

"Did Joel seem excited?"

"Extremely. He'd seen the show and loved it."

"Doesn't that strike you as odd?"

"What?"

"That he'd get an invitation to be on a showcase of sorts, ninety minutes with a big name and influential audience, and he decides the best way to celebrate is to kill himself?"

There was a pause on the line. Ellie parked her car and turned off the ignition. She picked up the phone and took it off speaker. "You still there?"

"Yeah, I am. You're right. Inexplicable. Maybe it was accidental. Prescription drugs?"

"Heroin, the cops think."

"Huh. He was clean. Sad he slid back into that habit."

I looked at the phone. The battery was almost dead. "Battery's going Kyle, I've got to run. And I think he had some help. Joel didn't kill himself. Somebody killed him."

"Really? Who in hell would want to kill Joel? He was harmless."

"Your guess is as good as mine, but he's been clean for three months and had absolutely no reason to kill himself. We had a three-month-clean party planned. This wasn't suicide, and I'll be damned if I'm going to let someone get away with killing him."

10

"It's Ross 'Melon-Head' Mellon coming to you live from Los Angeles, the city of Angels. And devils. And trolls, troglodytes and scuzzbags. But today it's just angels. With us tonight, hopefully for the full two hours, is a fellow Aussie, aspiring actress and good friend Ellie Bourke. You told me earlier, Ellie, that you were quitting this place, turning your back on a very promising career and heading back to our sunburnt country. You probably don't know Ellie's name, folks, but you'd recognize her if you saw her. She's tall, almost six foot, has long blonde hair and a dazzling smile that is absolutely captivating.

"But there's no smile today. What's going on, Ellie? Why are you quitting this cesspool of malcontents and ego-bruisers?"

"I don't want to talk about me tonight, Ross. I'm not leaving because of me. I'm not even sure now if I am leaving. Something has come up in the last hour that has changed things for me."

"That's great news. We need more real people here."

Ellie smiled. "That's nice of you, but I'm probably only delaying my departure. I know you know Joel Sampson. He's been my roommate for the last six months. We became very close, in a platonic way, like brother and sister. I was like an older sister to him. I'd been here longer and helped him settle in. Not much longer, but every day here ages you like a month anywhere else."

"I do know Joel. He's a very talented stand-up comic. I expect to see more of him. Tell us what this has to do with your decisions."

"He killed himself yesterday. Our landlord discovered him in the tub with a needle stuck in his arm. It was an overdose. And it was tragic."

Ross interjected. "If you or anybody you know is feeling helpless and don't know where to turn, please call the Suicide Prevention number here in L.A. on 1877-7CRISIS, or 1-877-727-4747. If you're listening to this back home in Australia, the number is 13 11 14. Don't waste a second. Life is too precious. Go on, Ellie."

"I was going to say it seemed strange to me. Joel was doing well. He was advancing in the comedy clubs. He was gaining the respect of his peers. I couldn't understand why he would do this."

Mellon jumped in again. "Sometimes the signs are subtle, possibly not visible at all. You can't blame yourself. And I'm not blaming him, either, but people need to understand there shouldn't be a stigma attached to mental illness. Reach out. There are people who want to help you."

"All good sentiments, Ross, but I found out just as I got here that his idol, the guy who inspires him, his definition of the pinnacle of success, wanted Joel to be on his talk show in a couple of weeks. Joel knew this and was supposed to confirm the timing with his agent the day he was killed." Ellie stopped and took a breath. "Yeah, I said the day he was killed, not the day he died. There's no way in hell—can I say that?—that Joel would do anything to jeopardize an appearance on that show. It would have been the catapult that launched him into every living room in the US." She sniffed and rubbed her eyes. "He didn't kill himself, and he didn't accidentally OD on drugs. Somebody killed him." She stopped talking and sat back in her chair in the studio.

Ross forgot for a moment that they were live and on the air. He looked at her for a couple of silent seconds before recovering. "Wow. I thought I had hard-hitting news before, but this is a first. We're going to continue this in a minute, but we've got to get a song on the air first. Here's Katy Perry and Eminem with their reinvention of that Ray Charles favorite 'I got a Woman'."

He pushed his mic away and stared at Ellie. "The cops know about this, yes?"

She shook her head. "I just found out in the parking lot outside."

"You could have warned me before we went on air. You've got to take this information to the police immediately."

Ellie fished a card out of her pants pocket. "I was interviewed at the scene by a cop. I've got his number here. I'll call him after the show."

Ross leaned over the console and snagged the card from her. "Who is this? Constable Larry Perkins. Constable? No Detective on this murder?"

"It's a suicide as far as they're concerned. And with the President coming in a couple of weeks, I hear they're flat out. I'll call him tomorrow and see what he thinks."

Ross smiled. "Bullshit. We're going to call him on the air."

Ellie grimaced. "No. You're going to get embarrassing, aren't you."

"I had that surgically removed. You can't embarrass me."

"I wasn't worried about you." She pointed at her chest. "Me."

The song was winding down, Katy and Marshall harmonizing on the final chorus. Ross stepped all over it with a definite look of purpose on his face. "That was Katy and Mathers crooning away like the lovebirds that they want to be. We've got some hot, breaking news here. The suicide prevention information I gave you all before the break is still important and valuable information to have, but it appears that our good friend Joel Sampson did not commit suicide. It is looking more and more like he was killed. By whom, why and other questions still need to be answered. Ellie Bourke is with me in the studio. Say Hi, Ellie."

"Hi Ellie."

Ross smiled. "Great. You are truly a natural." Ellie cracked a small smile. "She has given me the business card of one of the policemen who attended Joel's death. We'll give him a call right now and see if we can prod the L.A.P.D. into action."

He dialed the mobile phone number and put it over the air. "Okay, the number is ringing now. I respect the work the L.A.P.D. do, but they are seriously overworked and it's not surprising things fall between the cracks. That's the second ring. There's no way I'm going to let a killer get off scot-free, though, just for expediency's sake. Here's the third ring."

"Perkins."

"Constable Perkins? This is Ross Mellon and you're on the air."

"Melon-Head? Love your show. What's this about? Did I win something?"

Ross cleared his throat. "You attended the death of a Joel Sampson yesterday, right?"

"Oh, hey, I can't talk about any cases. I'm not the official spokesperson for the L.A.P.D. You need to call Nancy Wilson at the main number for any official statements."

"That's a fair comment, Constable. You can't officially talk to us and I respect the rules you need to live by. We all need to live by rules. So I'm going to ask you to just listen, okay? New information has come to light in the death of Joel Sampson. Information that almost certainly precludes suicide as a cause of death. Not even accidental overdose. I'm going to ask Ellie to explain this to you." He pointed at her and mouthed "hit it".

"Okay Constable, so Joel had no reason to kill himself. He had found out that morning that he was lined up to be interviewed by one of his idols. It would launch his career beyond anything he could have hoped for. There could be nothing more positive for him. He had no reason to take his own life. He was about to reach his dreams."

There was silence. "Constable are you still there?"

"Melon-Head, Miss Bourke, if you think you have information pertaining to this case, I strongly suggest you come by and tell us in person. We can take a statement from you and direct our investigations appropriately."

"That sounds like a blow-off Constable. You're going to whitewash this, aren't you?"

"We handle each case on its merits. Miss Bourke should come by the station tomorrow and make a statement, and if she has more information, we'll take it under consideration. Sorry, I can't really say any more than that. I still love your show, though. Bye."

Ross pushed some buttons on the console. "Well it appears we've lost him. Ellie, are you going to head back to Australia now? Or are you going to hang around and help the police solve this crime?"

"I can't leave. Not knowing somebody out there killed him. I don't know how long I'll stay, but I'm not heading back tomorrow like I had planned."

"That's a girl. Our very own Australian Nancy Drew." He gave her a wink. "Lily Allen is back with a song so crude we've had to bleep more than half of it. We'll take your calls, Sydney, right after that. Remember, 131666 is a toll-free call from your lounge to my studio in hell. Call me."

He dumped his audio and turned to Ellie. "You okay with taking some calls?"

"I guess. Rescue me if they go overboard, okay?"

"The plug will be pulled." He raised his hands like Moses. "I. Have. The. Power."

Ellie chuckled. She was feeling a bit better. "I'm glad I came. I wasn't going to."

"I am, too. Song is ending," He switched on his mic, "and the boards are lit up, Ellie. And they all want to talk to you. You ready?"

"Fire away."

"This is Mellon-head with Sarah on the line from Collaroy, on the beach in New South Wales. Sarah, what do you have to say to Ellie?"

"Hi there. I listen to your show all the time. I think you should get more up and rising stars on more often 'cause, like, we really support them."

"Ellie is here waiting for your question, Sarah. Or comment. Anything to say to her?"

"Oh, Ellie, hi. I loved you in *Beast of Bondi*. That was the scariest movie ever and you were excellent in it. Too bad you had to die near the end. Are you going to be in the sequel?"

Ellie laughed. "Hi Sarah. I didn't know there was going to be a sequel, so I guess I'm not in it. Since I died in the first one, it's unlikely I'd be in any more anyway, right? Thanks for calling though. It's great to hear from my fans."

Ross chuckled. "Maybe you could come back as a ghost. Or your twin. Stranger things have happened." He looked at the screen. "Giovanni is calling through for you. Giovanni, you're on the air."

"Ah, miss Ellie, you are a goddess. Do not leave Los Angeles. You should be plastered on billboards and the walls of buildings all over the city. If I could guarantee you jobs in movies I would, immediately."

Ross shook his head and raised an eyebrow. "Sounds like you've got a stalker there, Ellie, listening on the Internet. So, Giovanni, any thoughts about the death, the unfortunate and untimely death of Ellie's room-mate, Joel Sampson?"

"Not really. I don't care so much. One less man for competition, I guess. Marry me, Ellie."

"Giovanni, I'm sure you're a fantastic guy, but I'm not going to get married, to you or anyone else, for a few years yet."

"Marry no one else. I will save myself for you."

"You do that." She smiled at Ross and made a cutting motion across her neck.

"Well, that was special. I think he'll last 48 hours, at most." He checked the board. "I was about to go to another song, a Will.I.am / Susan Boyle mashup, but there's someone on the line I think you should talk to. Go ahead, sir."

"Hey, Ell, it's me."

"Dad?"

"Cancel your flight home and find out what happened to your friend. It's more important than coming home to see me."

"Great to talk to you too, dad. Why didn't you just call my phone?"

"This is a free call, hon. None of us are rich. Yet. Don't quit, okay? Your mom would be incredibly proud of what you are doing."

"I'm flopping. I haven't had a successful show since I got here."

"Then I guess the stuff I read in the local news is a pile of crap. You are doing well. You'll do better. Nobody leaps to the front of the line and stays there. You need to put in the hours to get the gravy. If you -"

"Whoa, Dad. You sound like you're reading off a bunch of those cheesy motivational posters. I get it. And I'm really glad you called me. We don't talk enough. Love you."

"Love you too, Ellie-babe. I'm putting some money together. I'll be flying out to visit in a couple of months, if that's okay?"

"Absolutely. Let me know when, exactly."

Ross jumped in at a break in conversation. "I hate to get between you two, but we've got to pay my salary. After this ad break we'll be doing that Will.I.Am - Boyle song. Stay tuned. You'll be surprised." He dropped his audio while the ads played. "You want to finish up with your dad?"

"We did. Thanks. I've got to go now, Ross. Thanks for the invite."

"No problem. And I want you back to tell us all what the outcome of this Nancy Drew-ness is, okay? Call me. You've got my number."

"You really think I'm as good as you say I am?"

He pointed at her. "That, exactly, is your problem. Remember the Winter Olympics a few years back where the Aussie girl was competing in the snowboard competition? Final run, she gets two attempts. On the first one, she stacks and lands on her ass. Lowest possible scores. She gets back up to the top of the pipe for the second, and final, run and she aces it. Highest mark in the comp, instant gold medal."

"Yeah, so?"

"Did she train between the first and second run?"

"Of course not."

"Of course not. It was 100% in her head. And you've got to get it 100% in your head. Do you want to be up on the screen or forever sitting in the audience? Eighty, ninety percent of the people in this town are getting beat in their heads. Let me tell you a secret: every time self-doubt crawls in to your skull, grab that mother by the throat and kick the ever-loving shit out of it. Trust me. You only succeed in this business when you know," he punched himself in the chest, "absolutely know in your heart you will succeed. It's like the guy says, if you think you'll win or you think you'll lose, you're right. Now piss off and succeed. I've got a show to do."

Ellie removed her headphones and waved to the producer as she left. Ross sat back in his chair and watched her leave. He depressed the mic button to talk to his producer. "I hope she stays, man. There goes one of the most genuine and talented people I know."

"I haven't seen her in anything. What's she been in?"

"This and that. Check her out on imdb.com. The biggest movie was a schlocky horror made in Australia by that Sweeney guy. She was actually pretty good in it. I saw it and hoped it would launch her to better stuff. Was not to be. But she's still young, and I think she'll come good."

He flipped the microphone back on as an auto-tuned Will.I.Am harmonized with Susan Boyle. "Well, they said it would never work, but I'm here to tell you that this duet beats anything Dolly Parton and Kenny Rogers have every done. My God, how do I know that? Anyway, we'll have Ellie back on as soon as she's learned more. If any listener knows anything about this apparent suicide, give me a call."

11

Ross was right, and I knew he was right, and even though I knew he was right, I still had a problem telling myself that I was all that. At least not without thinking myself a total twat. I must have lain awake for hours thinking about that after the show.

Perkins' card had an address off Devonshire. I got to the station just after 9:00 hoping there would be someone there on a Sunday morning who could help. The station lobby looked early DMV. A chest-high counter separated me from the office drones, all in police uniforms, some with guns. I caught the attention of a person sitting at a desk near the front of the station proper. "I need to talk to someone about a case Constable Perkins was working on yesterday. A suicide at Bart Sweeney's house."

She checked a roster list and smiled up at me. "Would you like to talk to Constable Perkins himself? He's in today. Pulling extra shifts. Like all of us."

My lucky day. "That would be good. Thanks. Where do I go?"

"Oh, you just wait here, doll. I'll get him to come out. Have a seat."

I sat. I didn't have to wait long. Perkins hustled out like he was expecting me.

"Miss Bourke, I was expecting you."

See?

I stood, a couple of inches taller than him. "Sorry about that call last night. You know Melon-Head. Likes stirring the pot. I hope we didn't get you in trouble."

Perkins laughed. "I told my boss about it and he congratulated me for keeping it close to the vest. Follow me. I want to hear more about what you were talking about last night."

I followed. We snaked through a maze of desks and cubicles until he held a door for me and motioned me to enter. If it wasn't for the uniforms it could have been any government office. Right down to the painfully uncomfortable chairs in the small meeting room.

"So, Constable, what more do you want to know?"

He sat across from me and opened a notebook about halfway through. "From the top, Miss Bourke."

"Call me Ellie, okay?" I took a breath and collected my thoughts. "I have known Joel for six months now, when he first arrived here from Boise. He went through a self-destruct stage when he first got here like a lot of people do. Then one day he ran into a comic who he admired, when the both of them were plastered. That was about three months ago. The next morning he woke with the memory of an idol of his being a complete and utter asshole, and he was in the same state. Like looking in a horrible funhouse mirror. He vowed to clean himself up. Tuesday would have been three months of sobriety."

Perkins flipped pages back and forth. "Yes. You've told me all that already. Makes no difference. Depression comes to sober and drunk. There was no evidence to indicate it was anything other than a suicide. And, frankly, a lot of evidence that it was a suicide. The scene was staged. There were candles all over the place and the lighting was low. He set the place up to go."

"Where was the note? There was no note."

Perkins sighed. "Only about 20% of suicides leave notes. And of those 20%, more are female than male. No note is not a negative indicator of suicide." He flipped through his damned notepad again. "Ah, as I remembered. There was no sign of forced entry. The door was locked when Sweeney arrived. He knocked twice and used his key to enter. It's a textbook suicide. I'm sorry."

I was getting frustrated. He was murdered. I knew it. "He was told the morning he was killed that the biggest show a comic could do wanted to book him. It would have been the culmination of all the hard work he'd put in, both in Boise and here. He worked like a dog. I can't tell you the hours he spent running through his routines with me, adjusting single words, changing where the emphasis was placed, messing around with the timing until he was completely happy with the act. He was so comfortable in his own skin that when he completely screwed the pooch on stage Thursday night he recovered with an even funnier bit." I shook my head. "He didn't kill himself. There's nothing you can say that will convince me he did."

Perkins chewed his lip and flipped through his book. I was getting really, really tired of that. "What are you looking for now?"

He closed his notebook. "I'm willing to admit there is one other alternative to suicide. It's possible that Mr. Samson merely overdosed on the heroin. It's possible that he was rewarding himself for three months of sobriety and this opportunity of a lifetime, which you described, and things got out of hand. He hadn't been using for three months, after all, and it's likely he forgot how potent this stuff was."

I was wasting my time. "Dammit, he was clean. Look, Perkins, I don't care that you don't think he committed suicide. I'm going to prove you wrong. Somebody killed him. He didn't kill himself, either accidentally or on purpose. If you guys are too freaking busy to do the leg work, I'll do it for you." I stood to leave.

"Sit, Miss Bourke."

I sat. "What?"

"You're going to end up getting in trouble and I'm going to have another case on my hands. I don't have time for another case. I'm flat out. We're running around like bricklayers in Baghdad. Stay out of this, and let us do our job."

"Yeah, well your job," I jabbed the table with my finger, "is telling you Joel killed himself. You're flat-out wrong. How do you expect me to accept that?"

"I'll tell you what. When my partner gets in tomorrow, we'll review all of the evidence. We'll talk to the medical examiner. I'll keep an open mind. But if I can't find any evidence that points to anything but suicide, you drop off, okay? You're a nice girl but already I'm getting tired of seeing your face. Go back to whatever it is you do—auditions, movies, whatever—and stay out of our way. I'm saying this with all of the kindness and compassion I can muster. Losing someone is difficult. Don't compound it by trying to make a conspiracy out of it."

Enough was enough. I stood quickly, tipping my chair and almost throwing it backwards. "Believe what you want. I'll let you know when I've got evidence." I threw open the door and stormed out, my ears deaf to his calls. I got halfway through the maze when it occurred to me that I had no idea how to get to the exit. "Son of a bitch. Can somebody tell me how to get the hell out of this place?"

I jumped when a hand took me gently by the elbow.

"Allow me, Miss Bourke." Perkins guided me to the door. I was front-loading all my embarrassments for the day.

"Gee, thanks."

He had a half smile on his face. "It can be a bit confusing the first time. Go home and get some rest. It's Sunday. A day of rest. Not that you'd know it by my schedule. You look like a good sleep would do you well."

And now the nice policeman was telling me I looked like shit. What was that thing Melon-Head said about self-doubt? There was a serious shit-kicking going on inside my skull right now. I was losing.

He stood at the front door and looked like he would tell me something, maybe lecture me again. Then he must have thought better of it because he just shook his head and held out his hand. "Best of luck, Miss Bourke. I hope you get your life sorted out."

I shook his hand and thanked him. For what I wasn't sure, but our social mores are pretty ingrained.

I stood in front of the station and took stock. I clearly wasn't going back to Australia. Not yet, anyway. I couldn't leave Joel, not as a suicide. And I couldn't leave his murder unanswered.

"Damn. What in the hell am I supposed to do now?"

In the movies, the detectives and the police went back over the victim's last movements, what he did and who he met the day before he died. Retrace their steps. I had no idea what Joel was doing the day he died. I left in the morning with him asleep on his sofa bed, sitting up with his headphones half off his head and Al Roker on the TV. I guess the best place to start would be his laptop and phone calendars. I hoped he was more organized than I was.

I was parked across the street, and as I jogged back to my car, a police lady was flipping open her ticket book.

"Wait, wait, wait. I'm here. I was just leaving."

She shook her head and fished a pen out of her breast pocket. "And I just got here. Your meter expired. I've got to write you a ticket."

"But I was just in there. In the station. I was talking to," I fumbled the card out of my back pocket, "this guy." I handed her the card. "Constable Perkins."

"Life-time Larry? What were you talking to him about?" She handed the card back. And closed her ticket book. Yes.

"Why "life-time"?"

"He's been a Constable since I was finger-painting in Miss Lawries Grade 1 class. He's been passed over for promotion so many times that I don't think he even tries any more. Lovely guy, though. What's he helping you with?"

I unlocked the car door. "My roommate committed suicide two days ago."

"Yeah, so?"

That was unexpected. "What do you mean?"

"Suicides aren't that uncommon in this city. Show business, right?" I nodded. "Too many to count. I think the rate here for you kids between, what, 18 and 25?" I nodded again. She was psychic. "It's damn near double the national average if you're in show business. So, what were you talking to Perkins about? How is he supposed to help? The kid's dead, right?"

"You're pretty callous, aren't you?" This lady was pissing me off, cop or no cop. "I don't think it was suicide. He had everything to live for. There was no note. He would have told me if there was something wrong. I just spent half an hour in there trying to convince life-time Larry that he should be investigating a murder, not a suicide." I was getting a bit loud, I think. I took a deep breath. "Sorry. He was a good friend. It's not right. I've got to go. Thanks."

I got in the car, fastened my seatbelt because she was watching and left as quickly as I could.

Shit. I was letting my anger get the better of me, but at least it was anger now. I was feeling the funk until I met Perkins and he transformed it to anger. I should thank him for that. Then the ticket lady amped it up a degree. I was pissed. Too bad I didn't know who I should be pissed at.

It wasn't much more than a five-minute drive back to the house. Sweeney wasn't there. The place was empty. I unpacked my clothes and re-hung them back in the small closet. It occurred to me that maybe I didn't have that many clothes because there was nowhere to put them. If, at the other end of this, I decided to stay in L.A.—and nothing was certain yet—I vowed to find a better apartment, closer to where work was. Driving an hour to an audition was just stupid.

I put on a pot of coffee and started going through Joel's laptop. Or tried to. He had a password on startup. I tried half a dozen different comics' names with no luck. I was getting tired of the password prompt shaking at me. I thought about it from his point of view. Or tried to. He didn't have a favorite pet that he told me about. I tried his parent's names, with no luck.

Then I typed in my name. I don't know why I did, but it worked.

And I started crying again. Son of a bitch. I was turning into a wuss. I sniffed and opened the calendar. It was empty. Not a single entry. Come on. I wiped my eyes and pulled the charging cable from the laptop to locate his phone. I swiped the screen to unlock it. Fortunately he didn't like passwords on his phone.

The calendar on that was just as empty. I checked his text messages, and aside from one from me telling him to pick up a pizza on the way home over two weeks ago, all of them were from his agent, Kyle Johnson. He was in Joel's phone as "Kyle the Douche". There were a bunch of text messages from Kyle the day he died, all of them saying essentially the same thing: "Where the fuck are you? I need to get back to them."

His "recently called" list was not much more help. He took a call from Kyle the morning he died, made one back to him, and then missed five incoming, all from Kyle. All in the late afternoon / early evening.

So I guess I'd have to talk to Kyle again. I used Joel's phone. He wasn't around to haggle about the bill.

Kyle answered after the first ring with a very tentative "Hello?"

"I'm not the ghost of Joel, I'm just using his phone."

"Ellie?"

"It is. Do you think he killed himself?"

"He did, didn't he?"

"That's not what I asked. Do you believe he did it to himself?"

There was a pause. "Not really, no. I placed a golden opportunity for him on a platter at his feet. No, to be honest, it doesn't feel right."

"Exactly. Try telling that to the cops."

"Is that why you called?"

"No, but it's great to get confirmation that I'm not crazy. Do you know what Joel was doing on the day he died? Before he died, that is. In the morning and early afternoon. I know you talked to him. Did he tell you if he was going to meet someone?"

"No. I just told him about the podcast invite, he flipped his gourd, and that was it. He called me a couple of hours later to double-check the date and time. I was led to believe he was rearranging his gigs on that day to make sure he could make it, and that he wouldn't be rushed to leave. I think the record is Eddie Izzard at 2 and a half hours, and he was looking to top that."

I nodded. "So he was excited. I would have thought so. That guy is his idol, although I don't know what he sees in him. Do you think he was so excited he'd get back into drugs?"

"You knew him better than I did, Ellie. You lived with him. But I don't think so, no. Do you?"

"Hell no. He was almost evangelical about his sobriety."

"So, who killed him then?"

Finally, someone else on the same page. "No idea, Kyle, but I'm going to find out if it kills me."

12

"You want a beer, George?" Bart held the fridge open and waited for a reply.

"Yeah, a lite. Thanks for agreeing to meet me. Steve and Bobby Bowens said they'd be here in five." George sat on the back porch and took a mouthful of beer.

Bart sat beside him. "So what's this about? Turning cold on the movie?"

George licked his lips and shook his head. "Far from it. We think it's a winner. We were talking about it last night, though, and I want to bounce a few ideas off you. You are still the owner of this project." He laughed at the worried look on Bart's face. "Cool it, man. This is a goer. Trust me. I've been around this place a long time. I know something good when I see it."

Bart sat back and took a deep breath. It was delicate times right now. The movie at this stage was nothing but an idea on 150 pages sitting in his bottom drawer. An idea supported by a few backers, but still not a concrete event. Contracts still weren't signed. Negotiations were still ongoing. He suspected George and his two buddies were going to alter the story just enough to get writers 'credits, bumping up their cut of the pie. That was okay. It was going to be a big pie. He could feel it. He'd gladly shave off a point or two to get the support he needed to push this across the line. Soon, if he played the game right, it would be caught on the wave of studio support and all he would have to do is gently steer it to its final destination.

"You want to talk about it now, or do you want to wait until the other two musketeers show up?"

"Let's wait." George took another pull on the bottle. "So, you're renting your guesthouse again? The girl left? Ellie?"

Bart shook his head. "She showed up on my doorstep at about noon. Said she changed her mind. She had something to prove to herself and wanted to know if she could continue living there."

"You let her, of course."

"Of course. Why wouldn't I?

George nodded. "Good. I didn't want to see her go. She's got talent she doesn't realize she's got. You going to talk to her about the girlfriend part?"

"You think?"

"Oh, definitely. Thought of her as soon as I heard the pitch."

"That's because she was sitting over at that table. You couldn't help but think of her."

George shrugged. "I actually think she could do it. But wait until the expert shows up. Steve thought the same." He put his beer on the table. "But what does he know, he's just a casting director."

"Yeah, whatever. I was thinking more along the lines of Emma Stone. But I'll let Steve do his part." He looked at his watch. "What time are they showing up?"

"Any minute now." George hesitated. Then, "So, you and Ellie. Anything ever happen between you two?"

Bart almost choked on his beer. "She's young enough to be my daughter. Good God, George. Besides, she plays for the wrong team. You know that, right?" A car pulled into the drive. "And perfect timing. The other two are here and maybe now you can tell me what this confab is all about."

He retrieved two more beer from the fridge and greeted his guests with cold bottles. Like a good host should.

"Talk to me, guys," he said, once they had settled in their chairs. "What's so important?"

Steve looked at Bowen and George who nodded for him to continue. "So, Bobby, George and I got together last night and were bouncing around some ideas." He held up his hands. "Still yours, though, Bart. We're not hijacking the deal."

"Would never have imagined that you would, boys. And I'm always up for constructive criticism. Fire away."

Steve rubbed his chin, a little nervously. "How dramatic were you planning on making this flick?"

"It's not a comedy, Steve. It's the struggle for survival with a love triangle/alien subplot. I don't see Russell Brand playing the alien, if that's what you mean."

"No, no. It's definitely not a comedy. But we were thinking we go more satirical than you were initially describing, going a bit overboard on some of the symbolism. Make it a quasi-political thing. Remember 'Wag the Dog'? It pushed everything just half a degree farther than reality. I think, in order to get the Oscar buzz for a sci-fi movie we've got to do that."

"Oscar buzz? We don't even have a finished screenplay. Jumping the gun a bit, maybe?"

George put his drink down and leaned forward. "Bart, we think the story is great. But let's put an edge to it. Make some people sit up. Don't play it with the straight sci-fi / love triangle. Get a dig at the current, or past administration. It doesn't matter which one if it makes people go "Crap, did they really just do that?" You know what I mean?"

Bart frowned in thought. "I think so. Pushing it will take someone who's a better writer than I am. Maybe a team of writers. I like it, though. The same essential storyline with an environmental cast to the story—the alien vampires don't want a man to travel to their planet because they've already screwed up Earth."

"Yeah, and the alien vampires are really behind the green movement." Bobby was spit balling.

"Maybe. Need to work on that a bit. I like the concept. It's going to require a reworking of the script." Bart laughed. "But it needs some rework anyway."

They sat nursing their beer and thinking about the project. Steve spoke first. "So, casting. I was hoping for Ellie in the girlfriend role, but since she's gone what do you guys think of Emma Roberts?"

"Too young." George shook his head.

"And too goody-two-shoes in her last roles. Nancy Drew? Give me a break."

"That was years ago, Bart. She's matured as an artist."

George laughed. "You've just got a woody for her, Steve. What about Emily Browning?"

"Huh. Australian." Steve tapped his nose. "If I'm not careful, you're going to take my job. Not a bad choice."

Bart rapped on the table. "Guys, you're jumping the gun. Ellie is still here. She didn't head back home. I was telling George just before you guys got here that she decided she had something to prove and wanted to stay in the house. I can talk to her about the part, if you all agree she's a good choice. I'm not sure myself now what with everything she's been through, but majority rules in this case."

Nods around the table confirmed it.

"Done. I'll talk to her when she gets back. I think she's getting some groceries."

Steve leaned back in his chair. "So if we can snag Colin Hanks for the vamp-alien, and Ellie for the female lead, who'd be a good choice for the male, non vamp-alien lead? The scientist. Needs to be nerdy." He looked around the table. "Anyone?"

"Jake Gyllenhaal." Bart liked the tried and true.

"Too old for the part. The LeBeouf kid?"

"Over-exposed. And nuts" Bobby thought for a second. "The kid who was in Harry Potter - what's his name?"

The three other answered in unison "Radcliffe?"

"Yeah. Him."

"I heard he's retired from movies and is just doing stage. At scale." Bart had heard no such thing, but he loved starting a good rumor.

They sat back and thought again. Finally, Steve leaned forward. "I'll have to run a casting call this one. I'm thinking of a younger Hank Azaria. Got to use your toilet, Bart. Same place it always was?"

Bart waved him in. "Of course. What do you think, I renovated and moved the bathroom to right beside the fireplace?" He looked at George and Bowens. "Azaria? Really?"

A few minutes later Steve came back out carrying two bags of groceries, Ellie by his side. "Look who I found. Ellie, have a seat. I'll put these away for you."

"No, that's fine. I've got them. Thanks." She took the bags from Steve. "You guys know that Melon-Head radio show?"

They nodded. Steve sat back down, his burst of chivalry depleted. "What about him? He's Australian too, right?"

"Yeah. I'm on his show. Just started. I've got to get inside and record it. Catch you later."

Bobby watched her walk into the guesthouse. "I don't get it. How can she be on the show if she's here? She calling it in?"

"It's a recorded program," explained Bart. "It's aired live in Sydney on their Sunday afternoon. That was last night our time. He rebroadcasts the for the local audience."

"We should listen. I want to hear her voice, recorded," said George. "Unscripted and natural."

Bart stood and flicked a couple of switches on his sound system. "I think I've got radio here."

The speakers crackled and Ross Mellon's voice flooded the back yard.

"If you or anybody you know is feeling helpless and doesn't know where to turn, please call the Suicide Prevention number here in L.A. on 1877-7CRISIS, or 1-877-727-4747. If you're listening to this back home in Australia, the number is 13 11 14. Don't waste a second. Life is too precious. Go on, Ellie."

"I was going to say that it seemed strange to me. Joel was doing well. He was advancing in the comedy clubs. He was gaining the respect of his peers. I could understand why he would do this."

"Sometimes the signs are subtle, possibly not visible at all. You can't blame yourself. And I'm not blaming him, either, but people need to understand that there shouldn't be a stigma with mental illness. Reach out. There are people who want to help you."

"All good sentiments, Ross, but I found out just as I got here that his idol, the guy that inspires him, his definition of the pinnacle of success, wanted him to be on his talk show in a couple of weeks. Joel knew this and was supposed to confirm the timing with his agent the day he was killed." There was a pause and some dead air. *"Yeah, I said the day he was killed, not the day he died. There's no way Joel would do anything to jeopardize an appearance on that show. He watched it religiously. This would have been the catapult that launched him into every living room in the US. He didn't kill himself, and he didn't accidentally OD on drugs. Somebody killed him."*

Bart sat back hard in his chair. "Shit."

"Did you hear that, Bart?" George was leaning forward in his chair. "That's insane. Someone broke into your guesthouse and killed Joel? Not a safe neighborhood, Bart. You should move."

Bart swallowed and licked his lips. "Relax, guys. She's mistaken. I saw the body. The house was locked up. He was dead in the tub. No way it could be anything but a suicide. The poor girl is losing it."

Steve got another beer from the fridge on the back porch. "She seemed pretty even-keeled when I talked to her."

"Well, she's obviously deluded." Bart sighed. "It's a shame."

Bobby waved his arms. "Quiet. They're talking again."

"...it appeared that our good friend Joel Sampson did not commit suicide. It is looking more and more like he was killed. By whom, why and other questions need to be answered. Ellie Bourke is still with me in the studio. Say Hi, Ellie."

"Hi Ellie."

"Great. You are truly a natural. She has given me the business card of one of the policemen who attended the death. We're going to give him a call right now and see if we can prod the L.A.P.D. in to action."

"Fucking lovely. She's getting the cops involved." Bart was shaking his head. He clenched his fist. "Why in the hell is she doing that?"

"What's the big deal? It was a suicide. If there even is an investigation, it would take less than twenty minutes, correct?"

"Cops tramping all over the place, reopening old wounds. It's not going to do her any good. That's for damn sure. And guys, we're about to kick off an Oscar-worthy movie. Last thing we need is a pointless investigation getting our names in the news for no reason." Bart rubbed his face. "Damn. Is that why she's not going back to Sydney? To play Nancy Drew?"

Steve put his hand up. "Hang on. It's the cop."

"Melon-Head, Miss Bourke, if you think you have information that pertains to this case I strongly suggest that you come by and tell us in person. We can take a statement from you and direct our investigations appropriately."

"That sounds like a blow-off Constable. You're going to whitewash this, aren't you?"

"We handle each case on its merits. Miss Bourke should come by the station tomorrow and make a statement and if she has more information we'll take it under consideration. Sorry, I can't really say any more than that. I still love your show, though. Bye."

"That's it?" Steve looked around. "Did you guys hear anything the radio guy said? I missed it."

Bart shook his head and turned off the radio. "It's all nothing. The kid offed himself. I don't know what she thinks she's going to find. She better be paying me rent while she's in there and not just running around chasing ghosts."

George tapped the table to get his attention. "Stop pacing and sit, Bart. Tie her to this show. Steve and I will work on Hanks. That's got to be a good draw for her, right? Poor girl needs work to get her mind off things. Steve, have you fed any info to her agent?"

"He's a lazy asshole. I'm going to bypass him from now on. There are a few things. Nothing big, aside from this project." He looked around the table. "We got a name for this thing yet?"

"Needs to have some zing to it, something hi-tech, yet earthy." Bobby thought for a minute. "Nope. I got nothing."

"Earth. Trees. Clouds. Hi-tech. Wires. Wire-cloud." Steve was stringing words together like a brain-damaged librarian.

Bart interrupted. "Got to get the vampire angle in there."

"Blood clouds?"

"What in the hell does that mean, Steve? Leave it." Bart sat back at the table. "We'll wait until the writers get on board, and we'll let them come up with something. Back to Ellie. What am I going to do with the poor kid? She's obviously deluded. I don't want another suicide on my watch. It's going to be hard enough to rent this place when she finally goes."

"She's going to go? I thought we had her for the girlfriend. We need a name for the girlfriend."

"Keep up, Bobby. We've been bouncing the idea around, but we haven't talked to her about it yet. Jesus. You had too much to drink already?"

Bobby Bowens scowled at George. "Piss off, George. We should attach her now."

Bart shook his head. "Give her a couple of days. If she persists on this damned crusade to find the killer of the guy who killed himself, she's going to be no good to us at all." He looked around the table. "Okay guys? We've got to stay focused."

13

Ugh. Why did I tell them I was on the radio? Bart's going to hassle me about that the next time I see him. He swears it was a suicide, I know it wasn't. And I sounded really nasally on the radio. I wonder if I always sound like that? I don't remember hearing that tone before. I was getting self-conscious again.

Joel's surfboard, a mid-sized Becker, leaned against the wall by the sofa bed. I coveted that board. It wasn't as good as the one in storage at my dad's place, but it was still a pretty sweet plank. I felt a little bit bad about thinking it, but I was pretty sure there was nowhere in Idaho this would get used. I logged a thought to ask Joel's brother if I could buy it from him. At a discount, of course. Hell, shipping it back to Boise would probably cost almost all of the $500 Joel paid for it. And it was hardly used. I don't think I spent more than three or four weekends trying to teach him to stay up without breaking his neck. Had a ball, though. He was a true blue Midwesterner.

Damn, I missed him. The younger bother I never had.

Well, if I was going to be detecting, I'd better get at it. The best person was Kyle, I think. He spent more time talking to Joel than anyone else did, as far as I knew. If there were any other candidates, he'd know. I didn't have his number though. I had to call from Joel's phone.

But Joel's phone was dead.

Again.

I plugged it back in and unlocked the laptop. The phone synched, sending a bunch of short files to the laptop. I plugged my headphones into his phone and called his manager-agent. "Kyle, me again. Ellie."

"You've got to call me from your phone. That's freaking me out. It comes up on my phone with Joel's name and face. And the ringtone for his number is his voice saying: "Dude. Pick up". Very freaky. What's going on? What can I do for you?"

"Making sure, first, that you're going to go to the funeral."

"Of course. When is it?"

I wasn't sure. "I don't know, but I'll let you know as soon as I know. It'll probably be Tuesday. His brother's coming into town. I think he's going to be here tomorrow, So I'll double-check with him. But that's not the reason I called. I'm trying to recreate his day before, you know, the killing. What time did you talk to him again?"

"I called him at 10:15. I woke him, by the sound of it. I think he was up late watching late night standup. He freaked. As you would."

"Did he say what he was going to do for the rest of the day?"

"Nothing specific." I heard him take a deep breath. "If I had known what he was going to do I would have told him to come over."

I shook my head. "He didn't do anything. Something was done to him. And there's no way you would have known."

"Yeah. I know. Still, terrible." A deep sigh. The poor guy was taking it pretty hard.

"So he called you back a couple of hours later?" I think I was coming across as nosey, but I needed to figure this out.

"On my mobile. I was at lunch, so maybe 12:30. Definitely before 1:00."

"Still sounded excited?"

"Yeah, still on a high. He had a gig on that Sunday and wanted to confirm the timings to see if it could be shifted to later in the day, or rescheduled to another day. He was going to have to reschedule, but it was no problem. He was seriously stoked. No doubt. You're good at this. Ever think of being a cop?"

"Right. Cagney. Or Lacey. Not likely." I would rather swim in surf filled with bluebottles. "You knew him pretty well, knew the other comics he knew. Were there any who wanted to kill him, strange as that may sound?"

"Joel? Joel was everybody's kid brother. He was under the wing of almost every established comic out there. And it was because he cleaned himself up really quickly and worked his ass off. Joel was old-school hustle. If they'd let him do four shows a day, he'd do four a day for months straight just to hone his act. This wasn't someone who others targeted. I know where you're coming from, but I can't think of a single person who would harm a hair on his head."

"Yet he's dead." I shook my head. "Thanks for talking. I'll put your number in my phone so I don't keep freaking you out, okay?"

I hung up and added him to my contacts. He was a pretty good guy. Maybe I'd dump my agent for him—thoughts for later.

I felt like I was wandering around like a kid lost in the woods. I stayed here to do something that now I didn't think I could do. Doubt, my old friend doubt, was camping in my skull. Maybe there were signs pointing to suicide. He was short-tempered a few weeks ago. Maybe that was the start of his downhill slide.

No. Hell no. I knew him as well as anyone. This wasn't something he'd do to himself. Or to me. I managed to stay in the house a little longer. Tolerance was building. But I had to get out again. I grabbed both phones and headed to my car. One thing that rubbed off on me from this city in the past year was the obsessive need to drive. All the time.

I still had my headphones plugged into my ears so I pressed the play button on them expecting to hear some John Farnham.

Joel's voice pumped through the earbuds, shocking me.

"Day 83. Went shopping with Ellie today. That sounds like a lame day, and for most it probably would be. But we had a blast. Shopping, for both of us, is primarily walking down Rodeo or, in today's case hitting Fashion Island at Newport Beach."

Shit. That was last weekend. Last Sunday. He kept an audio diary.

"I couldn't afford to buy shoelaces there. Not yet, anyway. We window shopped at half a dozen places, getting kicked out of a few for loitering with intent, whatever the hell that means, then Ellie sprung for food at Cali Pizza. Excellent food and a very reasonable price. That would be free for me. Too bad Ellie isn't a guy. Too bad I'm not straight. We make a great couple. Anyway, perfect day. Some gigs next week that I'll be telling you about, dear diary, and hopefully they'll be good news."

Oh, great. This was going to make me bawl. I needed to get out on the road and drive. But I wanted to keep hearing his voice. I got in the car, plugged his phone into the charger and listened to the next audio file. Hearing his voice made me miss him even more, but I couldn't stop listening. I must be some sort of masochist.

"Day 84. Mondays suck, don't they? Even in this business where Monday is usually a day I don't work. A reminder to all of those happy people listening to this, I didn't used to be famous. Note to self: get famous so that last sentence doesn't sound particularly twatish. Second note to self: Thank Ellie for the word "twat". A better word I've never heard to describe some of the - ahem - twats around here. Where the hell was I? Oh yeah. Twat. Not just the past tense of tweet. Ass-hat himself came on to me again today. It doesn't matter how many times I explain to him that I'm not just saying I'm celibate - I actually am - he thinks I'm just rebuffing him. And he showed up with a beer. Hello! Celibate and sober, dickwad. Which of those don't you understand? Oh yeah. Both of them. Soon, I will be well off enough to get a place in the hills. Not looking forward to not living in the same place as Ellie, though. She makes a damned good omelette.

"Okay. Vent vented. Third note to self: This is the genesis of what will no doubt be one of my funniest bits, recorded here for future reference. James Lipton may one day play this audio while I sit on stage, looking vaguely embarrassed and immensely pleased. Here's the bit: Women in this town are addicted to Botox. They make needle appointments like they make hair appointments. They walk around with semi-paralyzed faces that have a plastic-like sheen on them. They look like they should be in a display box at a - no scratch that. They look like they could pass for mannequins - from the chin up. Their hands, though, are right off the crypt-keeper. And then I had this vision of the first woman to Botox her hands, numbing injections in the wrists and back of the hands. 'Oooh, I can't feel my hands!' "

I laughed. He'd gone into his falsetto, Mrs. Doubtfire-from-the-Valley voice. That always cracked me up.

"And then, for the bit, I flop them around like they're completely out of my control and "accidentally" smack myself in the face a couple of times. "At least I can feel that."

"So, Mr. Lipton? Whaddya think?"

I could hear his smile in his voice.

And that explained Tuesday. He did that bit for me for almost half an hour, refining it as he went along. I hurt from laughing for hours. A good kind of hurt.

"That's all for today folks. A warm up gig in Tustin tomorrow night. Hopefully Ellie will give me a lift because if I have to use public transportation to get there I'm going to have to leave now, twenty-four hours in advance. It makes sense, though, I guess. A city so in love with cars would be doing everything they could to discourage the use of public transport. If I want to go to a place just a couple of miles from here I need to make two transfers, travel on three buses. Redickalous. Note to self number 4: Thank Ellie again for all of the schlepping me around that she's been doing."

I sniffed. I had been driving aimlessly, on autopilot. I took stock of my surroundings. I was near the top of Topanga Canyon Boulevard near the 118. Rock climbers were assaulting the boulder there, which served as some sort of testing area for the local climbers. I guess you had to have a hobby. I never understood why people did that. I tried it a bit when I was younger and fell completely and thoroughly out of love with it the first time I fell off the face, about 6 feet up. I only hurt my pride, but it was a massive pride bruise.

I continued under the 118 on to this little cow path called Bella Vista Place. It was still rough out here, like Aussie bush land. There were not many people, but there were still plenty of rabbits. I pulled over and reset the audio file back to the beginning of day 84. He was angry about someone hitting on him.

I listened to the audio again while I sat on the side of the road and watched two rabbits play. I'd never seen rabbits play before, just eat, run or boink each other. These two were playing tag or something in the grass on the side of the hill.

I re-listened to the part about the "twat, ass-hat" a couple of times. I wondered who it was. Joel was very open about the fact that he was on a journey of cleansing, no sex, no drugs and only a healthy diet of rock and roll to maintain his comic rock star lifestyle. And once that journey was communicated, he had no patience for people who disregarded it. It was the one area where he wasn't funny.

I started the car and made my way back south on Topanga Canyon and home. His circle of acquaintances wasn't that large. There were the comics he ran into on his rounds. I knew some of them from my times driving him to gigs and being his support and sometime foil in the audience. There was his agent, a happily married man and father of a deliriously funny two-year-old. There was me, and I couldn't think of anyone else.

My phone rang. I answered and spoke into the headset. "Ellie speaking. Hello?"

Crap. The headset was still plugged into Joel's phone. I held the steering wheel in place with my knees and moved the headset to my phone. "Hello?"

"Ellie, it's Hanson here. Sorry for calling you on a Sunday, but I've got an audition for you tomorrow morning. I just checked my email and the notice came through Friday night."

"Damn, Davie. Aren't I lucky to have you as an agent? What's the part call for? A four foot tall gypsy?" I really didn't want to think about work now.

"What? Why would it be that?"

"That sit-com thing you sent me on last week was for a bimbo. Big tits. You remember what I look like, right? Your tits are bigger than mine. I'll pass on this one, thanks."

"What?"

"Have you been hitting the sauce again, Davie? Pass. I'm not in the mood."

"You really shouldn't pass on this one. The part's made for you."

I sighed. "Fine. What is it?"

"Modern Family. Foreign tutor for one of the families. The goofball father family. The Dunphy guy. You're teaching the oldest daughter, and he hits on you, and hilarity ensues. Seriously, the part is made for you."

Well, I loved that show. "Okay. Give me the details."

"Tomorrow morning at -"

"I'm driving. I can't write this down. Send it to my phone, okay? I'll let you know how it goes. What time tomorrow?"

"Starts at 11:00. Might go to as late as 2:00. Why? Your day filling up already?"

"Text me the details, Dave. Thanks." I hung up and almost immediately heard the thunk of an arrow sound, indicating a received text message. I'd read it when I got back. Modern Family might not be too bad.

If I stayed.

Sweeney was still out in his back yard with his cronies, sitting around the table going on about something. They watched me a little too closely as I walked into the guesthouse. I gave them a wave, and slid the door shut behind me and locked it. They were creeping me out. Middle-aged men perving on me. Middle-aged, overweight and well into their drinks at 3:00 in the afternoon. My skin crawled at the thought.

This place was seductive. Less than twenty-four hours after absolutely positively committing myself to returning to Australia and I was accepting auditions from my shitty agent. I should have turned it down. I had detecting to do.

14

"You think she's been detectin'?" George did a very passable Bush impression.

Bart laughed. "Detecting what? Seriously? There's nothing to detect. The kid killed himself." He was getting a bit boozy. "I'm ordering pizza. Meat lovers." He laughed. "Are you guys meat lovers?"

"Not as much as you are, man." George drained his bottle. "I've got to drain a man about a snake. Or something. Be right back." He swayed a bit as he tacked toward the back door. "I'm bringing beers back with me. Who else wants another?"

"Bring us all one, George, thanks." Bart belched. "Well, guys, I think we're getting all of our ducks in a very nice row here."

Steve shook his head. "Not good enough yet. We need to secure Hanks. He's the keystone to this."

Bart made like he was checking his pockets. "Damn. I don't have his number on me." He cocked his head and looked at Steve. "Do you?"

"As a matter of fact…" He took out his phone and placed it in the middle of the table.

"For real?" Bobby lifted his head off his arms. "You've got Hank's number?"

"You're awake, are you Bobby? I thought we lost you a couple of beer ago." He tapped his phone. "Not Colin Hanks directly, but I've got his agent's number. Obviously. That's what I do for a living."

"So call him."

"Not so fast. What do we want to achieve here? What do we *expect* to achieve here?"

George returned with four bottles. "Achieve with what? What are you talking about?"

"Steve here is going to call Colin Hanks' agent." Bart took a beer and twisted off the top. "Thanks. So what do we expect? Well, I'd love to get commitment to the project from him."

"Come on, Bart. Be realistic. We don't have a finished script, we don't have a title—"

"Yeah, but we've got a hell of a concept."

"You can't even wipe your ass with a concept." Steve rubbed his chin. "At this juncture, the best we can hope for is a strong expression of interest and an agreement to meet with us and the first draft of the script."

"And I thought we agreed on a title."

Bobby looked up again. "Which one did we agree on? Blood Stump?"

George laughed. "Hell no. Sounds like a spin off from the Saw franchise. "Blood Thunder", wasn't it?"

"It really doesn't matter." Bart looked at the phone. "So. We make the call?"

"We make the call." Steve dialed the number, put the phone on speaker and placed it in the middle of the table.

"Is this the famous Bond, Steve Bond? What can I do you for?"

"Marty, long time. You're doing well, I hope?"

"You know I am. Am I on speaker? Who else is with you?"

Bart interjected. "Bart Sweeney here, Marty, with Bobby Bowens the cinematographer and George McPherson. And Steve, of course."

"Hey George, how's the beautiful Daphne?"

"Still beautiful. Thanks for asking. And thanks for taking the time to talk."

They heard paper rustling on the other end of the line. "So, guys, what is it? I've got a pretty full plate right now."

"It's Sunday," said Steve. "Quit trying to blow us off, buddy."

Marty laughed. "Cut to the chase, Steve-o. What do you want?"

"We—Bart, Bobby George and I—are putting together a project with your boy Colin written all over it."

"No, no, no. You're looking for an anchor for a shit project. I wasn't born yesterday, boys. Good talking to you."

"Wait! That's not it." Bart rubbed his eye. "Look, Marty, yes, we need an anchor. We need a high profile attached to this to make it fly, but it's gold. Seriously, gold. The first draft is written. We've got a team of the top writers coming in next week to tweak dialogue and smooth the edges. The concept is a winner."

Marty sighed, hollow sounding over the speakerphone. "Fine. I'll bite. What's the concept?"

Bart smiled at his colleagues. Step one. "Vampires. They're—"

"Oh, hell no. They're dead. That's a meme whose course has run. Not interested at all."

"You didn't let me finish, Marty. The vampires are not the traditional, Romanian Vlad the Impaler types."

"I don't care. They're vampires. They're old hat. Even the glittery ones."

"Not these ones. They're aliens who have been here since the Industrial Revolution, keeping an eye on us. They have an energy source on their planet, just at the edge of where man can currently travel in space, that they know we would kill for. After watching us for the four hundred years since the Industrial Revolution—"

"Three hundred years."

"Yeah, whatever. They've been watching us to make sure we aren't going to invade them. Just keeping an eye on us. They know we don't ask nicely or negotiate; we tend to take what we want. There's a love triangle, environmental subtext and the usual high techie stuff you get with aliens."

George stepped on Bart's explanation. "And it's going to be a satirical view of the green movement, infiltrated by these aliens."

They listened to the tap-tap-tap at the other end of the line. Then a deep breath and Marty spoke. "Interesting. Not what I was expecting. I'll bounce it off Mr. Hanks. What role were you looking at him for?"

Bart smiled. Step two. "The hero / anti-hero alien vampire. He's perceived as the bad guy initially, but by the midpoint of Act Two, the audience starts pulling for him. The love triangle between him, the scientist whose advances allow earthlings to reach the alien vampire planet and the scientist's girl, a translator for the UN," he looked at the other guys around the table and shrugged, "tilts so the girl starts falling for the Hanks character. A bit of a message movie with mankind learning about planet care and the military complex getting slapped down." Bart was just making shit up now, but it didn't matter because the movie that hit the screen wouldn't have much in common with the discussion they were having today.

They could almost hear Marty nodding. "Yeah. I like it. I definitely like it. Is the script complete?"

"Yes, yes. The first draft is. About one fifty pages. Needs to be trimmed a bit, but it's workable."

"That sounds good. Send me a treatment, and I'll get in front of Colin. Let me know when the script is in better shape. Or when it's story-boarded. Remember, he's not attached yet, okay? You can say he's showing interest. You can say he's in discussions, but he's not attached until I tell you he's attached. Understand?"

"Absolutely, Marty. I'll get something to you tomorrow morning, okay?"

"Sounds good, Bart. Talk to you tomorrow. And then I'll talk to Colin. Make this work, guys." Marty hung up.

There was a few seconds of silence, then George let out a whoop. "Hot damn, Steve. You came through." Then he looked at Bart. "Translator? That just come to you?" He smiled. "Nice touch. So, how's the treatment?"

"How many pages in a treatment?"

"What? You kidding me?"

"I'm a director, George. I'm not a writer."

"So get whoever wrote the script to do the treatment."

Bart put up his hand. "I wrote it. It's probably shit, which is why we need some real writers to come in here and fix it up."

Bobby shook his head. "You're flying this by the seat of your pants, aren't you? You're going to crash and burn. If our names are attached to something responsible for drawing in one of the biggest film dynasties in this city, and fails them miserably, we'll all be living in cardboard boxes under the Santa Monica Pier."

Bart sat back and snorted. "That's never happened before, and I can guarantee you that it's not going to happen now. This is nothing. The story's already written. I can put my head down and get the treatment out in twelve hours. I won't sleep tonight. Sleep is for the dead. Fuck it. I've been in worse situations. So have you, for that matter. To the victor go the spoils and all that. You can't hit what you don't shoot at. Who said that?" He snapped his fingers. "That hockey player guy."

Bobby shook his head. "Gretzky said, 'You miss 100% of the shots you don't take.' I think that's what you're talking about."

"Exactly. That's what I meant." Bart looked at the other three around the table. "What's the biggest gamble you guys made? The farthest you've gone to achieve a goal?" He tipped back his beer then put the bottle on the table and grabbed a new one. "Bobby?"

"I'm a camera guy. I point the camera where you director types tell me. I'm pretty by-the-book, pal."

George laughed. "You're pretty boring, Bobby. I've had my share of ledge walking. Producing is not all martinis and parties. There was this time we needed to get this actor, who we all know well, on set for the final day of shooting. There was no way we could replace him, and we were running out of time and money. The idiot had spent the night with his girlfriend and her twin brother, going through more opiates and alcohol than I've seen an entire football and NBA team go through. And, apparently, plenty of sex and I don't want to know who was doing what to whom."

Steve chuckled. "You get any pictures?"

"Maybe I'll show you later. That's not the ledge I was talking about. Remember, this was the last day of shooting. We didn't have the location beyond the day, the scene was critical, and we would have blown the budget if we tried to recreate it." He held up his hand. "No, I won't tell you the location. It'll give away the movie and the actor. I don't feel like getting sued. Comes time to shoot the scene, and he's comatose."

"So how'd you get him to the set."

"You see *Pulp Fiction*?"

"No way. The adrenaline scene?"

George laughed. "Dead on. He was flat on his back in his apartment - included in his rider, by the way, an apartment instead of a trailer, and aside from a very weak pulse, he was gone from this world. Didn't want to get a doctor involved, didn't have the time, anyway, so I acquired a syringe full of adrenaline and drove it through his chest bone, into his heart and gave the mother fucker a jump start."

The other three were laughing at this point.

" 'Acquired'?" Steve asked.

"Yeah, another don't ask. I still don't think, to this day, he remembers what happened to him. He complained about the bright lights and the pain in his chest the rest of the day. He hasn't mentioned it since."

Bart laughed again. "Nice, but I've got you beat. What about you Steve? Anything in your past that spells risk?"

"Nothing. Not much risk in my job at all. I find people for other people. The most daring my job gets is sending a brunette when the producer asks for a blonde. And sometimes I do it because I know it cranks you guys up." He laughed and looked at Bart. "So spill it. You've got George's adrenaline in the heart story beat, do you? You going to tell?"

Bart put his beer to one side. "I think I better switch to coffee. This is going to be a long night."

"No, pal, you can't start this and not follow through. Spill the beans."

Bart looked at Bobby and held his gaze for a few seconds. Then the same with George and Steve. A small smile formed on is face. "We're in business together with this movie, right?" They nodded. "The four musketeers, right?" More nods. "So I'm going to tell you the lengths I will go to—have gone to—to make sure that ends are met. I am the poster child for the ends justifying the means." He licked his lips, taking a perverse pride in the story he was about to tell. They wouldn't soon forget it.

"Out with it." Steve drummed his fingers on the table. Bowen yawned.

"You guys know I made *Beast of Bondi* in Australia, right? That B-grade horror, surfer slash flick?"

Bowen snorted. "You're generous calling it B-grade. It barely made it to that level."

Bart smiled. "I bought this house with DVD royalties. There will always be teenage boys willing to fork over their paper route money to see tits and gore." He rubbed his hands together. "So, we're in rehearsals for this movie. Maybe a week all up, and the entire week I'm badgering the lead psycho about his limp. The character was supposed to have a pronounced limp. It informed his motivation and was essential for the audience to recognize him in Act 2 when he was in disguise."

Bart looked at them and continued. "He couldn't limp for shit. We already signed the guy—couldn't get out of the deal without killing the movie, and the asshole couldn't limp."

"Put pebbles in his shoes."

Bart waved that idea away. "We did that, George. We tried everything. Whenever he tried to turn on the limp he walked like Richard Dreyfuss' Richard the Third in *Goodbye Girl*."

There were blank stares around the table. "How fucking old are you, man?" Steve shook his head. "A little more info?"

"Like a gay hunchback of Notre Dame. For a horror movie he was the funniest man on screen."

"You couldn't shoot around it? Bring in a stunt limp?"

"No time and no money. Last day of rehearsals, and I pulled him aside and spent, oh something like four hours working with him. He was a great terror, an ugly face and horrible teeth. He'd shaved his head. He worked out for six weeks before rehearsals and was Wolverine-ripped. But the fucker couldn't limp."

Barry frowned. "I saw that movie, I'll admit, and his limp looked fine. It looked very convincing."

Bart nodded. "We worked on him right up to the end of the day on Sunday. We started shooting on the Monday. I was seriously screwed. So I figured if I couldn't teach him to limp, I'd force him to limp."

"What, you bound his feet?"

"Technically speaking, I'd only have to bind one, but we had already tried that." He looked at the three of them. "This stays between us, okay?"

"Spit it out, Bart. Wouldn't want anything to happen to the guy who's behind this movie, would we guys?" George looked at Steve and Bart, the three of them looking like this was a good joke.

"Okay. So I brought him to my place - I was renting a house in Collaroy while I was there - and loaded him with every mind-altering substance I had. He was paralytic. Completely blotto. He couldn't stand at all. He was slumped in a chair in the kitchen. He had, by my recollection, a spoonful of smack, a couple lines of coke and almost half a bottle of Jack. He had no fucking idea where he was."

"Smack? You're a junky?"

Bart waved away the suggestion. "I had some habits in my youth." He rubbed his chin, looked at the guesthouse and lowered his voice. "I'm not a user now, but I was. Keep that between us too, okay?"

"You and everyone else in this business. Not a big surprise. The limp?"

"Yeah. Not exceptionally proud of this," said Bart, though his face seemed to contradict that statement. "I had a meat tenderizing hammer in the kitchen. I slapped him on the face a couple of times to make sure he was well and truly out of it, then I broke a couple of bones in his foot. Four, I think the x-ray ultimately said. We shot scenes the next morning with him hopped up on painkillers, none the wiser. He had no idea how he hurt his foot, and still doesn't know to this day."

Bart sat back and looked at his partners' reactions. He regretted telling them already, not because he was ashamed of what he had done —secretly, he was proud of his ingenuity—but because he had exposed a secret that could be used against him sometime in the future.

Steve broke the silence. "That is seriously fucked up, Bart. Seriously. Don't tell us any more stories like that. Don't you have a treatment to write?"

Bart chuckled. "You need big balls in this business Stevie. You need to do what needs to be done. I thought you knew that."

15

I didn't like waking up in the morning and not hearing Joel snoring on the sofa bed. It was a reassuring sound that couldn't be replaced. I showered and did the things I needed to do to sort out the day ahead of me. Good ole Davie had defied all expectations and had set up the dream audition for me, a possible recurring role in a show I loved. I couldn't be late. Definitely had to be prepared. I had to be ready.

And I needed a Joel fix.

I dialed up Day 85 and hopped in my car for the drive to Glendale. It was good to hear his voice, but I was sad it was a one-way conversation.

"What is this, day 84? Nope. 85. An emotionally seesaw day. Woke up tired and seriously missing bro. I honestly haven't missed him since I got here which is probably strange, being that we're twins and all. Anyway, almost called that ugly asshole three times today. But I resisted. I vowed that I'd do a full year here on my own, no family help and dammit, I'm going to wait the year."

I sniffed. His brother would be here today, I think. Joel didn't make it through the year. Not even half.

"So, anyway, enough about Jacob for now. That was the down side of the seesaw. I showed Ellie the flopping, Botoxed hands bit today and I think she liked it. I'm saying I think she liked it because I almost had to give her CPR she was laughing so hard. Let a bit of pee go, I think. I'll need to practice it a bit for a couple of days, get the pacing and the rhythm tighter, but it's got legs.

"I have to say, though, that I'm getting a bit worried about my buddy Ellie. I don't think she's had a good gig in a month or so. That can't be making her feel good. I might see if Kyle can help her out. Her guy is a bit of a jackass. But enough downer shit. Ellie and I had a good laugh today, stayed away from booze and etcetera and I'm ready to crash. And that's the way it is on Tuesday, day 85."

I laughed. His Cronkite was terrible. And I possibly had a good gig coming up. I pulled into the parking lot at the studio and joined the crowd of girls all vying for the same part.

What was it Mellon said? Absolutely know in your heart that you will succeed. And that stuff about kicking the crap out of self-doubt every time it crawled in to my skull. Strangely I felt Joel had my back. The audio was helping. We had been close, but I didn't realize how close. It felt good knowing he had been thinking about me. Again, strange, but true.

I checked in with the PA. I recognized her from the sit-com audition fail the other day. I pointed to the closed door, behind which we'd bare our souls and hope like hell for some glimmer of validation. "Steve Bond back there? Is he running this thing?"

The PA smiled, plastic and insincere. "Mr. Bond is the Casting Director today. You'll get your chance when your turn comes. Please take a seat and make yourself comfortable."

I nodded and smiled and thanked her and sat in a plastic chair by the wall. I still wasn't sure whether it was better to be first, middle or last in these things. I sure as hell wouldn't be first today. There were a good dozen girls ahead of me, most of whom I recognized from other auditions, including Charlotte, my waitress from last Thursday at the Improv. I smiled at her and gave her a wave. She got up and sat beside me.

"Hey Ellie. Small world."

"No it's not, Char. Small world would be me hiking in the hills of Peru and running into you. This is almost a ritual. Your agent and my agent must live together."

"I guess. So what are you doing for work?"

"I had a part in a TV movie about a month ago that paid pretty well. There's that Horse Riding Center commercial. It's national. Nothing since then, though. The wallet's getting pretty thin."

"No, I meant non-acting work. You know, like mine, waiting at the Improv."

I looked at her and was a little surprised at the question. "Nothing. Just acting."

"Wow. You're doing well. Everybody I know here is working a non-acting thing to keep food on the table." She looked at the growing crowd. "Most of them, anyway. How do you do that?"

I hadn't thought of it much. My costs were fairly low. I didn't think getting one gig a month a month was "doing good". "I don't know. I hit the same auditions as you do, I think. Maybe a few more than you do."

She smiled and shrugged. "It's a catch-23, or something."

"Catch-22."

"Whatever. I can't get to some of the auditions because I have to work."

"But, you want to have a career in acting, right?"

"Yeah?" Charlotte, the poor girl, looked confused.

"So you've got to take the leap, right? Commit. All or nothing."

Charlotte winced. "It's the nothing part of 'all or nothing' that scares me."

"You're young. What's the big deal? Fall flat on your face and get up and try again."

"I'm playing it safe. So are you, really."

That surprised me. I never thought of myself as playing it safe. "What do you mean? I *am* all or nothing girl. You just said I was doing well. Where's the safe? I'm not schlepping pizzas or working as a car dealership model."

Char smiled one of those I-know-I-really-shouldn't-be-saying-this smiles. "You *are* sleeping with that director. From that movie you did in Australia."

"Bart? Oh, for fuck's sake, you think I'm sleeping with Bart?"

"You aren't?"

"Jesus, Char. He's older than my father. And gay. And ewww. No. Most emphatically not. How many other people think this?"

"It's, like, common knowledge." She looked apologetic now. The bitch.

"Oh my God. Am I getting parts because people think this? Is that what you're saying? Shit." I turned sideways in my chair and looked at the expressions on her face. Regret, embarrassment, a smidgen of fear, maybe. "Who started this rumor?"

"It's just assumed. He directed you in Australia, you're living in his house. Who wouldn't think it?"

"Someone who actually had a brain in their fucking heads, that's who. Do you know what he's done that's memorable? Anything? He's schlock with a capital S. And I'm not living in his house. I'm living in the guesthouse in the back. If anything, I'm getting parts despite being associated with that - that, asshole." I was steamed. No way to charm a casting director. I needed to cool off. I took a deep breath. There was no point in being angry with Char. She was just passing the story along.

And was too stupid to know any better.

"Look, Charlotte do me a fave?"

"Sure. What do you want?"

"Tell people, as many people as you can, that Bart is an overweight, stinking alkie who I wouldn't sleep with if his was the last dick on earth, okay? Spread the word." I took another stabilizing breath. "Now if you'll excuse me, I've got to get in the right frame of mind for this audition." I looked at Charlotte. "I've met the casting director in a non-work environment. Do you think that gives me an edge?" I paused. She opened her mouth like she was going to answer. "No, never mind. I was just pulling your leg."

She smiled, closed her eyes and did whatever it was she did to prepare. I had to do the same. I needed to drop the adrenaline to normal levels and calm the shit down. I grabbed my headphones and pulled my phone out of my back pocket. It was Joel's. Craptastic. It wouldn't have any of my music. I checked anyway, we had similar tastes in tunes. I checked his playlists to see if there were any looking like pre-gig pump ups. There was one called "writing music"; nothing but a single artist I hadn't heard of before. Zoe Keating. The picture on the album cover made her looked like Jennifer Garner with Sideshow Bob's hair.

From my experience you needed calmness to write, so I put the ear buds in and dialed it up. A slow heartbeat throbbed in my left ear for a few bars followed by the deep resonant sound of a cello layered over itself. I was sucked into an almost trance state. Repetitive, but beautifully melodic cello music swept me to a forest glen, an open field, sunlit meadows, soaring canopies. This was wild. And incredibly focusing. And calming. I checked the artist information and made a note to get her music.

I was in another world, eyes closed, head leaning back against the wall behind me, my heart rate probably in the sub-sixties. This was entrancing.

The elbow to the ribs, not so much so.

I opened my eyes and prepared to launch at Charlotte for interrupting my Zen only to see a short, green-eyed redhead looking at me with a concerned face. "You're Ellie Bourke, right?"

"What of it?"

"They've called your name twice now."

"Shit. Thanks." I stuffed the iPhone into my back pocket and hustled to the table at the front. "Ellie Bourke?"

"No, I'm Trudy Wells."

I shook my head. "I'm Ellie Bourke. You called my name."

"Oh, I'm sorry but that was a few minutes ago. You missed your turn. You'll have to wait until the end now."

"No, I can just go next, then the sequence will be okay." I was told by someone much smarter than me to never piss off the person between you and what you want. Like the counter clerk at a car rental agency. Bitch about the car you get and they'll make sure you get the one with the shimmy at 60 and a funny smell in the back seat. I smiled at her, as sincere as I could fake it. "I'm really sorry about the mess up. My best friend died a couple of days ago and I'm still a bit out of it. The auditioning process is supposed to help me deal. This is my first one since he died. I'm afraid if you put me at the back of the line I'll chicken out and never come back to acting again." Cue puppy dog eyes, with a hint of tears. The tears were actually almost real. The music mixed with the memories of Joel had my emotions on edge.

She looked at me like she was trying to gauge whether I was full of it or not. "Okay," she looked down at the sheet, "Ellie, either that was true or you're one of the best young actresses I've seen come through here in a very long time. You're next. Don't fall asleep again."

I was about to refute the sleeping accusation but then thought better of it. I got what I wanted. Best to keep my big mouth shut. I nodded and stood against the wall near the door to the second office. As good as that music was, I wasn't going to miss my chance again.

After a few short minutes the door opened and a visibly upset Charlotte almost ran out, Steve right behind her. "Better luck next time, Miss Webb." He saw me and smiled. "Oh, you are still here. When you missed your time slot I thought you'd backed out of this. Ideal for you, I think." He held the door and motioned me in to the audition office. A camera was set up and some sides were lying on the table. A middle-aged sparrow of a woman was seated behind the table with her glasses halfway down her nose and a sheet of paper in her hand. "This is Cathy. She'll be reading everything you're not, and she can't do voices so you're going to have to pay attention. Cathy, this is Ellie Bourke."

The woman took her glasses off and looked closer at me, then back to Steve. "This is the girl?"

Steve looked annoyed and cleared his throat. "Not now Cathy. Hand Ellie a side to run through."

"This is what girl, Steve? Are you telling people I sleep with Sweeney, too? For Christ's sake, I don't believe it."

Cathy laughed. "No, honey, it's not that, thankfully. He told me about your roommate and the unfortunate death. Nobody who knows Bart takes that other rumor seriously."

"It's out there that far? Shit. Help me shut it down, will you? I don't want that following me everywhere." I took the side from Cathy and walked back to the mark for the camera. "What is this scene?"

"Dave told you the show, right?"

"Yeah, he did. Fantastic. Don't know how he managed to pull his head out of his—" I looked at Cathy. "You did this, didn't you?"

She smiled and held up her hand. "Guilty as charged." She nodded at Steve. "The boss has been telling me about you. I gave your lazy asshole agent a call and told him if he didn't get you to this we wouldn't use any of his actors in anything we did for the next five years. Got his attention."

I was a little pleased at that. "Okay. The scene?"

"You're just hired. You're sitting at the kitchen table with the oldest daughter trying to teach her how to speak French when the father walks in."

"I speak French."

"I know. I thought of you as soon as I saw the script."

"Just the one episode?"

Steve shrugged. "Who knows? Depends on how well the audience likes you. You might end up being Mork."

I chuckled at that. "Would the character need to actually be French, or just fluent."

"What do you mean?" Steve flipped through the script. "I don't think it says."

"So I could be a traveling Australian, who just happens to speak French who gets hired to tutor the girl in French."

He shrugged. "No reason why not. Use it if you'd like."

I took my place and we ran through the lines. The script was hilarious—but I was biased. I always liked the show. I had a huge smile on my face, as did Steve and Cathy when I was finished.

"That was great Ellie. So far you're at the top of the pile. There are still a dozen or so to go through, but that was good."

"Thanks. This was fun. So why did Char go running out of here like she wanted to hurl? Or cry. Or both."

A kind smile from Steve. "You know her? She and I had a disagreement over the French abilities a tutor should have. She was insisting she could fake it. The producers aren't having anything to do with that. There's plenty of talent around this town—you being a prime example. I told her she didn't have a snowball's chance in hell of getting the part. She wasn't that happy."

"I saw. So, what's next?"

"For you? Enjoy the rest of your day. For me, another twelve hopefuls to traipse through the door to get their dreams steamrolled by me, 'cause that's what I do." Steve dropped his pages on the table. "You have any other plans for the day?"

The door cracked open before I could answer. Bart, of all people, poked his head in the door. "Steve, buddy, when are you doing lunch? I'm right next door."

"Hey Bart, you couldn't call?"

"The Nazi at the front desk wouldn't put any calls through."

"My mobile, you ass?" Steve was smiling as he spoke. Somehow he had a way of insulting people to their face and getting thanked for it.

"Whatever, Steve. Lunch?"

"I was just checking with Ellie here what she was up to."

Bart looked around the edge of the door. "Oh, Ell, didn't see you there. Lunch?"

Not with him. "Oh, I'd love to, guys, but I've got to call Perkins and see if they are re-opening the investigation into Joel's death. I think I gave him pretty good reason."

Bart came in to the room and closed the door behind him. "Don't do that."

"What?"

"Don't keep pushing. He killed himself. It's a sad, but undisputable fact."

"Indisputable." People who don't know how to speak their native tongue annoy the hell out of me.

"So you agree."

And a sub-normal I.Q. "No, Bart, I was correcting your English. He didn't kill himself. I know he didn't. I need to convince the cops he didn't, and I think Perkins is receptive."

Bart squared off in front of me, his finger raised. "I strongly suggest you back off from this. It can only go bad for you."

"What in the hell does that mean, Bart?" He was about an inch shorter than me. This was surreal.

He faltered and backed up a half step, squinting. "Only that you are going to screw up what could very well be a great career if you persist on spending your time tilting at these water wheels instead of focusing on your craft."

I looked at Steve and shook my head. "Windmills, Bart. Windmills. Steve, call me if you want to see me again for this, okay?" I pushed past Bart. "I've got to go see a guy about a thing."

16

Bart watched the door close as Ellie departed. "She's a bit snippy today."

Steve chewed on his lip. "She's been through a lot. You of all people should know." He looked back at the table. "Cathy, we're going to grab some lunch. We'll start again in an hour. Your time is your own."

She pulled a book out of her bag. "No problem, boss. See you then. If you want my opinion, and that's why you hired me, this one was the best by far today."

"I agree." Steve opened the door and held it for Bart. "See you in an hour, Cath." He followed Bart out. "Trudy, it's lunch. Let the young ladies know we're having an hour break."

Steve and Bart left the offices into a brilliant sunny L.A. day.

"Where did all the smog go, Steve? How can this be L.A. without smog?"

"It has it's days. Where are we going?"

"Damon's. The other two are meeting us." He smiled at Steve. "Things are coming together."

"So I take it you got the treatment finished." Steve inspected Bart's face. "You don't look like you were up all night."

"Pharmaceuticals, my friend. Can't live without them." He caught the look on Steve's face. "Legal, doctor prescribed pharms. Relax. I'm not going down that path."

"So how did Marty like it? When's he showing it to Colin? Why are we walking?"

"I'll tell you the answers to the first two questions when we get to the restaurant and are with the others. I hate repeating myself, Steve. And we're walking because the place is just around the corner."

Bart introduced himself at the door and was escorted to a nice corner table, quiet, subdued lighting and out of the way of regular foot traffic. Bowens and George were already there, well in to their drinks.

Steve and Bart slid into the booth. Bart picked up his menu.

"So," Steve took the menu from him and placed it on the table. "What happened this morning?"

Bart picked the menu up again, looked at Steve and checked the specials, smiling. "I think I'm going to have the T-bone steak. And a beer. You guys order yet?" He waved the waiter over.

Steve placed his hands flat palm down on the table. "Spit it out Bart. What happened with Marty? You emailed it to him, right?"

"I didn't email it to him." He held up his hands to stop their inevitable interruption. "Or fax it. I dropped it off in person and waited while he read it. It was pretty rough, being my first treatment, but I had a few lying around from other projects and basically copied the format. Not rocket surgery, guys. He was halfway through reading it and he was smiling and nodding and I knew he was hooked. He thought it was a great idea and is showing it to Colin," he looked at his watch, "as we speak. He said he'll text me after the discussion."

"So it was positive sounding then?"

"What's it sound like Bobby? He loved it. Thought Hanks would too. Called it one of the few original ideas he'd read in a long time." Bart was wallowing in this and fought hard to keep control. This was better than he had expected it would be. He had to stamp his ownership in this fast, before any of the others around the table tried to usurp him. "So I haven't showed you guys the script yet, so why don't I give you copies of the treatment?" He used his Blackberry and forwarded the document to his three friends. "You all should have it now." He placed his phone on the table as theirs all started vibrating almost simultaneously. They grabbed for them and opened the mail and attachment. Bart laughed. "Looks like a convention of doctors."

The drinks arrived and they sat back and read while they waited for their food.

George finished first. "Not bad, Bart. Not too bad at all. Didn't think you had it in you."

"Thank you, George. Really." Bart yawned. "Sorry. Been busy. As you can see. Writing and drinking and burying bodies. Literary bodies, of course." He turned and looked over his shoulder at the wait station. "What in the hell is taking our—" He stopped when his phone started vibrating. He received a text message. *"He's interested. Wants to see the script. When will it be available?"* Bart looked up from his phone, his face telling the story. He handed the phone to the left, to Steve, who read the message and passed it on. By the time he received the phone back they all were chatting animatedly among themselves.

The waiter arrived with their steaks. Bart grabbed him by the arm before he left. "Pal, can you bring us a bottle of bubbly, best you've got? We're celebrating here."

"Don't you think that's a bit premature," asked Steve. "I mean, we don't have any commitments for money or actors and you yourself admitted the script needed an overhaul to clean it up and make it workable. There are still many hard rows to hoe."

Bart patted the waiter on the arm. "Don't listen to Janice here, just get us a bottle and four glasses." He turned back to the table and held up his phone. "Do you guys realize the impact of this text message? We can go to the money people and tell them, hand on heart, Colin Hanks is in discussions to be the lead. We can sign other actors, get a crew lined up. This is a go, gentlemen." He slapped the phone back on the table. "Almost too good to be true, eh?"

"Let's hope you don't have to break Hank's foot to close the deal." Bobby looked at the other two. "So, while Bart here tries to find some writers to polish this thing we need to find the rest of the main characters. Line up crew." He looked back at Bart. "It's key you get a good script in front of Hanks as quickly as possible. There are good writers and there are bad writers in this city and if you can't tell them apart, let me know if you need help. I know a couple of good guys who can polish fast."

"So Bobby wakes up. I was beginning to doubt you were interested in this."

"Bart, baby, I wasn't. Not until you got the thumbs up from Marty. If we get Hanks attached to this we can get it on the screen. It may be shit, but it'll get on the screen."

George finished his drink. "It's our job to make sure it's not going to be shit."

The champagne arrived and Bart poured out a glass each. "To Bloody Thunder."

"Blood Thunder."

"Whatever, Bobby. To Blood Thunder. Our chance of a lifetime."

The chorus sounded around the table: "Hear, hear." "Let's do this." "It's on."

Steve took a small sip of the bubbly and slid the glass back. "I'm going back to work auditioning actresses for a small role. It should be the last time I do anything unrelated to this project. We need to think about a casting call for the rest of the parts." He sipped his juice. "Bart, have you talked to Ellie about the female lead? The translator part?"

He sighed. "We've talked about this. She's not right in the head. I'm seriously considering buying her a ticket myself and sending her back to Australia."

Steve leaned in on his elbows. "Are you crazy? I auditioned her this morning for a role in a weekly sitcom and she was perfect. On pace, funny, great timing. You should reconsider. Based on what we talked about, and what I've read in this treatment, she would be perfect for the role. A smart, funny, strong female lead will draw the 18 - 25 male and female market. And she is definitely that."

Bart shook his head. "You saw her for, what, thirty minutes? She's living in my back yard. She's messed up in the head. That Emily chick— anybody know how to reach her?"

"No, no. Bart, you agreed that Ellie was the best choice yesterday. What changed your mind? It was not even twenty-four hours ago."

"Steve, that wasn't agreement so much as an acknowledgment of majority opinion. I think I did express some reservations then, and I have even more now. So, Emily Browning? Who's her agent?"

George made a note in his phone. "I'll track her down but only as a back up. I think we need to put this in front of Ellie first. Oh, and by the way, no Daniel Radcliffe. He really does have a thing on stage for the next six months."

"Maybe we go for a new face then. Launch some young actor's career. Have you seen anybody lately who can do scientist and action anti-hero?" Bart tried to swing the conversation away from Ellie.

"I'll look around. We're going to have to do a cattle call. A new face. Not a bad idea. I still believe Ellie's our best first choice for the female lead."

Bart was about to answer when his phone rang. "Shit. It's Marty." He shushed the table and answered. "Marty, what can I do for you?"

"I've got Colin here. He's eager to get his hands on a script. The first draft is good enough."

"I couldn't. It's really rough. It may change in the rewrites."

"We expect it will. We're not novices. Can you send it today? Don't worry about the roughness of the draft. You've been banging around this town long enough. I'm going to text you my email address and Colin's address. Send it to us this afternoon. I'm keen on moving this forward. And quickly. There's a small window of opportunity in Colin's schedule and we want to make sure we grab it."

"Absolutely. Just know it is first draft. I've got some writers lined up—"

"Don't worry about writers. We know some."

"But—"

"Relax. You get writing credit. These guys are fixers. They will be so far down the credits the only way anyone sees their names is if we put a cookie at the end."

Bart looked at his colleagues watching him, his phone stuck to the side of his head. "Okay. I'll send it this afternoon. We'll be looking for financing shortly. A positive reaction by Mr. Hanks would be very helpful in that regard."

"I'm sure it would. He mentioned that if the script was as good as the treatment was—or at least has the potential to be as good—his father would like to come in as an Executive Producer. Hands off, of course, but a good name to have on the page when you're wandering around with your hat out."

Bart blinked. "Tom?"

"He only has one father. I need to run, Bart. I look forward to getting the draft this afternoon. Thanks. Later." He hung up.

Bart sat with the phone to the side of his in stunned shock before he mumbled "bye" and placed the phone on the table.

"What about Tom," asked George. "I heard you say Tom. Hanks?"

Bart nodded. "I need to get a draft script to Marty and Colin this afternoon." His phone vibrated and he checked the contents of the incoming text. "That's Marty's and Colin's email addresses."

"Colin Hanks? You're going to send him a script directly? I thought you said it was too rough."

"They're insisting and have a couple of fixer writers standing by. If he likes it he's in, and since the treatment is just a condensed version, and he liked that, I think we're sitting pretty."

Bobby nodded and smiled. "Sounds like it's clicking. What. About. Tom?"

Bart blew out a breath of air. "Yeah. The Tom of the Hanks clan has said he'd like to get on board as a hands-off executive producer if his son likes it."

Steve banged the handle of his knife on the table to drown out the hubbub after that remark. "Hey, calm down. This is good news whether he's hands-off or hands-on. His name attached is pretty much a guarantee of box office success."

Bart felt funny. This was the biggest single thing that had ever happened to him, and it was his baby. He spawned it, and it would place him firmly in the company of A-list directors and producers. Not only would he be the director, he'd be the credited writer and one of the producers.

He took a deep breath and addressed the table.

"Guys, this is huge. We don't do things halfway for this. I'll be going back to my place to give the screenplay a final once over before I send it out. I want someone to come with me and sanity check it."

"That'll be me." Bowen raised an eyebrow. "I've got an English Lit degree from USC. Should be a bit of help."

"That's great, Bobby. Appreciate it." Bart scrubbed his hair with his fingertips. "Listen, guys, this is a do or die opportunity. Having the Hanks on board is a double-edged sword. If we don't do this professionally and with a very high degree of quality, we're screwed. If we do this halfway and embarrass ourselves in front of them, we might as well pack it up and move to Idaho and farm potatoes. One hundred percent all the way, all the time." He looked around the table and smiled. "I told you what I did to get the movie in Australia made, on time and under budget. Believe me when I tell you I will stop at nothing to make sure this goes off without a hitch. Nothing."

Bobby grunted. "Dude, if you break one of Colin Hanks' feet for this movie I'll gladly move to Idaho and farm potatoes. Under an assumed name."

"Fuck off, Bobby. It was an illustrative story. But I will do anything at all. As long as I don't think I'll get caught."

George interrupted the laughter. "If the Hanks are involved, we take them with us to get money. I say we leave the financing until it's confirmed and start lining up cast. Email me a copy too, Bart, and I'll break down the characters we need to fill and go over it with Steve after he's finished his auditions this afternoon. You up for that Stevie?"

"Yeah. Let's assume we've got Colin for argument's sake and use him to line up the rest. We can always backtrack later if we have to. The female lead and the scientist need to be the top two on the list after the young Hanks, and I want to toss Ellie into the ring one more time."

Bart vigorously shook his head. "That will be one of those unprofessional things I was talking about. We can't afford to do that. There are rumors all over the city that I'm sleeping with her, to start with, and the whole Joel-didn't-kill-himself thing marks her as stark raving mad. I say give her a wide berth."

Steve sighed. "I give up. I'll track down Emily Browning, but I'm not convinced. She's got the looks but I don't see "action start" in the way she moves. We need more athleticism than she brings."

"Kiera Knightly?"

"Pregnant. She's taking a year off after the birth, so her window of opportunity is just a mirage it's so far out."

"Who else is in that age group? Emma Watson?"

"At university. Two more years."

"Emma Roberts?"

"We talked about her. I think she's way too sweet for this. The female lead needs to be tough mentally and physically. I don't think she can pull that off."

"Remains to be seen. She might surprise you. Any other Emma's you know?"

Bobby thought. "Not off the top of my head. Why does it have to be Emma?"

"It does't, Bob. Just joking. Wait, there was that movie about the English girl's school that Brand was in."

"You mean 'St. Trinian's'?"

"Exactly. Who was the lead in that?"

Steve snapped his fingers. "Talulah Riley?" He thought about it for a minute. "She might work. Look, this is my area of expertise and if we can't have Ellie then I'll make sure we find someone almost as good. I've got the bill. Let's get the hell out of here. We've all got work to do."

17

Wow. Three hours later and I was still buzzing. That was one of the best auditions I'd ever done, here or in Australia. Bittersweet, though. Joel should be here to share this.

I took a deep breath. It was slowly sinking in that he was well and truly dead, and it didn't matter how it happened, he wasn't coming back. I popped the ear buds in and dialed up day 86. I liked this exercise. I think I might get someone to put them together and take the funny bits and put some kind of CD together.

"Day the 86th. Can't say this is going to end up in my top ten all time favorite days.

"Slept in and missed a meeting with my agent. Now he's usually pretty good about that kind of thing, but he was a complete asshole about it today. I discovered that I'm a validation junky. The crap he spewed at me was downright hateful. Comparing me to Pauly Shore. Shit, that was low. And then Carrot Top. I may need to find another agent.

"Anyway, I've got an ethics question for you, imaginary listeners. I overheard a fairly respected comic deliver a joke this afternoon that was, as a joke, not too bad, but as a "delivered" joke it was the stinkiest pile of cat vomit I'd ever heard. I know, I know. You can't hear cat vomit. But if

you could, it was this joke. I want to steal it. I know I can deliver it better. Hell, Pauly Shore could deliver it better.

"Can these recordings be used as evidence in a court of law? Don't know. Don't care, really.

"So the bit goes like this: This pirate walks into a bar with a ship's wheel attached to his groin. The bartender says, 'Hey, there's a ship's wheel attached to your groin.' The pirate nods and says, 'Yeah. It's driving me nuts.' "

I chuckled. So that was the genesis. And this time he didn't screw it up. He laughed on the recording and continued.

"Funny, right? Well the delivery that I heard was as flat as the cornfields in Nebraska, had the pacing of a one-legged man and was so quiet that I could barely hear it. I don't know if he was ashamed of the gag, or just afraid he was going to screw it up. Doesn't matter, really. There was dead silence after the delivery.

"Decision made: I'm stealing it. Nobody can do it better than I can. I'm assuming. And if this recording is used as evidence against me, my defense will be that the original guy killed it within an inch of its life and I revived it. Plus, finder's keepers and the salvage laws of the high seas."

I liked his logic. Not that it mattered any more. He exhaled and continued talking.

"That's all. Humpday over. Gig tomorrow night at the Improv, a little later in the night, which is good. Ellie is providing transport, which is even better. I'm designated driver which owns several levels of suckery, but sober is as

sober does, or some such shit. I think I'll open with the pirate bit, see how it goes.

"This brings episode 86 to a close. I'm here all week. Try the veal and tip your waitress."

That was that. I had been absently cleaning while I was listening. All of Joel's clothes were folded and packed away in his suitcase. The room was cleaned. His personal possessions, save his phone and laptop, were stacked in boxes ready for his brother to pick up when he arrived.

I then had one of those out of body, surreal experiences that I think are called cognitive dissonance.

I turned away from the pile of clothes I had just finished folding and looked out the window and saw Joel. Vertigo, a mental vertigo where my thoughts hammered into each other, knocking me off balance. Basically, I fucking freaked out. It took a couple of seconds before I realized I was looking at his brother. The two of them were identical, except for hair length. Jacob's hair was a bit shorter, but seriously, if I didn't know he had a twin I would have sworn on a stack of bibles I was looking at the ghost of Joel.

I stood rooted to the spot, in front of the kitchen sink, looking out the window as Jacob slowly walked through the yard. He seemed a bit lost. He was heading for the back door of the main house.

"Shit, Ellie. You're being an idiot." I slid open the front door and called out. "Jacob? Jacob Sampson?"

He changed course and came toward me. "I'm in the right place then? I'm Joel Sampson's brother. I'm here to make the funeral arrangements and to pick up his stuff. And who are you?"

I touched his face like I was a freaking basket case. "You look exactly like him. Except his hair was longer." I pulled my hand away. "Sorry."

He looked surprised. "Were you his girlfriend? We hadn't heard much about him while he was here. Something about needing to do this completely on his own so he knew it was real."

Girlfriend. Well, they clearly didn't communicate that much. "We both lived here. Come in and sit. I think we need to talk." I stood to one side and let him in, feeling a bit embarrassed about the hand on the face thing. "I'm not a total trog. Sorry for touching you like that. It took me by surprise, seeing you. You really are identical. Except for the hair."

Jacob's smile was kind. "He let it go, did he? Rebelling against the folks. Don't worry about the touch. It was sweet." He sat on the sofa. "What's your name?"

I sat sideways in the chair at right angles to the sofa so I could look at him in the eye. It was spooky. "I'm Ellie Bourke."

"He didn't tell me he was living with a girl." He raised an eyebrow. "If I'm honest, I'm a little surprised. I would have bet money he was a little bit, you know." He wiggled his hand back and forth in a seesaw motion. "So how long had you been seeing him?"

"Oh, Jacob, your brother was definitely gay. He and I are—were— just very good friends. I was living here, and he moved in as a roommate about six months ago—"

"—when he got here. Okay. So." He frowned a little bit. "Like I said, I suspected as much. And frankly it makes no difference to me, but I'd like it if you wouldn't share that with our parents if you meet them, okay?"

"They have a problem?"

"We're from fairly religious family." He sighed. "I really don't know if they will have a problem with it or not, and the suicide is enough of a controversy. If you don't mind, I'd like to just keep this quiet. I can tell them later, when it feels right."

The idea of hiding a part of yourself from your parents didn't sit right, but it really wasn't my decision. Jacob knew his parents better than I did. I might drop some hints, though, and see if they picked up on them. Joel would love that. "I'll keep the fact Joel was gay to myself around them. If I meet them." I considered if I should take the next step. And after about one second of consideration, did. "I don't think it was a suicide though, Joel."

"I talked to a Constable Perkins who informed me all of the markers for a suicide were there."

"Except there was no note, and his career was really taking off."

Jacob shook his head. "Less than—"

"—I know. Less than twenty percent of people committing suicide leave notes which seems ridiculously low since all of the suicides in every movie and TV show I've seen leave a note. Still. No note. And then there's the career."

Jacob sat back and tucked a leg under his butt. "Career? He was doing well?"

"For the length of time he was here, yes. I take it he was the talk of the town in Boise. Before he left, I mean."

Jacob shrugged. "He was okay. It is Boise, after all. Not the comic breeding ground he may have made it out to be. He had a regular gig Tuesdays, Thursday and the weekend at the Funny Bone. Frankly, I was a bit concerned about him. We weren't completely surprised to hear he died. This city chews people up like toothpicks. He was starting to get in with some unsavory characters, dabbling in some drugs and getting pretty hammered during his weekend sets. I assumed it would escalate when he got here."

That explained a lot. "Yeah, it did. Until about three months ago. He had one of those flashes showing him what he would turn out like if he kept it up. Ran into an idol of his acting like a babbling fool. He stopped all booze, drugs, cigarettes and, for reasons he never did explain, sex. He's been clean ever since."

"He says."

"I lived with the guy. We were very, very open with each other. The last night he was alive he did a gig at the Improv and absolutely killed it. I was there and had three double scotch. Couldn't feel the end of my nose. He was stone, cold sober, drove me home and crashed watching late-night comics on TV." I shook my head. "No, he was sober. Three months today, if he was still alive." Ah, shit. If I wasn't careful I was going to start crying again.

I changed the subject somewhat. "I'm surprised the funeral is going to be here. I would have guessed you'd take his remains back to Boise and have the ceremony there."

"Nah. He loved it here. Since he was twelve he said he wanted to come here. We'll have a ceremony at the crematorium tomorrow, then I'll take his ashes up the hill behind the Hollywood sign and leave them there."

I sniffed. Now I was going to cry. "He'd like that, I think." I grabbed a tissue and wiped my nose. I was going to hell. "You really think it was a suicide? Is depression common in your family?"

"I don't believe so, no. But I don't think there's a genetic link to it, is there? Look, Ellie, I'm a Detective in Boise. If it wasn't a suicide then it would have to be either an accidental death, or a murder. I don't see it being either. If he were as clean as you say he was, the drugs wouldn't be recreational. He would have intentionally overdosed to kill himself. And as for murder, so far I've seen no motive, no suspects, and the guy was alone in a locked building. That's the kind of thing Agatha Christie has to figure out." He shook his head. "Occam's razor leaves us with suicide"

"Who's razor? What do you mean?"

"Occam's razor. The simplest explanation is the most likely one. For whatever reason, Joel thought the only solution to whatever problems he had was to kill himself. I've never felt that way myself and can't imagine what it must have felt like, but he must have been in some kind of pain to do this." He leaned forward and took my hands in his. God, he looked like Joel. "I know you've been a very close friend of Joel's. Don't beat yourself up. Frequently there are no overt signs. It's unlikely you would have noticed anything out of the normal, and less likely you could have stopped him once he made his mind up. I'm sorry."

I pulled my hands back. "Well, that is a load of shit. My mother committed suicide when I was ten and I knew a week before she did that she just wanted to go away. I was ten. You think I'd forget that look? Joel was happy. He was succeeding. He was coming up with some pretty fucking funny jokes. You obviously didn't know your brother very well."

"You're upset. Imagine how I feel, Ellie. My twin, the person closer to me than any other person could possibly be, is dead. Gone forever. We had a good relationship until our mid-teens when we drifted apart, but that doesn't mean I didn't love him."

"You're a cop. I would have thought you'd take my concerns a bit more seriously." My frustration levels were increasing. "Your Occam's razor theory is a lazy man's approach to a problem. The fact is, Jacob, Joel did not kill himself. I want to thank you for coming by, though. I was beginning to doubt it myself, but this discussion has strengthened my belief that something stinky happened with your brother. If you loved him as much as you say you do, you'd believe me." I was about to cry, and I was damned if I was going to do in front of him. "Take Joel's stuff and get out of here, okay? I need to be alone right now."

Jacob stood and rubbed his hands on his pants. "Look, Ellie, I'm sorry. I'm not too good with interpersonal things."

"You're a public servant. A cop. I would have thought it went with the territory."

He smiled sheepishly. "I'm with the K-9 unit. I related to dogs much better than people." He looked at the personal belongings I had piled together, all that remained of Joel. "I want to leave things here until I head back to Boise. Is that okay? I can take it now, but I'm staying in a very small hotel room."

I stood. "Leave it here. I'm sorry if I'm coming off like a bitch, but you're wrong. Perkins is wrong. Sweeney is wrong. You're all wrong. Joel was not suicidal and he wasn't on drugs and I'm starting to sound like a crazy lady."

"Who's Sweeney?"

"My landlord. He found Joel in the tub." I swallowed. "I'm serious. I need you to leave. I'm about to lose it and I can't do that in front of you."

At least he was a gentleman about it. "Okay. I'll give you a call later." He turned to leave, then turned back. "I don't have your phone number."

I took his phone and called mine. "Now you have mine and I have yours."

He thanked me and walked back out to his car and left. I watched him go from the kitchen, watching through the kitchen window. I was both sad and glad to see him go. He was a carbon copy of his brother in looks, but his outlook on life, his soul, couldn't be any more different than if he planned it that way. Where Joel was outgoing, boisterous and full of life -

bad choice of words - Jacob was a repressed tight-ass. Hard to believe they came from the same egg.

Just before I turned away from the window Sweeney's car pulled into the driveway. He levered himself out and a shorter, rounder person jumped out of the passenger's side. They were all smiles, briskly walking to the house, in through the back door. Then it was silent again.

I sat back in the chair. I had lost the audition buzz like it had never happened.

18

Bart and Bobby sat across from each other, sheets of paper spread across the table.

"This isn't too bad, Bart. A bit loose. Kind of wordy in places, but a good story. I thought you were bullshitting us earlier. I mean you clearly failed English. Your spelling and grammar are remarkable."

Bart laughed. "That's what editors are for, right? Can you get this together?"

"Give me a soft copy and an hour or so and it's done."

Bart pointed to his computer. "Right over there. If you want to clean it some, I'm going to start fishing for money."

Bobby raised an eyebrow. "I'm your secretary now?"

"You'll get writing credit."

He laughed. "Right. So, what was it you told Marty the female lead did for a living?"

"Translator. I think I called her Susie, right? Generic name. Haven't given it that much thought."

"It's got to be Jackie. Good hard name with a hint of hot. She can be Jacquelyn during the romantic, sensitive scenes, and Jackie when she needs to be hard."

"Love it, Bobby. You're a master." He smacked him on the shoulder. "Can you believe it? We've got Hanks interested in this, with his dad as Exec." He shook his head. "Too fucking good to be true."

"Just cool the exuberance until there's a signature on the bottom of the page, okay? It's looking good now, but it can tank at any point. Tell me you haven't heard of a shot movie, in the can, sitting on a shelf in a warehouse somewhere, never to see the light of day."

Bart shrugged. "Not one with Colin Hanks in it."

"Have you seen his signature on a piece of paper yet?"

"His agent is pretty positive." Bart shook his finger at Bobby. "You stop with the doubt sowing, okay? Think positive, dammit. You do the writer thing and I'm going to round up cash and distribution." He turned, then stopped. "Any idea who made his last movie? What was it, "Lucky", I think?"

"Mirabelle. Ten/Four. Some finance company. You going to try them first?"

"Maybe. The movie did well. Type words. I'll call."

Bobby grunted and turned back to the screen. "Good luck. Get some money for me."

Bart looked around his small office. "This may be the last project developed out of this house." He bought it with the proceeds of *Beast of Bondi* and some other forgettable movies. At least he hoped people forgot them. This house was the best he could afford. Malibu, Hollywood Hills, Brentwood were all out of his financial reach, but he never revealed that as the reason for moving to the Valley. He wanted to be "away from the noise of the business" where he could "clear his mind". All bullshit. He would have grabbed a place on a Malibu cliff in a heartbeat if he could have afforded it.

But the Valley it was.

Bart flipped through the Rolodex on his desk, a testament to the time he had been in the business. Any and all numbers he had acquired in the twenty years he was working the movie biz were in that aging piece of yesterday's technology. He flipped and flapped the thumbed cards until he found what he was looking for. Using his desk phone, leaning back in his chair, feet on his desk he started calling numbers, looking and trying to feel like a mogul of old. In his experience, you couldn't win unless you truly felt like you deserved to win.

All he needed was a cigar. Too bad he was out of them.

As the phone rang on the other end, another thought passed through his mind — a success like the one he was imagining would afford him the wherewithal to acquire, somehow, a case of very nice Cubans, *Totalmente a mano*. He smiled at the thought.

The phone answered at the other end. "This is Harvey."

"Harv, it's me, Sweeney. What you been up to lately?"

"Making money, unlike you. What are you looking for?"

Bart laughed. "You haven't changed a bit. And I have an opportunity sitting in front of me that will make you even more money.

"Bart, when's the last time you made a significant amount of money on anything? Let me rephrase that–when's the last time a project you've been attached to has made a significant amount of money. You, personally, seem to be able to squeeze enough dollars out of the financial people to last as long as you have, but your projects tend to tank."

Bart couldn't disagree with that assessment. It was a matter of some pride that he could set the finances up in his favor in almost every project he organized. This, however, could be something else all together, a deal orders of magnitude better. "Harv, I called you first because you've supported me in this crazy business over the past twenty years—"

"Stop reminding me how old I am."

Bart laughed again. "You're still young. And after I tell you about this, you're going to jump around like a spring chicken."

"So tell me already."

"I've got Colin Hanks attached to an environmental sci-fi picture that promises to be Twilight and Avatar combined, with his father as Executive Producer."

There was a hesitation from the other end of the line.

"Attached? As in John Hancock on the dotted line? That kind of attached? Who wrote the script?"

"As good as attached. He's read the treatment, is very interested and wants to see the script. I've got a word doctor buffing out the rough edges as we speak. The script will be going to him within the hour. The treatment was written after the script was complete, and since he likes that, there's no way he's not going to like the script." He paused for a breath. He was getting even more excited about this himself the more he talked. "I'm giving you the opportunity to be the first one in on this. This is going to be a blockbuster. It explores the true origin of what we call vampires, has a sizzling love triangle between an alien-vampire and an earth couple, and I see it as a more realistic world view—more District 9 than Star Trek type of gritty."

"What were Hanks' exact words?"

Bart smiled. The hook was set. "I've been going through Marty, his agent. I'll be talking to Colin directly after he's read the script."

"Marty's a good guy. No bullshit around him, unlike some other people I know. Marty said he was interested?"

"Marty loved it."

"No, you misunderstood me. Did Marty say Colin Hanks was interested?"

"I had Marty on the phone while Colin was in the room with him. He told me, in front of Hanks, that Hanks was interested and that if the script was as good as the treatment his father would want to come in as Executive producer. Exact words."

There was a pause on the line. "Tell you what, email me a copy of the treatment and when the writer doc has buffed out the first draft, send that to me too. I'll have an answer for you an hour after I get them. Okay?"

"An indication now would be helpful Harv. You know how these things work. It's a house of cards, as easy to blow over as the little pig's house of straw until the money comes in as glue."

"How much glue are you talking about?"

"I back of the enveloped about 250 mill, but we might be able to get it down to 200 if we trim some of the space externals. You're the glue Harv."

"Not yet I'm not, but you've got me interested. If it's as good as you say, and Hanks gives the official nod, I can get the money together."

Bart blinked. He was expecting a bit of resistance at the cost. He cursed himself for not going higher. "Okay, I appreciate where you're coming from. I'll email the treatment now and the script within the hour. Your email address still the same?"

"Hasn't changed in the last fifteen years, Bart. Send it now."

"You're a champ, Harvey. It's on its way." He hung up and smiled. "Bobby, how's it going?"

"There are more words spelled incorrectly than there are not. Give me a bit of time here."

"Yeah, sure. You've got forty-five minutes, but you need to stop and send the treatment to Harvey first. He says he can pull together enough investors to do the deal if we get him the words, and Colin Hanks, today."

"He's not asking much, is he," muttered Bobby.

"What was that?"

"Oh, nothing. What's his email address?"

Bart wrote it down and dropped it on the computer table. "Send the treatment now, and as soon as the screenplay is presentable, send it too."

"If you've got Marty's email address, we can send it to him, too."

"Oh, hell no. It gets printed and we give him a paper copy, face to face. Enough chitchat. Let me know when it's ready. I need to think about some stuff."

Bart left out the back door, grabbed a beer from the fridge and sat in the back yard musing on next steps. Steve could sort out the other two leads. It didn't really matter who they were as long as he was clear about who they weren't. And there was no way Ellie was going to be the female lead. She was causing him enough stress already. There was absolutely no way he could survive with her around all the time going on about the kid getting killed in his own guesthouse. If she couldn't get rid of that idea, he'd have to get rid of her.

He put the beer down on the table and walked over to the guesthouse. It was time to settle this once and for all. He rapped on the doorframe as he entered.

"Ellie. Are you in here?"

She came out from the back, from the bedroom. "Bart. You usually call first."

"Yeah, well, I own the place, so I guess I can come and go as I please. And I think it's time you went."

"What? Went where?"

"Back to Australia. Or anywhere, actually. I don't want you around here anymore. You've been upsetting a lot of people by persisting with this stupid idea that your buddy was killed. He offed himself. He was a two-bit comic who couldn't take the pressures and finally gave in to the inevitable."

Ellie shook her head. "That's where you're wrong. He wasn't a two-bit comic."

"I saw him. He wasn't that great. I've got some huge things happening, and I can't have you around here disturbing the flow. So, pack up your things and get out of here by the end of the day."

"What the—? End of the day? There's a two week notice period in my lease."

"Tough. You told me you were leaving the other day. I'm taking you up on that. I want you out of here by sundown."

"Bullshit. I'll leave in two weeks after you give it to me in writing. There are tenancy laws in this country. What turned you into such an asshole?"

Bart stood his ground. "I said today. Two weeks is not today. I'm tired of you moping around here making outrageous statements about unsubstantiated murders in this house. I can't have that. I've got a 250 million dollar movie in the works and I won't stand for wrinkles like this."

"Fuck you Bart. I'm here for two weeks from today per the agreement we signed when I moved in a year ago. If you want to get me out of here sooner, then you'll need to call the sheriff. Now get out of my way. I need to get something from my car." Ellie picked up her keys and pushed passed him.

He followed her out to the car. "Don't ignore me young lady."

"Fuck off old man. I'm not your daughter. I'm not your girlfriend. I'm not anything you may think I am in your fucked up head and I'm most certainly not someone you can intimidate out of here. I will make you wait until the last second before I leave this place."

She turned back and proceeded to her car on the street. Bart stayed in the driveway and blocked her way on her return. He leaned in close and spoke low.

"You're making a huge mistake. I have weight in this industry. I command respect. I am brokering a movie that'll gross a billion worldwide after DVD sales. You, you fucking piss-ant, are nothing more than a pain in my side. Get the fuck out and don't come back or I'll do to you what I did to your asshole boyfriend."

Ellie's eyes widened. "What do you mean? Joel? What did you do to him?" She smacked him on the chest. "You fucking killed him, didn't you. Why?"

Bart grabbed her by the wrists. "Shut up bitch, or you're next. Get on a plane and get the fuck out of here. I have friends. They'll never find your body."

Ellie moved in close to Bart and kneed him in the groin and ran back to her car. She heard him yell something behind her but couldn't make out what he said. "Shit, shit, shit." She fumbled with the lock, looking over her shoulder. Bart was doubled over, but slowly straightening. She finally got the door open and the car started. As she pulled away from the curb, not knowing where to go, Bart limped down the driveway after her, murder in his eyes.

19

Holy crap, this changed everything. I slammed my palm on the steering wheel. My first thought was to get as far away from that place as I could. *"Don't come back or I'll do to you what I did to your asshole boyfriend."* Nothing ambiguous about that.

And what the hell? They'll never find my body? He's been reading too many bad scripts. The asshole.

I took a deep breath. But this meant I was right.

All along, I was right. Joel didn't commit suicide and he didn't get back on drugs. At least I had that. I pulled into a fast food parking lot and turned off my car. I needed to figure out what to do next. There was no way I could let that asshole get away with killing Joel. I needed more information. I needed a witness to him admitting what he did. I needed something to convince the police.

And I needed somewhere to stay.

A hotel was out of the question; I was getting low on cash and I didn't know how long this was going to take. I hadn't made many close friendships since I came here. Most of the girls I met I was friendly with, but I didn't know any of them well enough to call and sofa surf.

But Bernie said he was coming back to town today. I fished out my phone and called him, fingers crossed.

"Bernie here, is that you Ellie?"

I heard Cathy in the background "Give me that." And then she was on the phone. "Ellie, get your ass over here. I heard what happened to Joel. We just got home and were going to go over there but I think it's better if you got away from there and came here. Are you okay, hon?"

"God, it's good to hear your voice, Cath. I was calling to see if I could come over. You're never going to believe what's going on."

"Stop talking and start driving. Bernie is cooking up some fish and I've got a cold bottle of white wine here. Where are you?"

I looked around. I wasn't really sure. "I'm in the parking lot of a Jack in the Box on Victory, I think near Fallbrook."

"I know the place. You're five minutes away. West on Victory to Berquist, then north. I'll pour a glass for you."

"Thanks Cath. A big one." I followed her directions and pulled up in front of their little bungalow five minute later, just like she said. Cathy and Bernie were waiting in front of their house. They were the perfect Southern California couple. He was a muscled six-foot plus gaffer, setting up the lights and power for TV and movie sets. Cathy was only a couple of inches shorter, short-cropped blonde hair and a body a younger Jane Fonda would have killed for. She had two glasses in her hand. I loved that girl.

I slammed the car door shut, locked it and took the proffered glass. "You have no idea what kind of day I've been having." I held up the glass. "Thanks for this. Can we sit down?"

Bernie stood to one side. "Ladies, food is ready in the back yard. And it's a lovely night for it."

I took his arm and walked back to the patio. Chairs were set around the table and broiled fish and a light green salad sat on serving platters. "I'm not exaggerating when I say you guys are lifesavers. You're not going to believe what happened."

"Oh, I heard. Poor Joel. Who knew he was feeling like that? It must be terrible."

I sat at the table, took a healthy drink of the wine and looked at the both of them. "You guys have no idea."

"Pretty shocking, wasn't it? You can stay here tonight if you want. Sorry we couldn't be here when it all went down."

"It all went down today, you two. Today was the most fucked up day I've ever experienced." I sipped the wine. If I wasn't careful I'd be plastered sooner than later. I licked my lips and sat back. "I'm not sure where to start." I cleared my throat. "Almost immediately after Sweeney found Joel dead I questioned the whole suicide thing. He was doing too well and he wasn't back on drugs so I knew it couldn't have been accidental. But Bart said he found him there, and had to unlock the doors to get into find him. So it had to be true, right?"

"So it wasn't suicide? How did the police figure it out?" Bernie served the portions of white fish and salad with a yummy lemony dressing.

My stomach growled with the smell. I was starving. I worked on a mouthful while I decided how much to tell them. It was unbelievable. I took another measured sip of wine. "They haven't figured it out. The police don't know. I'm still trying to figure out how to convince them."

Cathy looked at Bernie and they both looked back at me. I recognized that look. Jacob gave me that look. "Ellie, how can you be sure? Really, all of the evidence, as you described it, looks like a suicide."

I shook my head. "I just ran from the house. Sweeney told me that not only did he kill Joel, if I didn't get the fuck out of here—his words—nobody would ever find my body." I ate and watched their faces. They clearly didn't believe me, but I was used to that. I showed them my wrists. "Check the bruises. I had to fight him off. Not much of a fight, I'll admit, because he's an old man and I grew up fighting off the advances of horny surfers, but he was absolutely bat shit." I picked at the salad. "I don't know why he killed him, and I suppose until I know that there's nothing to really take to the police. They're not going to believe me. They'll think I'm just rambling." I nodded. "Yeah, you think I'm rambling too. But it's real. And that's why I was calling you. Sweeney threatened to kill me if I didn't get out of there. So I got. I don't have anywhere to stay, though. Can I stay here?"

Bern and Cath, to give them credit, didn't act like I was a complete nut job, although I'm sure they thought it. "Absolutely, right Bernie? You can crash here until all of this is sorted out."

Bernie looked puzzled. He scrubbed his scalp with his fingertips. "I'm having a hard time following all of this. Why did Sweeney kill Joel? How? I'm confused Ellie. Of course you can stay here, but you're going to have to explain this a bit more. Is all your stuff in your car?"

"I got nothing but the clothes on my back and my mobile phone. And my car." I smiled at the two of them. "And my friends." I took a deep breath and tried to sort out the insanity from the reality.

"I still can't believe what my ears heard and my eyes saw tonight. But I can't say I'm that surprised. He's been acting a little weird lately. And that whole 'the door was locked so it must have been suicide' thing makes perfect sense. He has a key."

Bernie shook is head. "I've known Bart for five years longer than I've known you. He's a bit on the eccentric side, but I've never gotten a violence vibe from him." He shrugged. "But I'm believing you. I don't know why, but I am."

"Thanks." I meant it. "I'm a bit messed up right now. I'm not sure which way is up."

Cathy topped up my glass. Probably not a good idea, but I wanted to be a good guest. "Ellie, you have got to call the police. Bart sounds like a total nut case."

"And tell them what? That he killed the guy that the police believe is a suicide victim? I don't have any evidence. If I tell the cops what he told me, Sweeney will just tell the police that I'm a disillusioned, confused homesick kid." I sniffed, feeling a bit sorry for myself. "And he wouldn't be that far off." I put my glass down on the table a little more forcefully than I had to. "No, dammit. I'm not going to the cops with nothing but bruised wrists. Sweeney would laugh me out of the joint and run me over the first chance he got." I rubbed my face with my hands. "Jesus, the crap I find myself in."

My phone rang. It was Jacob. "Ellie, I told you I'd call when the arrangements were made and I completely forgot. I'm sorry. I hope it isn't too late?"

"No, it's okay. I'm up at some friends. What's going on?"

"There's going to be a small service at a crematorium in Glendale. I'll be taking the ashes to spread them after that. We'd really like it if you came. Bring some of his friends too, if they want to see him off."

"Where? And when?"

"Tomorrow afternoon at 2:00. I'll send the details to your phone, okay? Are you going to be okay?"

"Eventually. Is it just you or are your parents here too?" I closed my eyes. Memories of my mother's funeral slid around in my head, not providing specifics, but more than happy to fill me with the memories of the emotions. Not nice emotions.

"Mom and dad came out too. Dad's taking it pretty rough. Can you not mention the lifestyle thing?"

That little bit rankled. "Yeah. I told you I'd keep it quiet. You are going to tell them later, right?"

"I will. I promise. They need to know who he was. I understand that."

"And they need to know he didn't kill himself."

"Ellie, we've been over this. The evidence doesn't support any other conclusion. You said it yourself. That guy, what's his name, Sweeney had to unlock the door to get in."

"That's because Sweeney killed him."

"More speculation, Ellie"

I closed my yes. I was getting tired of the constant challenges. "No. He told me. And then said he'd do the same to me if I didn't leave the country."

"Seriously?"

"No, I'm fucking joking, Jacob. I joke about this kind of stuff all of the time. Of course I'm serious. No, I don't have any proof and yes, I'll see you tomorrow. You can be my bodyguard in case the psycho shows up." I hung up and tossed the phone on the table. "That was Joel's brother. The service is tomorrow afternoon at two at some place in Glendale." My phone vibrated. "And that would be the where."

"You're going?"

"Of course I'm going. Joel was the one constant support I had here. I can't believe how happy he could make me feel. It's tough without him, but I have to do this for him. You guys should come too. You knew him almost as well as I did." I picked up my glass. My empty glass. I didn't remember finishing it. I waved for the bottle and refilled. "Cath, you're almost the same height as me, right?"

"You've got an inch on me."

"Can I borrow a dress for tomorrow?"

"You're a lot skinnier than I am. I'm what you might politely call "big boned"."

"I'll belt it at the waist. It'll be fine. I really appreciate it."

Bernie leaned forward. "You want me to go back to your place and pick up your stuff? Sweeney doesn't worry me any."

Cathy patted him on the arm. "Big brave man. Maybe you can go tomorrow. I can sort out our Ellie tonight. You've had a bit too much to drink to drive."

"Damn. I'm itching for a fight."

"Down, boy. Save your energy for later."

I looked away. It was getting a bit sappy. "Get a room, guys."

"We've got one already. We'll try to not keep you awake, okay?"

"Ha." As I reached for my phone it rang. "Shit." I checked the caller ID. My lazy-assed agent. Working at 9 at night. Inconceivable. "Davie, what the fuck?"

"What? Can't an agent call a client to let her know about a short notice audition?"

"I'm booked up tomorrow, if it's that short notice." I was walking slowly back to the house. I think Bern and Cath were going to crawl in to the hot tub and I didn't want to be around when that happened. It was awkward enough as it was.

"What about tomorrow evening? It's between 5 and 7 in Glendale. Steve Bond specifically asked if you were available for this one."

It was starting to sound like I had a Rabbi. A thin, balding WASPy as hell Rabbi. "I won't turn it down if he's asking for me specifically. I'm not that dumb. Can you send the info to my phone?"

"I will. And he's got a couple of sides he wants you to prepare with. I'll email them to you."

My laptop was still at Sweeney's. All of my stuff was still there. I could retrieve the email with my phone, but the thought of reading it on the small screen kicked in a sympathy headache. But it's not like I had a choice. "Okay. Email them. Did he say what it was about?"

"Some national commercial for a well-known brand of soft drink. It seems you've got an angel."

"Thanks Dave. Maybe I'll end up making some money for you after all." I signed off and stopped at the door. I didn't know were I was going to sleep. I turned to head back to the yard and almost plowed into Cathy.

"I heard that. You have an audition tomorrow night?"

"Remarkably, yes. I now have an agent who is actually trying to find me work."

"Oh. Did you fire that Dave guy?"

"No. Same guy. He just seems to be coming up with stuff lately. Listen, Cath, I'm exhausted. Can you show me where I can drop my head? And I hate to ask this, but do you have a big t-shirt or something I can wear? And I need to have a quick shower first."

"That's why I'm following you while Bernie sits in the hot tub unattended and frustrated." She smiled wickedly. "He can wait for a few more minutes. We've got a small guest room you can use. And sleep in tomorrow, okay? Things always look better after a good sleep."

I thanked her and headed for the shower. It was going to have to be one hell of a sleep to make any of this look better.

20

Bernie's skin had started to prune by the time Cathy got back. "She okay?"

"I think she will be," she nodded. "She's tough."

"Aren't all Australians? You just going to stand there or are you coming in?"

"I thought maybe you'd like another glass. Was I wrong?"

Bernie leaned back in the spa and smiled at his girlfriend. "Hit me."

"You're such a fucking romantic. I don't know how I can keep my hands off you."

Bernie laughed. "Don't fight it, babe."

She shushed him. "She's crashed. I think she was asleep before I was out the door." She stepped into the warm water and handed Bernie a glass. "She looks wrecked."

"She looked good to me."

Cathy slid in beside her boyfriend of five years and snuggled in close. He draped an arm over her. She looked up at him. "What do you think about what she's saying about Sweeney? You've worked with him before. Does it strike you as something he'd do?"

Bernie shrugged. "It's not like I worked directly with him. He directed the actors. I worked with the cinematographers." He shook his head. "But no. From what I saw, Sweeney was a glad-handing, fake-smiling ass-kisser."

"So, typical movie jackhole."

"Hey, I resemble that remark."

"No. You do real work. That's why I'm more concerned about what Ellie is saying than I normally would be. I like her. She's one of the real people in this town, even though she's in front of the camera. She seems to really believe this. Either she has slid down the slope to completely certifiable nut job or Sweeney's got an evil streak in him that everyone has missed all these years."

Bernie splashed at the water with his fingertips. "I have heard some stories about black-hat Bart back in the day. Nothing ever proven. More like anecdotal, friend of a friend stuff. Some say he was a nasty little fuck in his early days." He took a drink of his wine. "I still think I should have gone back to her place and picked up her stuff. A confrontation with Sweeney might have cleared some of this up."

Cathy swung a leg over her boyfriend. "And miss this? She's fine for tonight. She's dead to the world in the guest room. We can help sort her out tomorrow. Tonight, I've got other plans. With you."

Jacob was in an eternal internal debate about whether and when he should let his parents know about Joel's sexuality. His father was not taking the death well. His mother seemed stronger about this, but no parent wanted to be in this situation at any time in their life. He was driving, his father in the passenger seat and his mother in the back. It was a five-minute trip from the hotel to the crematorium. Five incredibly long minutes. "You okay pop?"

"What the heck do you think? Of course I'm not okay. One of my sons is dead. You always hear people say, 'the kids shouldn't die before the parents' and until you actually experience it, it seems like a stupid thing to say. Of course they shouldn't. But this isn't the way I expected to feel. You'd think I'd be sad, right? No. Angry. Pissed off." Jacob looked at his father. He never wore. "Yeah. Pissed off. If he hadn't moved to this insufferable city he'd still be alive now. Don't tell me he wouldn't."

Jacob didn't have an answer to that. His father was correct. "I don't know if it makes you feel any better, pops, but he was doing really well here, and loving it. He was starting to get the attention of some people high up in the business—"

His father snorted. "Business? That's a business? Brakes and mufflers, that's a business. Aluminum siding. Road paving. Those are businesses. Standing on a stage and making wise cracks and having people who've had too much to drink laugh at you, that's not a business." He punched the dash of the rental. "At least you've got a real job."

"Come on. Don't do this pops. He was doing what he loved and apparently was doing well."

"And how would you know that? He didn't have the decency to even talk to his family for the past six months. Like we weren't good enough."

"I was talking to his - girlfriend. They were living together in a guesthouse. She told me he was doing very well. She'll be at the service today, I think."

His father looked at him for a good ten seconds before replying. "Girlfriend? Do you really believe that? Are you telling me you didn't know your twin brother was a homosexual?"

Jacob pulled into the parking lot. "You knew?"

His mother piped up from the back seat. "We're old. We're not dumb. Or blind. Of course we knew. Is he dead because of this?"

Jacob took a deep breath. The things you don't know. "I don't know, mom. The police say it was a suicide. I can't see how it can be anything else. Apparently there were no signs. I really don't know why he did it. If there's a place in this country where his sexuality would be accepted, it would be here, so I doubt it had anything to do with his death."

"You don't sound like you think it was a suicide, son."

Jacob shook his head. "I don't know, pops. Ellie - the girl Joel lived with - seems convinced he was killed. She told me last night the guy who killed Joel threatened to kill her." Jacob shrugged. "It's hard to say with her, though. She's kind of flakey. I'm hoping she shows up here tonight so we can talk face to face."

"Still with the girlfriend thing. Your mother and I have known he was gay since he was fifteen. We're okay with it. He was our son. We loved him no matter what. We love you even though you seem to have no life outside of your job, and your job, as near as we can tell, involves playing with dogs."

"I run the K-9 unit. You know that."

"Lighten up Jacob. I'm pulling your leg. You do good work. I guess. Your mother and I very proud of how you turned out." He took his wife's hand. "And we were proud of your brother, too. He found something he was passionate about and went for it. Too many people are afraid to do that and your brother, give him credit, went 100%. It would have been nice if he had let us in on what he was doing and not shut us out, but I think I understand why he did."

His mother grunted. "I don't. I never will. Let's go into this place and get this done."

The walked into the place and met the minister. Pleasantries were exchanged and an agreement on what the sermon would be. It was an hour before the service would start.

"Come on Bernie. We're going to be late."

"I'm coming." Bernie slid on a suit jacket and walked out of their bedroom. "How long is this going to take?"

"It's just a couple of hours to support our friend."

"Where is Ellie?"

"She left about ten minutes ago. Seemed pretty subdued."

"As you would. You know where we're going, right?"

Cathy slipped a piece of paper out of her clasp. "Right here. You drive. I can't in these shoes."

"Let's go then." Bernie looked at the address. "Only five minutes from here. She'll be there already. She's going to need a lot of cheering up after. Any ideas?"

"I should get a board under her. Some surfing will take her mind off all this shit she's going through."

Bernie nodded and started the car. "Good idea. Girls afternoon out."

Jacob sat in the small chapel on the aisle, beside his mother and he father. Few people were there. A couple of younger guys who Jacob assumed were colleagues from his comedy circuit stopped in to pay their respects. Jacob thanked them, in a bit of a fog, not catching their names or really hearing what they said. He saw Ellie come in and sit in the back pew. He considered approaching her and then reconsidered it. There would be time to talk to her later. She looked like she needed to think in peace.

The service was simple. When the pastor asked if anyone would like to talk on Joel's behalf, Ellie strode purposefully to the pulpit and addressed the small crowd.

"I've only known Joel Sampson for six months. Not even six months. When he first moved into my guesthouse - the guesthouse I was staying in, I didn't really own it - I was a little put off at the interference in my life. That lasted about a day.

"The next morning I woke up to pancakes, bacon, fresh squeezed orange juice and a hot pot of coffee. It was heaven.

"It was also the last time it happened."

There were muted chuckles from the pews.

"He made me laugh. He made me cry, with laughter. He made me cry with some of the stories he told me about -" She paused and looked at Jacob and his parents. He gave her a slight nod. "- about the bullying he had to put up with as a teenager when he became aware of his sexual orientation. But there were far more laughs than tears. He was the complete party animal and I'll be the first to admit he probably got into the drugs and the alcohol a bit too much.

"But three months ago he ran into a comic who he admired as a teenager. This guy was a drooling, babbling mess. His speech was so slurred that he was incomprehensible. Joel left that meeting a changed man. He had nothing to drink since then, swore off drugs and even quit smoking. I was great for me; I had a live-in designated driver. And he stuck to it, religiously." Ellie looked around her surroundings. "In a manner of speaking.

"The last six weeks I watched him hit his stride as a performer. His confidence grew, his audience grew and the quality of the people looking to book him grew. He was on the threshold of success.

"So when I came home last Friday and heard he was dead, that he supposedly committed suicide, I couldn't believe it. I still can't believe it. It didn't happen like this." Ellie wiped away a single tear. "Joel was killed. I know who did it, but I don't know why or how. He shouldn't be dead. If it's the last thing I do in this city I'm going to find out what happened." Ellie stepped away from the pulpit and laid her hand on the casket. "I loved you Joel. I'm not going to let him get away with this." She kissed the casket, paused for a second and strode down the aisle and out of the chapel.

Bernie leaned over to Cathy. "What the hell was that all about? Very moving. And very weird. She seems a little freaked."

"Who wouldn't be freaked? Her best friend was killed."

"You're going with the not-a-suicide angle?"

Cathy nodded. "I am. What she said makes sense. There was no reason for him to kill himself. I'm going to help her. Are you?"

Bernie shrugged. "Why not? It's been a bit boring around here."

In the pew in front of them a similar conversation was taking place.

"This Ellie not-a-girlfriend seemed to know my son pretty well. A mother's supposed to know her son better than a girl who just met him six months ago." Joel's mother sniffed. "And what was she was saying about a suicide? Of course it wasn't a suicide, right? The police said it was a drug overdose. Wasn't that the case?"

Jacob patted his mother's hand. "I'll talk to her later tonight and see what she's talking about, okay? Let's not worry about it now. "

"What, we wait until he's in an urn? No way. You're a policeman. Find out what you need to do to investigate his death further. If this little girl, who spoke so lovingly about my boy, thinks there is something strange with his death then I want you to check it out, okay?"

"But mom…"

"Do as your mother says, Jacob. I've been married thirty years to this woman and you can save a lot of time by surrendering to her now. Trust me."

Jacob looked at his parents and sighed. "Fine." He stood and talked to the crematorium operator and arranged for his brother's remains to stay in cooling for a couple of days. He didn't give an explanation, just a check to cover the delay.

"Okay, it's done. Joel will stay on ice while I try and sort things out."

His father cocked an eyebrow. "What are you waiting for?"

Jacob excused himself and followed Ellie out of the chapel.

Bernie leaned over the back of the seat in front of them. "Excuse me, are you Mr. and Mrs. Sampson? Joel's parents? That was his brother who just left, right?"

"Yes. This is Mrs. Sampson and I am his father. And who might you be?"

Bernie stuck out his hands. "Friends of Ellie and Joel. I'm Bernard. Bernie. This is my girlfriend, Cathy. Sorry for your loss."

Joel's father shook his hand. "This Ellie friend of yours appears to be determined to turn over stones for reasons that aren't as clear to me as they seem to be to her."

"Ellie's a good girl. She's got an idea in her head and she doesn't want to let it go. So what's going on? I thought there was a service and cremation today. It seems like we just got through part of the service and it all went to -"

"It did," interjected Mr. Sampson. "It did. Jacob, Joel's brother, is a detective in Boise. He's going to talk to the local police and see what assistance he can give them in determining the real cause of death of my dead son."

Bernie nodded. "My condolences. Cathy and I need to find out what Ellie is up to and see if she needs any help."

"Please, do that. She sounded like someone who cared very much for Joel."

Bernie and Cathy excused themselves and left the chapel, running into Bart Sweeney at the front step.

"Is the service over? Joel's? I was running a little bit late. Have I missed it?"

"Yes, you have, Bart. Late, as usual."

"It's Bernie Boswick. Isn't it? I didn't know you knew Joel. Were you special friends with him?"

Bernie looked down on Bart, a good foot shorter than him. "Sweeney, you know how to get under a guy's skin, I'll give you that. I know Joel through Ellie. You know Ellie? His roommate? Your tenant? Or used to be until you kicked her out."

Bart's face darkened. "That girl is deluded and dangerous. You'd do well to steer clear of her. She'll just drag you into more trouble than you care to be in."

Cathy held on to Bernie's arm, physically and psychically holding him back. "She's staying with us until she finds her feet. You put a scare into her, Bart. That wasn't necessary. It was mean."

Bart snorted. "She's a menace. And I'm not going to talk about it any more. If you'll excuse me, the service is over and there's no point in me hanging around. Good day." He made an about-face and left.

Cathy hugged Bernie's arm closer to her side. "I don't like that guy, Bern. Let's get the hell out of here."

21

I ironed my only clothes, the shorts and t-shirt I was wearing yesterday when Sweeney chased me off. Bernie and Cathy pulled into the driveway as I sat on their front step. I waved at them and leaned my head in my hands, elbows on my knees. I had to be at an audition in an hour and a half and had no desire to go.

I sighed. I needed to get the guesthouse and get my stuff and wasn't sure how to pull it off. And Joel's stuff. I called Jacob.

"Is that you Ellie? Are you okay? I tried to follow you after the service, but you lost me."

"I couldn't stay any longer." I ran my fingers through my hair and weighed the decision, then went for it. "I've got to sneak back into the guesthouse tonight and get my stuff and maybe you can come with and pick up Joel's stuff. You should get it anyway. I can sneak in your shadow."

"You shouldn't have to sneak. Do you want to meet there now?"

I felt some relief that he didn't hesitate to go with me. "No. I've got an audition I've got to go to. I was requested specifically by a friend. I couldn't let him down. But thanks for not putting up a fight about this. Can you meet me at the house around 8:00 tonight? I don't want to face him alone."

"Yeah, that's not a problem. See you then."

I thanked him and hung up.

Cathy came around to the front of the house and sat on the steps beside me. "Are you okay, sweetie?"

"Define okay. My bestie's been cremated, my landlord has threatened to kill me and I've got an audition I feel like I have to go to, but could care less about whether I got the gig or not." I straightened. "A bit of self-pity creeping in there, Cath. Can't have that, can we?" I scrubbed my face with my hands. "I'll be back in a few hours. I'm going to the audition. Steve specifically asked I be there and I'm not a complete idiot. Then I'm going to meet Jacob and get my stuff from the guesthouse. I'll be damned if I'm going to let an over-the-hill, paunchy asshole like Sweeney determine what I can and can't do."

Cathy rested her hand on my back. "Don't do anything stupid. Bernie can go with you if you want."

I shook my head. "Jacob should be enough. He's a cop. I appreciate the offer, though. I'll see you tonight, okay? Wait up for me. I think I'm going to need another bottle of that vino."

"We'll be here. Be careful."

I thanked her and drove to the audition. I had read the lines they sent; they were very corny and made little sense. Maybe in the context of the scene they'd be better. The waiting room was as crowded as any other I've been in. I approached the desk. Trudy wasn't working it this time. "Ellie Bourke here. Steve Bond asked that I attend personally."

She smiled a practiced plastic smile. "Thank you for dropping by." She held out her hand for my headshot and resume. "Mr. Bond is not here. He got tied up on another project. His associate, Johnny Engle is here covering for him. I'll let him know you're here."

"Okay, well Steve called my agent and specifically asked for me."

"I'm sure I don't know anything about that. Have a seat, and I'll call your name when it's your turn. You know the lines, right?"

I didn't understand. "There are three lines. How could I not know the lines?"

"Okay, then. That's excellent. Have a seat, and I'll call you shortly."

I saw a few girls I knew from other auditions. To say I knew them wouldn't strictly speaking be true. I recognized them. I'd chat with them while we waited the interminable wait for judgment passed on our acting skills in a fifteen-minute snapshot. About half the chairs were occupied. I found one as far as possible from everyone else. I wasn't in the mood for chitchat.

That didn't stop someone who was vaguely familiar from getting up from their seat and sitting beside me. I knew her from somewhere, but I couldn't place it.

"We were both in that show, in the bar scene. You know, where we had to throw drinks in the guys' faces and then walk out. I'm Patti."

Ah, now I remembered. I pasted on a smile and was pleasant. It was a habit. You never knew in this business who could help you in the future. "I remember. Have you been keeping busy since then?"

"Meh. As busy as possible, I guess. I've gone back to school. Advanced hair and makeup. There's not as much time to do these auditions anymore. I'm glad this one was in the evening. Listen, I came over because I heard about Joel. That's terrible. I know you two were close. Are you okay?"

"I'm not now, but I will be. Thanks for asking." I had to change the subject. Bubbling rage threatened to erupt every time I thought about what Sweeney said, and I needed to stay collected. "Do you have any idea what this audition is for?"

"You don't know?"

"I wouldn't be asking if I did, right? I just got a call late last night from my agent. Told me to be here. Emailed me some notes. I can't make heads or tails of it."

"Really? I've known about this for two weeks now. It's a tie-in with that new Benicio del Toro movie and the soft drink company. Whoever gets the part will be opposite Benicio, reenacting half a dozen scenes from the movie, rewritten to include the drink. And the girl. I'm kind of excited about this. I've worked with him before. Well, as an extra in one of his movies, but we talked and seemed to hit it off really good."

Right. "Well, good luck with that. I need to focus my energies and get in tune with my inner self now, so if you can excuse me." I closed my eyes, took a deep breath and tried to sit cross-legged in the chair. I wasn't focusing on anything and the only tuning I wanted to do was on Sweeney's skull. I just needed the bimbo to shut up. I could bullshit as well as anyone in his city.

"Absolutely. I understand completely. I do the same thing, almost exactly. We're almost like sisters."

I tuned her out. This had better not take too long. I needed to get Joel's stuff from the guesthouse. And I wanted to take another look around. I must have missed something. Sweeney wasn't smart enough to kill somebody and not leave a trace. I was trying to visualize the place as I had seen it the last time I was in there when I was tapped on the arm. I almost broke a leg standing. "Damn. Sorry." Patti was looking at me, concern lines all over her face. "You look like you need a couple of jabs." I pointed at my forehead, just between my eyebrows. "Right about there. Are you okay?"

"They called your name. You seemed to be so peaceful, I was afraid to disturb you, but, you know, they did call your name."

"Thanks. I'm fine ,and thanks for asking. And for waking me from my daydreams."

I hustled to the desk. "You called Ellie Bourke?"

"I did, and you just about missed your place." She nodded toward the door. "They're waiting for you."

On the other side of the door stood a tall - at least three inches taller than my six foot - thin blonde guy. He smiled, thousands of dollars of dental work on display. "You are the Ellie that Steve talks about so much. I am Johnny Engles"

I bit the inside of my cheek to keep from laughing. Either he was doing a piss-take on the Swedish chef, or the Swedish chef had the Swedish accent down pat. I held out my hand. "Yes. I'm Ellie Bourke. Steve talks about me?"

"He says you're the best new thing he has seen in a long time. He told me to tell you he is sorry he couldn't make it here, but he is sure you will do well." The guy smiled and raised an eyebrow. "I think he is trying to influence my decision, right?"

I smiled. "So, how do you want me to do this?"

"You have the sheet with the lines?"

"My agent emailed them to me last night." I tapped the side of my head. "They're in here."

"Okay. Maybe we get to that in a minutes. You know what the commercials we are making are?"

I half expected a "yorp-dy morp-dy meatballs" to come out of his mouth. "A tie-in with that movie and a soda. Reenacting some scenes or something?"

"Exactly. And because of the reenacting part, we need to make sure the actress who gets this role can do some basic stoonts. Nothing dangerous, you understand, but enough to make it believable. There are only so many things we can convincingly fix in post."

This piqued my interest. I loved 'stoonts'. Considered being a 'stoontman' as a kid until some smart-assed 12-year-old boy told me they were stunt*men*, and if I hadn't noticed, I wasn't a man. It took me years to get over that,, and by the,n, the modeling career had taken o,ff, and I was contractually forbidden from doing anything remotely dangerous.

"That's cool. What are we going to do?"

Johnny pointed to the back wall. I hadn't noticed when I came in, but it was a rock-climbing wall. A rope and harness were hanging from a loop near the top and large, burly man was holding on to the free end. "We're going to put this harness on you, for safety, and then we want you to run and yump and hold on to the wall and start climbing."

I didn't hear him right. "Excuse me? Yump? I don't know what you're saying."

The big guy in the back of the room started quietly laughing. Johnny looked at him, shook his head slightly and turned back to me, smiling. "He laughs at my accent, but if I asked him to say anything in Swedish he would be completely stoomped. I meant yump." He jumped up and down a couple of times. "You know, yump."

"Ah, jump. You mean like this?" I trotted a few steps forward, eyeing the possible handholds and gathered speed as I got nearer. When I was about four or five feet away I launched myself upward and got both hands and one of my feet on holds. I was about four feet off the ground. Not a huge height, but with the right camera angles I could be miles up.

Johnny clapped his hands and laughed. "You Australians. There is a harness there for a reason. We don't want you to hurt yourself doing this.

When we make the commercial, we will have to do this scene maybe fifteen or twenty times. Even Tom Cruise wears a harness, you know."

"Tom Cruise is a pussy." I let go and dropped, landing with my knees flexed, only a slightly bit flushed. "There are probably harder things on your list for me than this. Although I am a natural-born klutz. It's probably lucky for all of us that I didn't break something." I brushed my hands off on the ass of my pants. "I rocked climbed a bit as a kid. This was pretty easy."

"As a kid? You are still a kid. But a very ballsy kid. I like that." He looked over some notes on his clipboard and shook his head. "This is actually the hardest stunt, unless you can't swim. But of course you can. You are from the land of Ian Thorpe and Stephanie Rice." He scribbled something on the paper. "We have your contact details? There is a way we can reach you?"

"Cell phone or email, okay? I've moved out of my house and don't have a new landline."

He scratched something on the pad. "Understood." He smiled again and held out his hand. "It was a distinct pleasure to meet you, Miss Ellie Bourke. You are a very unique character. I am glad you came by."

I thanked him and made to leave when he stopped me with a touch on my arm. "Has Steve talked to you about the movie role he is trying to get you for?"

I shook my head. "I haven't talked to Steve since the Modern Family audition. He's looking for people for a horror movie?"

"Not at all. He's one of the guys putting together a pretty big budget movie."

"And Steve told you he wants me for it? But he hasn't contacted me at all."

"Apparently, he's getting a bit of pushback from Bart Sweeney, who thinks you're not right for the part. In fact, Bart told me that he doubted you'd show up here, that you were on your way back to Australia."

"He told you I was going back to Australia? The shit. Sorry, I don't know if you're friends with him, but he's a grade-A asshole." I wasn't going to talk about what he said to me. There were no witnesses to that and I'd said enough to other people. I didn't want it getting around I was making unsubstantiated accusations like that. He could sue me for slander and I wouldn't have a leg to stand on. "He kicked me out of the guesthouse I was staying in. Seems to think I might be a little unbalanced."

"You live in L.A. By definition, you are unbalanced." He checked his watch. "I need to get to the rest of the hopefuls out there, Ellie, but I think I will be calling you back to do some scenes with Benicio to see if you work well together."

I grimaced, not a pleasing sight and a face I keep trying to avoid, but this time it was warranted. "I'm taller than him, I think."

Johnny looked at my sheet. "Almost six foot." He shrugged. "I don't think so. He's over six foot. He just looks shorter on the screen. So no problem. Besides, these are action scenes, you won't be ballroom dancing with the man. I don't think your height will be a problem."

"Fingers crossed."

Johnny laughed. "I tell you what. If nobody else comes in here and spontaneously yumps at the rock wall without a harness, the part is yours. That was the best thing I've seen in a long time. Thanks for coming by."

I thanked him and left. That was probably the second-best audition I've ever had.

Patti intercepted me on the way out. "How was it?"

"Oh, I don't know. They're looking for a damsel in distress, girly-girl. More you than me I think. Good luck in there." I can be such a bitch, can't I?

I checked the time. Damn. I had twenty minutes to get to Sweeney's house and meet Jacob. It was thirty minutes away. I was going to be late.

22

Bart leaned back at the desk in his office, eyes closed, fist around a tumbler of half-decent scotch. The only light in the house was the lamp on his desk. The sun had been down for well over an hour now. Marty had the script and if he was to be believed, Colin Hanks, and no doubt his father, would be reading it right now. It didn't matter how long he had been doing this; the thought of someone else reading his work or watching the movies he directed got him hard. He was hanging himself out for all to see, at least the veneer of himself he let people see. It didn't matter to him whether people loved it or hated it, as long as they weren't bored with it.

The more controversial the better.

Waiting for the reaction only intensified the feeling, pushing him to the brink. He looked at his watch. It was 8:03. Marty, and by extension, Hanks, had the script for five hours now. More than enough time to read it and make a decision. He took another drink and looked at the glass. If this played out, he wouldn't be drinking the mid-range stuff any more. It would be Glenfiddich all the way; the older, the better. There was a 50-year-old bottle he heard went for over 15 grand. It would be interesting to see how that kind of drink went down.

Bart was just settling into a half stupor when his mobile phone vibrated and rang. "Sweeney."

"Bart, this is Marty. Mr Hanks likes the screenplay."

"Likes as in he will do it, or likes as in, 'Gee, that was nice and what else is there?' "

"He is more than willing to do it. We need to work out some financial issues before he's officially signed, but his father can help with the financing."

"He's putting his money in?"

"Don't be stupid, Bart. He knows people with money who would be willing to invest on his word." There was a pause. "There will need to be some changes."

Bart sat up. "What kind of changes? I'm still directing this."

"Of course. And we know of a good AD who can assist." He paused again. "The script needs some tightening. I think it's about ten pages too long. Again, you will still get writing credit. The fixers will be way down on the credits. They're mercenaries. They do it for money."

"Again, no problem. We should meet. Face to face. My guys and your guys. Hash everything out."

Marty grunted. "Great idea." Bart could hear the flipping of pages and thought how archaic it was that the guy had a paper diary. "I'm swamped for the next four days, unfortunately."

Bart shook his head. "No, I think that's too long. We need to strike while the iron's hot, and all that. I'm available at any time, day or night. And I speak for the rest of the group also."

"The only space I have open is late tomorrow. Really late. Are you up to meeting at 10:30 tomorrow night?"

"Any time means any time. I'll see you tomorrow night at ten. In the meantime, I need to know how I can define Mr. Hank's relationship with the picture."

"Colin or Tom?"

Bart shrugged. "Either. Both.

Marty paused before answering. "In both cases you can say they are in advanced discussions, with a commitment pending financing. We can discuss numbers tomorrow. But the only thing holding them back from saying they are committed is an agreement in principal on the package. By the end of our discussions tomorrow I expect they will both be committed."

Bart smiled. "Great. So my place tomorrow."

"No, that's not going to happen. I'm not going into the Valley. You can come here." He gave Bart an address in Malibu. "Meet us at 10:30. Everyone will be here. I don't usually work that late, but I think you've got a great property on your hands. I want to tie things down as quickly as you do."

Bart thanked him and hung up. "Excellent." He padded barefoot through the dim light to the bar and refilled his glass. "Abso-fucking-lutely excellent." As he returned to his recliner a movement in the back yard caught his eye. "Fucking dog."

He stumbled through his dark house to the sliding door and realized he had a two-legged intruder. A second shadow followed. "Shit. Two of them." He stepped away from the window and reached for his phone as the halogen streetlights bounced light beams off a tall blonde's head. "That bitch." Bart quietly slid the door open and stepped out on the back porch. The guesthouse was about a hundred yards from his patio, and the porch and grounds were dark. He could barely see the two people in the backyard, but he was dead certain one of them was Ellie.

"That god-dammed bitch," he muttered. He slipped out to the back yard - his back yard, he thought to himself, his eminent domain - and tried to sneak up on the trespassers. It was difficult. The ice in his scotch clinked with every painfully slow step he took. He stopped and scooped out the cubes and threw them on the grass.

By the time he reached the guesthouse, both parties, as he had begun to think of them, were inside the premises, as he had begun to think of the guesthouse. He wondered what the law was. They were trespassing. Could he kill them in self-defense? Did they have to attack him first? Was their presence enough to justify deadly force? Where did he leave his gun? What did he have handy he could use as a weapon?

The bathroom light in the back of the guesthouse came on. He carefully unlatched the side gate and walked around to the back, wincing as he stepped barefoot over the decorative gravel. "Shit, shit, shit," he whispered. He almost fell on his ass. He downed the rest of the scotch, looked around for a place to put the glass and ended up stashing it in his robe pocket. He leaned over a low hedge, placed his fingers on the window ledge and looked through a gap in the opaque screening on the window. Ellie was in the bathroom collecting her feminine stuff. He had no idea what it was and didn't care. At least it looked like she was finally getting out of L.A. She was a danger to him if she hung around, but in Australia she was a nothing. He heard her call out to the other person. "Hey, what about the board? Mind if I keep it? You won't get any use out of it where you're going."

The answer must have been in the affirmative because she gave a fist pump and mouthed a "yes". "Okay, I'll be a couple of minutes and I'll help you with the rest of your stuff." He watched her pack up a small box, look around the bathroom, collect her mobile and slide it in her back pocket and turn off the light as she left the bathroom.

A lamp clicked on in the bedroom. The windows were covered by a cheap venetian slat blind. He got down on his hands and knees and crawled under the bottom of the window until he reached the other side. A gap in the venetian slats gave him a better angle into the room. He watched Ellie fold some clothes and put them in a small suitcase.

The second person entered the room and stepped in front of the lamp, casting a shadow over Ellie. She looked up and smiled. "Thanks for the board. It's beautiful. It would have gone to waste. I could have given lessons until the L.A. River ran full of water, and it would have done no good. I'll think of you every time I ride it."

"No problem. It would have been too hard to take it with me anyway. And I agree. No use for it."

Bart fell back on his ass. He knew that voice and it was impossible. His head swam as all of the blood left it for regions unknown.

"No. No way. What the fuck is going on?" He crouched at the bottom of the window and looked between the slats. The second person was half turned away from him so he couldn't confirm the face. The physique was the same though. He couldn't forget that. And the voice. That flat, nasally Midwestern voice.

Then the second visitor turned and faced the window, and Bart.

"Joel?" Bart growled under his breath. "Not a chance. No goddamned way. You were dead. How can you not be dead?" He squinted through the window.

Jacob hefted the box. "I think I've got all of the stuff here. Not sure, though, so if you come across anything let me know. I'll be around for a few more days."

Bart didn't hear Ellie's reply. His heart was pounding. He regretted that third scotch. He really wasn't thinking clearly. He shook his head, throwing himself off balance into the sharp gravel.

The talking inside stopped and he froze, taking shallow breaths, his heart pounding in his ears. After a few seconds of silence, they went back to their conversation.

Bart remained sitting on the ground, reviewing the events of the previous Friday afternoon. "No, I'm positive I killed the guy. The fucking ambulance took him away in a body bag. There was no way in hell he could possibly still be alive". He grabbed his chest. "Oh my God. Maybe I'm dead and this is hell. No. Fuck. What the hell is going on?"

He scrambled backwards over the gravel. "Shit. I'm losing it. I've got to get a grip. I can't be seeing him. I'm hallucinating." He got back on his feet and ran back inside his house and locked the doors.

"But if I'm hallucinating, why in the hell did it have to be that? Why dead people? Fuck. Okay, Bart. Take a deep breath and calm your shit down. I need some weed. Fuck, where did I put the weed? This is the last thing I need to go through. I need to be on top of my game tomorrow and hallucinations do not fit into the top-of-the-game scenario." Bart ripped his study apart. There was a bag somewhere. It might be a bit dry, but he reasoned that would make it burn better and better meant faster and faster was exactly what he needed in the getting-the-pot-into-his-system plan. He found the stash, appropriately, behind the Keith Richards autobiography that he hadn't cracked yet. There were two already rolled and a couple of ounces of grass in the bag.

He lit a joint and returned to his recliner, puffing furiously, inhaling and holding the THC rich smoke in his lungs as long as he could. He felt the buzz hit and the mellow surge. It had been a couple of months since he smoked pot, and the effect was magnified as a result. Half way through the first joint, and Bart was a much more relaxed person. He walked out to the front porch, on the opposite side of his house from the guesthouse, and sat in a lounge chair and finished his joint in the dark.

He sparked up the second one as Ellie and who he had to assume was Joel's ghost walked down the drive, both with boxes in their arms. "Sweet Jesus, I'm still seeing him. I've lost my mother-fucking mind." He looked at the lit joint in his hand. "Shit, did I put acid in these? I can't remember." He slowly placed the joint in an ashtray and ground it out. He took a couple of tentative steps off the porch onto the tree-lined walkway. If he was imagining this, then theoretically, they wouldn't be able to see him. That seemed, under the circumstances, a reasonable thought. He could hear their conversation as he got closer. They didn't seem to be noticing him, bolstering his belief they were both figments of his imagination.

"You need to keep in touch, okay Ellie? I want to make sure you settle yourself. Too many big shocks to the system and you might start feeling like there's no hope."

Bart squinted. Joel was a very solid form for a ghost. He shook his head and took a few steps closer.

Ellie placed the box she was carrying in the back seat of a car parked at the curb. "I'll let you know how the board goes. I think I've got some time later in the week. I'll take it out to Zuma. I'll get Bernie and Cath to video my skills and I'll send you a copy."

Bart squinted harder, this time in disbelief and anger. He started muttering to himself again. "Zuma? Later this week? So she's not leaving L.A.? We'll see about that." He cocked his head to hear the response.

"That would be great. I need to get going. My parents aren't comfortable in the big city. Off to go protect and serve."

Ellie laughed and threw a mock salute. "Officer Jacob Sampson on duty. Thanks for coming here with me. That asshole Sweeney could have tried something. I've got to get back to Bernie's house."

"You tell Sweeney I've got my eye on him and if anything happens to you, even a scratch, Detective Sampson will see that he pays."

Bart backed into the shadows. "Jacob? A fucking twin? Who saw that coming? And the asshole's a cop. And Ellie isn't planning on leaving. What else can she do to piss me off? Son of a bitch." Bart stood in the shadow of a large oak and watched as Ellie and the cop hugged and Jacob drive away in a rental. "I should have seen that before. Obvious now." He watched Ellie as she watched the car pull away and around the corner. She sighed and then walked back up the driveway to the guesthouse, relaxed, with not much urgency in her step.

"We'll see about that, the bitch." Bart climbed the steps into the front of his house, shedding his robe and exposing a neighbor across the street to therapy inducing ass crack. "This is over tonight. Where the fuck are my clothes?"

23

They were as different as chalk and cheese, but they were the same. Jacob drove away and it felt like someone I had known all my life was leaving. I watched as he turned the corner and then headed back up the drive to the guesthouse. I had almost everything I needed packed and so far not a single Bart encounter. Things were looking up.

Things change.

Bart came barreling out of the back of his house with a full head of steam. There was a bit of a wobble to his stride. This didn't look like it was going to end well. I slid the door shut and locked it. I ran to the back door and locked it, too. Fantastic. Was he waiting until Jacob left, or was this just another coincidence?

I sat on the sofa while he hammered on the door, yelling at me to open up or else. The only 'or else' I could think of would have him breaking the glass, a distinct possibility if he kept hammering that hard.

"What the hell do you want, Sweeney?"

"I told you to get the fuck out of here, and I meant it."

"I'm going. I've got a few things here that I own and two weeks left on my rent. You can't just kick me out."

I hated confrontation, but I'd willingly stick a fork in this asshole's eye. I picked up my phone, then felt my back pocket. Shit, I still had Joel's phone. I needed to get that back to Jacob before he left. Bart rapped on the door again and I jumped. "For Christ's sake Bart, what in the hell is wrong with you?" I had enough of his bullshit. I ran to the front sliding door and faced him through it. "Seriously, what in the hell has gotten into you? A week ago you were my champion and now you've killed Joel for reasons I can't understand and you're threatening to kill me. What the hell? Let me pack my shit and get out of here and I'll be out of your hair forever." Until I figure out what you did.

His face was turning a nice burgundy, veins in his throat and forehead throbbing. Spittle built up at the corners of his mouth. "You just don't leave well enough alone, do you? What is it they call it in your country? You're a sticky-beak. Tell me you are going to Australia and getting out of my hair forever and I won't have to kill you."

I took a step back. He was feral. I'm sure the booze and whatever drugs he took were doing a lot of the speaking for him, but he was frightening. "The guy who just left is Jacob Sampson. He's a detective with the Boise PD. He knows I'm here and if anything happens to me he will know it was you did it. Just let me get the hell out of here."

Bart scrubbed his face violently with his hands. "Jacob. Right. I though it was Joel. Thought I was losing it. Thought maybe I was hallucinating. Freaked me out. He's his brother, right? A twin? You could have warned me. I almost lost it."

That was rich. If he weren't so homicidal I'd be laughing. It was kind of funny. "Freaked you out, did it? Think how I'm feeling now. I've got a lunatic keeping me from leaving here, threatening to kill me if I don't go back to Australia. How is that normal in anybody's world?"

I turned and went back to the bedroom. I couldn't face him any more. I knew he wouldn't break the door glass - probably couldn't - and I was pretty sure I could outlast him. I sat on the bed and pulled a pillow on to my lap and leaned my head on it.

But I didn't want to have to outlast him. "Screw him." I threw the pillow against the wall and walked back out to the living area. The door was clear. He'd left. I sighed in relief and reached to unlock it when I heard breaking glass behind me. The asshole was coming in the back door.

I eased the front door open quietly and quickly and slid it shut behind me. I would leave, but I needed to get some stuff first. No time for all of it, but I could come back for the rest. He couldn't stay here all the time. He had a job. I didn't.

I ran around the back of the small guesthouse. He would be coming through the living room looking for me. If I stayed behind him I should be okay. I needed my phone and Joel's phone. The rest could wait for later.

And there would be a later.

I carefully stepped over the broken glass as I eased into the bedroom through the back door. I dare him to take that out of the security deposit. I could hear him fighting with the sliding front door. He must be plastered.

"Ellie, you bitch. Where in the hell are you? Hell, Ellie, we need to - talk."

The emphasis on the last word told me it was the last thing he wanted to do. I found Joel's phone but I couldn't see where mine was. I tossed the bedclothes and the pillows. Nothing. I popped into the bathroom and found it lying on the sink cabinet. Excellent. And I still wasn't discovered. Now I just needed to get out the back door, around the front of the guesthouse and to my car without being caught.

Piece of cake, right?

I couldn't bake a cake if my life depended on it.

I stepped over the glass again on the way out. The path behind the house around to the front was narrow, bounded by the wall of the house on my right side and a hedge on my left. The hedge was some kind of prickly thing that always tore at my sleeves when I left the back way. It tore at my arms if I wasn't wearing sleeves. It was no-win, either way. I cursed to myself, softly, and made it to the end of the walkway. I turned the corner, heading to the front of the house, and came face to face with Bart.

"Shit." I started to back up and ended up pressing into the hedge, little thorns digging into my back. "Bart, just let me get the hell out of here."

He grabbed me by my wrists. "I don't like you much. You were a bit of an ego in Australia and you're an even bigger one here."

"Occupational hazard, Bart. I can't do my job otherwise and what in the hell does that have to do with you holding my wrists and not letting me go?" I tried to pull them free but his grip was pretty strong. And he moved a step or two back from me, protecting his nuts. He clearly remembered the reach I had with my knee.

"I think, Ellie, that you are going to leave the country."

"I don't really feel like it Bart, you creep."

He squeezed a bit tighter. "There will be no point in you staying here. I am going to call every casting director, producer, director, agent, whoever in this fucking town and tell them I caught you - " he paused.

"Caught me with what, Bart? What could I have possibly done that you haven't already?"

"It doesn't matter, really. I have the ear of the Hollywood elite right now. I've got more power in this city than you could ever hope to have. It would take me at most an hour of phone calls to completely ruin you. And after you've lived in six months of obscurity I'll kill you, drop you off a cliff in Malibu maybe, and make it look like a suicide, too."

This was really freaking me out. He was talking about killing me again like I could do nothing to stop it. I pulled against his hands and as he pulled back I pushed. He let go of my arms and tried to break his fall. He hit with a grunt and sprawled there like the drunk he was. I hesitated. I couldn't get past him; there was no room. He'd snag my leg. If I ran back around and went through the back door he'd cut me off at the unlocked front door. There was a solution, though. And Bart wouldn't like it.

"Sorry, pal." I leaned in and stepped on his groin and put all my weight into it. I'm only 115 pounds - okay, maybe pushing 120 - but it was all focused through the small heel of my shoe. I stomped twice, too fast for him to react and grab my leg, and hightailed it to the back door. I was banking on the fact he'd be incapacitated for the short time it would take for me to get out the front.

Again I traversed the threshold, avoiding the glass, this time at a much faster pace. I didn't need to be quiet; I just needed to get the hell out of there. I stopped at the sliding front door and listened. I could hear Sweeney wheezing. He didn't sound good. I peered around the corner and saw him curled up in a ball holding his sack. "Hurt much, mate?"

He looked up at me. "You fucking bitch, I will ruin you."

"Not as bad as I just ruined you."

"I know where you're staying. You are dead." He rolled on to his knees and stood, shaky from either the pain in his groin, which I assumed to be acute, or the amount of substances he had coursing through his veins. Not that I cared much which it was.

"You've made too many shit movies, Bart. You're repeating the dialogue."

He staggered toward me. I kept backing away, enough to keep a ten or twelve foot gap between us. "You don't seem to realize the power I have in this city now, young lady. I am finalizing the financing on a $200 million movie. I could have put you in it. Others actually wanted you. I squashed it. I can squash any and every thing you audition for. You're going to starve to death here. Go back to dingo land because if you don't, you will become even more accident prone than you already are."

I shook my head. "I used to respect you. Now look at you. You're a fat, old pathetic man trying to scare a little girl." Succeeding, I didn't bother telling him. "Karma is a bitch, Bart. People will turn their back on you when I tell them what you've done."

Bart laughed, hocked up some phlegm and spat into the shrubbery, a trail of it sliding down his chin. "Nobody's going to believe the ravings of a homesick, drug-addled bimbo like you."

I smiled at that. "My tits aren't big enough, Bart. No way you'll convince anybody I'm a bimbo." I walked quickly up the drive to my car. "I will be back."

Jesus, now I sounded like Schwarzenegger. I wasn't feeling too good about this. Again, not big with confrontation. That's why I had an agent. And even then, confrontations with him upset my stomach.

I reached my car and looked back up the drive to the guesthouse. Bart was standing by the front door watching me. Dollars to donuts he would be pawing through everything I owned as soon as I left. Same odds he wouldn't lock the place up, or fix the window he broke. I'd be lucky if any of my stuff was still there when I came back, and for goddamned sure I was coming back. If I had to stake out the place like I was in a bad cop movie then I would, and as soon as he left I was collecting all my stuff.

I sighed. It wouldn't be happening tonight. I still just had the clothes on my back and not much else. Lovely. It was coming up on midnight. I would deal with it later.

I pulled in front of Bernie and Cathy's place with the headlights off and quietly closed the car door. I crossed my fingers that the back door wouldn't be locked. They were helping me more than they realized and I didn't want to over-extend my welcome.

I tiptoed up the back steps and slowly eased the door open. I was about half way in when a voice startled me. "That better be you Ellie, or I'm calling the cops."

I poke my head around the door. "Cathy. It's late. Sorry if I woke you. Things went pear-shaped at the guesthouse."

"Pear-shaped. I love your Australian terms. And no, you didn't wake me. I've been waiting for you. I told you I would, didn't I? I was a little concerned after that exit at the chapel and Bernie's run-in with Sweeney. Glad to see you in one piece. Can I get you anything?"

I dropped into the chair across the kitchen table from her. "I'm suddenly having a craving for cheesecake."

"I've got raspberry. Like a slice?

"You're a lifesaver."

"Coming up. You pregnant by any chance, with strange cravings and all?"

That was funny. "Not a chance, unless there is some divine intervention involved. I just need some pie."

Cathy placed a plate of cheesecake in front of me. The glaze of raspberry on the top and a glass of red wine looked perfect. "Enjoy. It's a fruity wine from Australia. Goes great with the raspberry." She pushed the plate another half an inch toward me. "You need to eat, hon. You're skin and bones."

I split a slab off with the fork. "I'm skin and bones purely for genetic reasons. But I do appreciate this. It looks delicious."

"Ah, hell. I'm going to have one too." She walked toward the kitchen and slapped her self in the ass. "Fortunately Bernie is fond of a bit of padding."

"Just a bit. Slice a piece for me, will you Cath?" Bernie wandered into the kitchen, rubbed his eyes and sat at the table in his tattered bathrobe. "You're sneaking in awfully late, young lady."

"Jeez, dad. I didn't know I had a curfew." I sipped the wine. Very nice. Clear, crisp, a lovely berry aftertaste. "You didn't have to get up, Bern."

"You didn't hear the conversation I had with Sweeney after you and Jacob left the service."

"Did he call you or you call him?"

"Neither. He showed up after the service, such as it was. It kind of ended after you left."

"He had the gall to show up, after what he did? He's a sociopath." I combed my hair back off my face with my fingers. "I'm falling asleep. Remind me to tell you guys what happened tonight."

"Did you get your stuff?" Cathy looked beyond me at the door, like she expected it to walk in behind me under its own power.

"No. Another run in with Sweeney. One more and he'll have no nuts left." I yawned. "Really. I've got to crash. If he shows up here and you guys can't handle him, wake me. I know his sore spots."

24

Bart's retching drowned out the chirping of the birds outside his window. Kneeling in front of his toilet, head in the bowl, all he could think about was that this was how it must feel to die.

He tried to recall what happened the night before, but his brain refused to function beyond the basics. And one of those basics seemed to be voiding his intestinal tract of everything that had been in it for the past three days. He retched again, his eyes watering. He wiped his face and looked at the results of his efforts. "When did I have pasta?"

He groaned and lurched to his feet. "Oh, my Christ." He rinsed his mouth out in the sink and gargled with some mouthwash. "What the hell? I'm not doing that again. Whatever it was that I did." He closed his eyes, fumbled for the package of high-octane painkillers and popped two in his mouth, swallowing them dry. He staggered to the kitchen and made a pot of coffee. While the machine was brewing he looked out to his back yard at the guesthouse. Parts of the night before started coming back to him. He subconsciously placed his hand on his groin and winced when he brushed against a bruise. "Shit. That bitch."

He opened his robe and looked down at a heel-shaped bruise at the top of his pubic bone. "I'm really, truly going to kill her, somehow, someday." He retied the robe and with a shaky hand poured a cup of strong black coffee. He sipped, winced and put on a pair of sunglasses before he walked outside. Memories were trickling back. The step on the groin, definitely. He sipped and winced again and walked just a bit unsteadily toward the guesthouse. He recalled hammering on the front door, close to breaking it with a rock, then remembering the back door. Easier to break into less expensive to fix. He squinted through the sunglasses and walked to the back. The broken glass. The rush through the house. Much of the encounter was a blur and he couldn't remember exactly what he had said to Ellie. The impression he had, though, was that she knew about the activities in the bathroom and was a danger to him and his plans.

Barefoot, he carefully stepped over the glass and went through the bedroom to the living area of the guesthouse. Her stuff was still scattered around the room. Joel's belongings seemed to be gone. He closed his eyes and thought. She said she was staying at someone's place. Someone he knew? The base of his skull was beating a counterpoint to the throbbing behind his eyes. Bobby? Barry? Bart knew it was a name he had worked with before. Bernie. Bernie Boswick. She was hanging out at his place.

"Bernie, Bernie, Bernie." Bart took his phone out of his robe pocket and scrolled through the contacts and dialed. "Bernie Boswick? I hope I didn't catch you too early."

"Who's this?"

"Bart Sweeney. We've worked together a few times. Do you remember me?"

Bernie paused. "Yeah. We talked yesterday at Joel's service."

Bart coughed and winced and searched his memory. Much of the past twenty-four hours was foggy. The talk with Bernie and his girlfriend started to swim into focus. "Yeah. Right. So you know who I am and what power I have in this town, right?"

"I'm not sure I know what you mean, Bart. Why did you call me and wake me up?"

"I know what you think of me. I've heard the talk. But I'm not B-list anymore, Bernie. A $200 million dollar movie I wrote and I will direct has been put together with some of the biggest names in Hollywood. I have pull. I can make or break you and anyone else I choose."

"Why would you want to do that? Even if you could, and I really don't think you can. Why are we having this conversation? I should be sleeping."

Bart kept his voice low. "Piss-ant, I can make or break anyone who gets in my way. Don't cross me, or there won't be a movie, play or TV show that will hire you or your half-assed actress girlfriend."

Bernie yawned. "You've completely lost me. I'm going to assume you're still drunk, or drugged, or deluded in some other way and for your sake I'm going to forget this conversation ever took place.

"I'm having dinner tonight with Colin and Tom Hanks. They are backing, and starring in my project. I can influence who they hire, and don't think I won't."

Bernie sighed. "This town is filled with nut cases. Where are you going with this Bart? You calling everybody in your phone to brag about how big your dick is now? Mine's bigger."

"Where am I going with this? You're harboring Ellie, a mentally ill person who has been falsely accusing me of things that are reprehensible. I've told her a number of times that if she doesn't leave the country I'm going to file slander charges against her. If you continue to harbor her you will be named in the lawsuit. And I will make sure anybody looking at you or your leggy girlfriend's resume knows about the litigation. Kick the Australian bitch out. If she's not gone within the hour I'll start spreading the news." He terminated the call without waiting for a response and dropped the phone in his robe pocket. She'd be back for her stuff. The guy's surfboard was still here. She wouldn't leave that behind. The rest of the crap, maybe, but the board was nice.

And when she came back, he'd make sure she was finished for good.

Jacob looked at the few belongings that now made up the entirety of his brother's life. This wasn't something he ever anticipated doing. His brother was the cool one, the class clown who made good. Joel wasn't supposed to be the guy who was buried while he was still in his twenties. He promised his parents he would look into what Ellie was talking about at the service.

He finished his coffee and dug the cop's card out of his wallet. He flicked the card with his finger. A Constable Perkins. "This is going to be a waste of time, I can feel it." He dialed the number and sat up on his hotel bed, back against the headboard and legs crossed in front of him.

"Constable Perkins. How may I help you?"

"Constable, this is Detective Jacob Sampson of the Boise PD."

"Boise? Like Idaho? What can I do for you?"

"I'm calling about the apparent suicide you were on last week."

"I had three. You're going to have to be more specific. So you have a - wait. Detective Sampson? We talked last week, didn't we? The suicide last week - just a second." Jacob could hear the small pages of a notepad flipping. "Yes, you're the brother of Joel Sampson. I'm sorry for your loss, what can I do for you?"

"I'm not sure it was a suicide. Things aren't sitting right with me. Would you have some time today to talk about the case?"

"Uh, Detective, there is no case. It's been closed. The determination was suicide."

"I'm going to have to ask you to re-open it. I've been led to believe there are some inconsistencies in the case."

"Oh, I see. You've been talking to -" flip, flip, flip, "- Miss Ellie Bourke, haven't you. She's adamant this wasn't a suicide. I'm afraid she's wrong. Sorry Detective."

"Listen, Perkins, I trust Ellie. She's not a flighty twit like most of the girls down here. She's got her head on straight. All I'm asking is for fifteen minutes of your time to see the case file and maybe ask a few questions. Where's the harm in that?"

Jacob listened to the silence for almost a minute. "How hard is it to say, 'yes'? Or 'no' for that matter, Constable?

"If you can get here in the next half hour I can spare some time, but I've got to get going after that. Do you know where the station is located?"

"It's on your business card, right? I think I can be there in less than fifteen minutes."

Bart, freshly showered and shaved, a double dose headache medicine providing targeted relief, felt like a million dollars. It was tonight. It had to be tonight. Those turning points in one's life - it was rare to see them coming at you with enough time to prepare. This was one of those points in time. If he aced it there would be more money than he knew how to spend thrown at him to make a movie that essentially started as a joke.

If it bombed, and that was a thought hardly worth contemplating, his career would be over. This was an all or nothing gamble. Smart men didn't gamble, though, and he had the rest of the day to make sure the cards were stacked in his favor.

The one wild card in the deck was Ellie. He had to sort that problem out once and for all. He inhaled sharply through his nose. "There's no fucking way that brat is going to screw this up for me."

Jacob sat in the chair in the police station usually reserved for perpetrators - or Richard Castle - and flipped through the case file of his brother's death. "There was no autopsy? Why wasn't there an autopsy? There should always be an autopsy."

"In suicide cases autopsies are at the discretion of the county coroner. There was ample evidence this was a suicide. And bodies are stacking up at the morgue like the battle scene in *300*." Perkins rubbed his forehead. "Plus we've got this presidential visit next week that's spreading us pretty thin."

Jacob shook his head. "You're not going to convince me my brother, a person who was doing what he loved, and succeeding at it, committed suicide. There was no note." He held up his hand. "I know the stats, less than 20%, but still. Everything to live for and his roommate had zero inkling of anything gone wrong."

"He was found behind locked doors. How else can you explain that?"

Jacob sighed. "Perkins, who has keys to the house?"

"Well, the deceased. And his roommate. But she has an alibi."

"And the owner. The guy who found him. Have you looked at him?"

Perkins flipped through his note pad. "That would be a Mr. Bart Sweeney. Owns the property. Discovered the deceased in the bathtub." He looked up. "We've got his statement, Everything seemed to check out."

Jacob closed the file and gently placed it on the Constable's desk. "As a family member I have the right to request an autopsy." He took a deep breath. "Re-open the case and perform an autopsy. I want to know how he died. Will that be a problem?"

"I was told the remains were cremated. That would be a problem."

"I delayed that. Please arrange the autopsy. I'll have my brother's remains delivered to wherever they have to go."

Perkins looked over the top of his glasses. "Really? Okay." He handed Jacob a card. "Here's the address. I'll call them and let them know you're coming. I have to advise you there may be a three or four day delay. It's been a busy few weeks."

Jacob slid the card into his shirt pocket. "Make sure the case is re-opened. I'll instruct the mortuary to deliver my brother to the morgue this afternoon. And I'm going to impress upon them the urgency of this. If foul play was involved, every day delayed halves our chances of catching the killer." Jacob had no idea if this was true, but it sounded good and Perkins looked like someone easily swayed by facts and figures.

He thanked the Constable for his time and left, checking the address on card for the mortuary, his next destination.

Bart had that excited and nervous feeling in the pit of his stomach. It was a feeling he rarely had, and he liked it. The culmination of his plans required some thought. Steve should definitely be at the dinner tonight, as should George. There as no question about those two. Bowens, on the other hand, he might be a liability. There was no doubt he was a brilliant cinematographer, but as a face to put in front of the talent, and the money, well, that was a different matter. He was boring. He was - brown. Everything about him was brown. His voice, his clothes, his personality. Bart shook his head. "Best to omit him from the invitations." He called Steve first.

"Steve, buddy, it's Bart. I'm hoping you're free tonight. Big meeting I need you to join me at."

"Sweeney, It's not even 9:00 in the morning. I didn't think you knew this time of day existed."

"Yeah, not my choice. Too many things yet to do today."

"I take it you've heard back. How are things progressing?"

"Marty called me late last night. The script was liked, although they want to trim it a bit. He wants to meet tonight in Malibu. I believe the Hanks will be there. I'd like to close off any issues so we can go forward from tonight with Colin Hanks actually attached."

"Shit, man. Excellent work. Have you told George and Bowen yet?"

"I'm calling George right after you. Not so sure about Bowen though. He's not the most charismatic character. Comes off like a wet blanket. I'm thinking we exclude him. For this meeting only, of course. No better lens man I know. Would definitely want him in on the picture."

Steve sucked air between his teeth. "He's part of the four. He should be there. He's not going to take it well if he isn't."

"But, man, he's a fucking bore."

"He is. No argument. And yet he's a proud person. He needs to be at the meeting. If you were an actor, wouldn't you like to know who's going to be behind the camera?"

"Yeah, well, maybe. Never thought about it before. But I think it's a bad idea and could screw the whole thing up. He's going to bore the pants off everyone."

Steve laughed and thought about it for a second. "Look at it this way, Bart. With Bowens there you'll look like George Clooney. He's the grenade, okay? You'll come across like the generous benefactor letting this guy in to your circle of friends. Am I right?"

Bart wavered. Steve had a point. "So, it's better I bring him along to make the rest of us look better? I hadn't thought of that. Not a bad idea."

Steve laughed. "Absolutely. We need a grenade." He didn't bother telling Bart that if Bowen didn't show up, Bart would be the grenade. They'd slice him out in a heartbeat if it wasn't his project.

25

I was starting to feel like I was getting somewhere. I still didn't have my stuff, but I had Bart on the ropes. I had a couple of really good auditions under my belt. It was sunny out. The positives just kept stacking up. Of course, the forecast was for rain later, but the sky was clear.

I was lying in the bedroom, the guest bedroom, sun streaming through my window and Melon-Head's radio station on. He was guest-spotting this morning. Apparently the regular guy had an ailment preventing him from showing up for work. I listened to these guys all the time. The ailments, as frequent as they were, were bottle related, if the rumors held water.

"G'Day, L.A.! Ross "Melon-Head" Mellon filling in for your regular morning man, Deadly Dave who is ah, under the weather. It wasn't the weather you were under when I saw you last night, Dave-o. Heh-heh-heh. Los Angelenos, it's one fantastic looking day out there this morning but don't be fooled. There's a bit of weather coming in later this afternoon. Hatches need to be battened. Special message for Paris Hilton. Two of them, actually. First, tie that dog down or it will end up with Dorothy and Toto and second, wear panties today, honey. Your skirt's going to get blown. Okay, PSA out of the way. Wake up to Pink and her seventh number one from her latest collection. If this doesn't wake you up somebody better be doing CPR on you."

I loved this guy. He always seemed to be in total control of everything he did. And funny as hell. I stretched and crawled out of bed. Another day.

And another chance to do Sweeney over.

Ever have one of those days where you feel uncommonly good? That was the way I was feeling, for no reason that I could figure out. The sky was blue, not hazy. There was a bird singing outside the window, and I could smell bacon cooking. Days like this, these feelings, I'd learned to ride as long as I could because they never lasted forever.

Maybe I was borderline bi-polar. Who knows?

I had a quick shower and wandered into the kitchen wearing Cathy's robe. "Smells good guys. Saved some for me, right?"

Cathy looked at Bernie and passed some kind of non-verbal message I couldn't quite interpret. But it wasn't nice. What ever he did, he was in serious shit.

I poured some coffee and sat at the kitchen table. "So what's up? Am I interrupting a fight between you two? Don't mind me. I can get out of your hair. I've got to go by Sweeney's place and wait until he leaves so I can grab my stuff. Let me fill my gut and I'll get out of here." I forked some bacon on my plate, two pancakes and a good pour of syrup. The tension was thick enough to - well, it was thick.

"These pancakes are fantastic. Who made them? You, right Cathy? Bernie's are thinner than this. Not as fluffy. Still, tasty, but these are Cathy fluffy. Right? Guys?" They didn't look good. I put my fork down and I have to admit, I was a bit worried now. "What's going on, guys?"

Cathy threw another set of visual daggers at Bernie, stood and leaned over to give me a hug. "Sorry," she whispered in my ear and gave me a final squeeze before she stalked - that's the only word I can use to describe it - back to her room.

"Sorry?" I watched her over my shoulder as she left. "What do you mean?" I turned back to the table. "What does she mean, Bernie, sorry? Sorry for what? What in the hell is going on?" I lost my appetite. The food smelled a bit off.

Bernie grimaced and shook his head. "You know I like you, right Ellie? We both do. But you're smart enough to know how things work in this city, right?"

"Where are you going with this Bernie?"

He cursed to himself and clasped his fingers together, leaning his elbows on the table and his chin on his knuckles. "Look, I'm really sorry it's come to this. Really. But I'm going to have to ask you to leave. Stay somewhere else. Really it's nothing personal, I've just got to get you out of the house."

Shit. So much for the uncommonly good day. And I was barely thirty minutes in. "What have I done? Am I freeloading too much? Would you like if I paid some of the bills around here? Jesus, Bern, I haven't even been here two days yet. Have I really overextended my stay that much? If you need some privacy, just let me know and I'll go for a swim at the beach and give you some privacy. Let's work out a schedule."

He shook his head. "That's not it. I got a call this morning. My career, such as it is, and Cathy's career hinge on you not being here. I'm sorry. I was threatened, but the guy can back up those threats and I won't have Cathy's career ended early."

Cathy yelled from the bedroom. "I can take care of myself. I'm not going to be intimidated by a middle-aged alcoholic asshole. I thought you had bigger balls than that."

I only knew one middle-aged, alcoholic asshole. "Are you telling me Sweeney is behind this? You're caving in to threats from that fat fuck? I agree with Cathy. I thought you had more stones than that." I shook my head. Sweeney was trying to run me out of town. I tended to resist that kind of pressure. He had no idea what I was capable of. "Tell me to my face Sweeney threatened you if I didn't leave this house."

He looked down at the table and muttered something.

"I didn't hear that. I can't believe it. Are you for real?"

He looked me square in the eye. "Bart is apparently on the cusp of a $200 million movie. The Hanks are involved."

"The Hanks? What in the hell is "The Hanks"?"

"You know, Tom Hanks. His son Colin."

"Involved in a movie Sweeney is making? I don't think so."

"It's true. I did some calling around. He's pitching hard. Looks to have some financing behind him. And he's pushing his weight around really hard about you. I don't have a choice."

"The hell you don't. Push back. Tell him to get stuffed. Stand up to the little asshole. I'm certain he killed Joel, so I'd call his bluff. He's probably too afraid I'll start telling people what I know. That might not send him to jail, but it would certainly destroy his reputation."

"You really think he killed Joel? And the police are doing nothing?"

"Nothing. They think I'm losing my mind."

"He seemed to be concerned you were trying to destroy him."

"I don't want to just destroy him. I want him to go to jail. To suffer." I looked at him. "So why do I have to leave?"

"He'll kill my career and Cathy's career if you stay. I'm really sorry. You need to go."

Cathy came storming out of the bedroom. "Pussy. You're a goddamned pussy. And he's an asshole. What's his number? I'll tell him myself."

"Cathy, calm down—Bernie's right. Sweeney will tank the both of you. I don't want that on my head. You're both doing so well. Let me get my stuff and I'll go."

"Right. Like I'd let that happen. You're like a sister. Sweeney can go to hell."

"Oh, I'm sure he will. Don't worry. I'm a big girl. I'll be out in half an hour."

And I was true to my word. It wasn't like I had much to pack. I didn't own much.

I didn't have anywhere to go. There was nobody else in this sprawling city who I felt comfortable enough with to cage a place to stay. This really burned me. I pulled into the same Jack-in-the-Box parking lot I was in before and called Bart.

"Sweeney here."

"You asshole. I would love nothing more than for you to crash and burn. I hope you rot a million lives in hell." I was on a roll. "You are nothing more than a sleaze-bag, wanna-be big shot with an over-inflated ego. You're hung like a hamster and smell like the ass end of an English Sheepdog. Karma is a bitch and I'm here to promise you right now this will all come back and bite you in you pasty, over-fed, white ass."

"Who is this?"

"You know who it is, Sweeney. You're half a bee's dick away from copping a murder charge, assault, attempted kidnapping and theft. Maybe it's you who should consider getting the hell out of Dodge before I start making a stink."

"You already make a stink. I've heard back from some of your auditions and you would have been better off if you hadn't turned up."

Oh, he knew where to hit. That stung. And while intellectually I knew he was bullshitting me, emotionally it was a slap to the face. Self-confidence is a gossamer web easily ripped to fucking shreds by nothing more than words. "Hey, bee's dick. Shut your gob. Know that I will take you down. I don't know how yet, but your days of glory are coming to a premature close, very, very soon."

Bart laughed, a phlegmy, throaty, hopefully cancer-indicating laugh. What a shit. "You're not going to do anything. You're incapable of doing anything. There are no levers for you too pull. You're too small. Nothing that you do, no influences that you have, or even think you have, would touch me. You're a speck of dust on my car. Bird shit on my windshield. Nothing more than an annoyance. Now Ellie, dear, I've got to run. I have some errands need tending to and they are far more important than whatever you are saying. Cleaning dog shit up the park is more important than you right now. Go get fucked and leave me alone. I expect you to be on the next flight out of this beautiful country back to your cesspool land of convicts."

He hung up before I could respond. Probably for the best since it was just devolving into full on trash talk. But it gave me an idea. If he was off to run an errand, as he said, I'd be able to collect my stuff. I still had not the foggiest idea where I'd put it, but at least I'd have it. Finally.

I oriented myself and pulled a U-turn. His place was about fifteen minutes away, and if I was lucky, he'd be gone before I got there.

He wasn't. I slowly rolled up the street until I could see down the drive. His car was still parked there. I drove past the house and around the corner, got out, and snuck back on foot. I could keep an eye on him from the grounds and get into the guesthouse when he left. I walked around to the back. There were some shrubs I could hide behind close to the house. From that vantage point I could see his car. I'd see him leaving. There'd be no mistake.

I was just settling in when he crashed through the door with a phone stuck to the side of his head. "No, you do as I tell you. I need some shit now. Not later, not in an hour, no, goddamn it. I'm starting to withdraw. I've got an A-list meeting tonight and I'm not going to go there strung out, do you understand me?" He stopped talking and listened. "No, you moron, not my place. Do you think I was born yesterday? In the hills. The usual place. In the open so I can see you're alone." He stopped and listened again. "A key. How much is a key?"

He paced his porch, and I thought the game was up for a second when it looked like he was staring right at me, but his gaze kept moving and he didn't change the pace of his step or his talking.

He took the phone away from his face and held it front of his face and yelled into it. "What? Are you shittin" me?" He put it back to his head. "You've got me over a barrel. You will get this on the comeback. Karma is a bitch."

The conversation interested me. If I could get him on video buying a kilogram of heroin I wouldn't need to prove he killed Joel. He'd be going to jail anyway. Not that a death sentence wouldn't please me, but fifteen years behind bars being some asshole's bitch would be just fine with me.

I waited until he finished his call and went back into the house. I ran back to my car, crouched over to stay below the window line. I started it and stayed just around the corner across the street. I'd be able to see him as he came out of the driveway.

This was a relatively big surprise. I knew he popped pills, but heroin was new to me. Of course, I was a naive foreigner in the big city. Aside from the odd time I could afford a good scotch, no mood altering substances passed my lips. After a year I was beginning to think I was way out on the very thin end of the Gaussian curve. At the other end were the John Belushi's of the world. I thought Bart was down on my end of the scale, but it was looking like he was much further up the line.

My phone had a digital zoom and a microphone but I wasn't sure how close I had to be to make an intelligible recording. I guess I'd find out soon enough. At least I knew I could outrun him. Even if I was wearing heels I could outrun him.

I heard his car start. It backed out of the driveway and turned to leave, away from the place I was parked. I was pretty sure I couldn't slide down in my car any further than I already had. He pulled away and I slowly sat up. I started my car and followed him. I could get my stuff later. Nailing this bastard to the cross got top priority.

26

Bart backed out of his driveway and smiled when he saw Ellie sitting in her car at the end of the block. He knew she would be back, but hadn't expected to see her so soon. "Fucking Nancy Drew. Thinks she can sneak around in my yard and not be noticed."

Catching her hiding behind the bush by the back porch was fortuitous. All he needed to do was bait her with the opportunity to trap him in some illicit act. A fake phone call to an imaginary drug dealer appeared to have done the trick. He knew exactly where he could take her, where there would be no witnesses and plenty of time and space to get rid of the nosy bitch once and for all.

The thought of luring a twenty-three year old woman to the scrub north of the city to kill her didn't strike him as odd. Or deranged. Or as something he should be at all concerned about. He checked the glove box again for the revolver then dialed up a jazz station, settled back in the driver's seat and started a circuitous path out of town. As long as she didn't figure out he was leading instead of her following he'd be okay.

The radio muted and his phone rang, the display on the dash indicating a call from George.

"Hey, Georgie, what's up? You ready for tonight?" Bart kept an eye on the mirror. He didn't want to lose Ellie.

"Hello, Bart. I just got off the phone with a group of investors who are incredibly positive on this deal. They want a representative at the meeting tonight. They are eager to have Colin and Tom involved. In fact, their involvement pretty much guarantees the cash. Do you think that will be a problem?"

Bart chewed on that for a second. "Money's popping up hand over fist. Hey, the Hanks are going to want to be paid well for their contributions, and I've got no problem paying them. I think it would speed things along. We could conceivably close this tonight. Damn, George, this is getting exciting. Are you getting excited?" He flicked his eyes to the rearview mirror. Ellie's Beetle was still tracking him.

"Nervous. Good things have a habit of falling apart at the last minute in this town. Don't get greedy or do anything stupid tonight, for my ulcer's sake, okay?"

Bart laughed. "Me? Do something stupid? Never. Just don't be late. I'll let Marty know there's an extra guest coming. I'm sure he won't mind. I'd love to know the commissions he takes off the Hanks kid. Must be rolling in it. See you tonight." He dropped the call and turned left onto Topanga Canyon Boulevard, heading north. He kept an eye on the mirror as he eased into traffic. Ellie was right behind him, like a good little puppy.

Cathy pulled her clothes off their hangers and stuffed them into her suitcase. "That's it. I've had it. You're a spineless asshole. I'm going to track down Ellie and we'll get ourselves a place. Together. Without you. Asshole."

Bernie leaned against the doorjamb. "I did it for the both of us. Sweeney could ruin us."

Cathy dropped the clothes on the bed and swung around to face the man who was about to become her first ex-boyfriend in over five years. "A week ago he was a laughing stock and now you're bouncing on the end of his strings. Are you a moron? He's a pompous ass with an over-inflated sense of self-worth. Stand up to the prick or stand out of my way."

"I've got bills to pay. I can't do anything else but what I'm doing. I can't afford the risk. Hey, Ellie will be fine. She's a strong girl. She'll land on her feet."

Cathy pushed passed him. "Move." She grabbed her toothbrush, hairdryer and a handful of other things from the bathroom and pushed him out of the way again coming back into the bedroom. "You're throwing a young, struggling actress, 8,000 miles away from home, under the bus so you can save your career. Running electricity and lights on sound stages. You are pathetic. I didn't really know you, did I?"

Bernie reached out and took her gently by the arm. "Cath, she's poison. If you help her he will tear you down."

She pulled her arm away. "You really don't want to touch me again. I won't be responsible for the number of bones that I break if you do." She zipped shut the suitcase and pulled it on to the floor. "I'll be back for the rest when I've found a place. By the weekend at the latest. I'll leave the keys on the counter. You'll probably not want to be here when I come for it."

"Cath, please, we need to talk about this."

"We just did. Good-bye."

Bart stopped at the red light at Saticoy. Ellie was three cars behind him. "Like a good little detective." The morning's blue sky was rapidly surrendering to an incoming bank of heavy, dark clouds. The wind picked up, steady from the west with strong gusts. The service center sign across the road was shaking under the force of the approaching storm. A horn behind him alerted him to the fact the light had turned green. He waved thanks to the Prius behind him and continued north on Topanga.

Oat Mountain was getting closer. Bart couldn't believe his luck. The approaching storm pretty much guaranteed he'd be undisturbed in the old covered wagon trials north of the 118. With luck her body wouldn't be found for weeks, another apparent suicide.

There was still one more thing to do before tonight's meeting. He didn't want to do it, but he didn't have a choice. He was out-voted. He called Bobby Bowens.

"Good day, Sweeney. What can I do for you?"

"It's what I can do for you, Bobby. I hope you're free tonight."

"Putting on another party? Thanks for the offer. Really appreciate it, but I'm staying in tonight."

"Oh no, you're not. Marty has invited us to a meeting tonight with some people very interested in getting our pet project off the ground. I need you there with the rest of us, in a shiny suit and with a smile on your face."

"When you say "some people very interested" are you talking about money people? Because I can skip that meeting."

"There will be a money guy there. Maybe three. They're showing up like rednecks at a rodeo. But that's not who I was referring to. The people who are very interested in our project are Colin and Tom Hanks." There was a long silence. "Bobby, are you still there?"

"Sorry. Mentally going through my wardrobe and I'm pretty sure I need to do some shopping before this meet. Do you have a where and a when?"

Bart laughed and gave him the details.

"Malibu? On the cliffs? There's a hell of a storm coming in, pal. I hope our hosts have one of the really solid houses. I'd hate to slide into the Pacific during the birth of our project."

"Relax Bobby. Just don't be late." He hung up and checked the rearview mirror. She was still there.

Cathy pulled into the parking lot of a Super 8 Motel. Not the best accommodations, but better than any place with Bernie. She sat in the parking lot and called Ellie. She didn't know where the Australian was staying, but maybe they could split costs. The call went straight to voice mail.

"Hey, Ellie, it's Cathy here. I've moved out. I'd apologize for rat-bastard Bernie, but that would imply I want anything to do with him. So I'll apologize for me. So sorry you have to go through this. I'm staying at the Super 8 on Topanga near Saticoy for a few days while I find a place. I'm thinking we should get an apartment together, maybe closer to where the work is, maybe even West Hollywood. Call me when you get this. You know my number."

She hung up, closed her eyes and leaned her head against the headrest. "Life is just chock full of slap-to-the-face surprises.

Ellie drove up Topanga behind her, too focused on her target to notice Cathy.

The wind ahead of the storm buffeted Bart's car. The sky was darker, the black clouds hanging low and heavy. The mood was set. Bart laughed. "This is like a fucking movie. I love it." He fought against the wind as gusts swept around Stoney Point. He was only minutes away from getting rid of the last burr under his saddle. Topanga kept rising until he was stopped by the traffic lights at Santa Susana Pass. She was two cars behind him and one lane to the left. The light standards were shaking like a 6.0 was hitting the area. He pulled through the intersection and lucked through a green light under the 118. Ellie got caught by a red. He pulled over on Mayan Drive and got out with a map, looking like he was wondering where he should be going. It was the only map he had in the car, one for the Santa Barbara City Center. He laughed. "I can act too, bitch." He couldn't keep the map flat enough to read. But he didn't need to stay there for long. When the first cars started coming through the now green light he hopped back in his car and continued up Mayan Drive. It wound along the base of the hills, dirt roads splintering off to the left every 100 yards or so. There was one particular road he was looking for. It had been a couple of years since he was last here and Bart was a little concerned that development may have stolen the opportunity from him.

His luck was holding. There was a gate across the road, but it was sitting half open. There was enough room to get his car through, and if there was enough room to get his car through then there was enough room for Ellie's car to get through. He bounced over the ruts of the dirt road and winced. The front end of his car felt like it was being shaken apart. "Consolation, Bart, old boy. Success tonight means you can buy that Bentley you've had your eyes on."

The dirt road switched back. He traveled along the ridge of a small hill back in the direction from which he had come. He watched Ellie pull through the gate and bounce up the same hill. "Her car may not actually make it. So do I have her shoot herself in the car, or out of the car? Out of the car would be easier, but I think in the car would be more convincing."

The road along the ridge went for less than a quarter of a mile before it dropped precipitously down the back of the hill to follow along the bottom of a little Valley. This is where the covered wagon trails were, a web of paths not fit to be called roads. Secluded, surrounded by echo-generating hills that easily masked the direction of gunshots, this was the place to sort out problems that couldn't otherwise be sorted out. Bart rode the brakes down the rutted road and as it bottomed out he took a sharp left and stopped. Ellie hung back on the ridge, probably afraid she'd be spotted. "Smart girl. For a dumb girl." He sat at the base of the hill until he saw the first edge of her front bumper, then proceeded slowly along the road. A couple of minutes later she reached the bottom of the hill and turned left. Bart figured a mile into the scrub and she'd be so far out of civilization it would be her skeleton that was discovered.

Bart looked in his rearview mirror again. Ellie had stopped. He slowed and was about to turn around in the narrow road when his phone rang. He thumbed the button on the steering wheel. "Sweeney here."

"You must think I'm an idiot."

"Ellie? Whatever are you talking about?" He watched in his mirror as she executed a three-point turn, hearing her grunt against the non-power assist steering.

"You set me up to follow you out here to the middle of nowhere." There was a crash of thunder and a wall of water dropped from the sky. The storm had arrived. And the Beach Boys were right. "What were your plans? Were you going to stick me with some drugs like you did to Joel? Or were you going to incapacitate me somehow and leave me out here to die? I don't think so, asshole. I'm on to you."

"You're crazy, Ellie. I'm in the parking lot at my local grocery store." The Beetle stopped in mid turn. It was too far away to see Ellie's face, but he imagined she was looking out the window at him. "I need to pick up some wine for tonight. Big meeting, you know. Want to impress my hosts."

"Sounds like you. You get the best vintage at Ralph's. I'm looking at your car, right now. You really do think I'm an idiot." She finished the three-point turn and sped back down the dirt road spraying up mud as the rain filled the holes.

"Bitch. Watch your back. You're not going to last the night." Bart hung up and wrenched the wheel into a U-turn, getting stuck in a mud hole. "Sonuvabitch." He grabbed the revolver from the glove box and leaned out the door of his car. She had to slow down to make the corner to go back up the hill. He fired a shot left-handed at the Beetle just as it made the turn. He thought he hit it, but couldn't be sure. It continued up the hill, so even if he had hit the car, it appeared he missed Ellie.

"Fuck." He got out of the car and was instantly drenched with rain. He steadied himself on the front fender and shot again, coincidentally timed with a clap of thunder. The back passengers-side window disappeared, and the upward progress of the car slowed for a brief second, then surged forward.

"Double fuck." He shook the water out of his hair and looked at the hole he was in. It wasn't that deep. He could rock the car out, but it would take five or ten minutes. By that time she'd be long gone. "This day better turn around and it better turn around pretty fucking fast." He kicked the tire mired in the mud and crawled back into his car. She was gone. That was twice now she managed to get out of his grasp. Third if you count the first day, when he didn't have much of a plan and copped a kick to the nuts. "I am going to hurt her so fucking hard she'll wish she never met me."

27

I wish I'd never met him. I caught on to the fact he was leading me into a trap of some sort at the bottom of the hill. The weather that was coming down, there wasn't a druggie in the world who would be out in this, in the bush, no matter what the profit.

I pulled out my phone to call his bluff and my battery was dead. So much for recording him. I needed a new one. So I called him with Joel's phone. Called him out on his plan and beat a hasty retreat, as they say.

I didn't know the asshole had a gun.

The first shot hit the body of my car. I'm not sure exactly where, but I felt and heard the impact on the back of the Beetle somewhere. The old girl didn't hesitate though, so wherever he hit wasn't an important part of the car. I turned back up the hill, hoping like hell the road was more rock than it was mud. By rights I should have been in a four-wheel drive to make it, but I had to make do with what I had. The adrenaline rush from getting shot at pretty much drove me forward.

Then, that clap of thunder. The lightning strike must have been just over the hill because the thunder was deafening. The brain does funny things under stress. At the same time as the clap of thunder, my back passenger-side window was shot out. Shards of glass flew into the side of my head and my right arm. My first, immediate thought was that the car had been struck by lightning.

As if.

I looked to my right and saw Bart leaning on his car with a gun in his hand. Shit. I pressed the pedal to the floor as hard as I could, almost driving it through the floorboards. The old car lurched forward, spinning a bit on the mud then gripping the surface like an old Army Jeep. I didn't feel any pain from the cuts, but blood was pouring down my neck and arm. Self-preservation dictated I get as much space as possible between me and the lunatic with a gun before looking at my injuries.

I headed west on the 118 toward Simi Valley, away from Bart's place. He would never look for me there. I don't think he knew Simi Valley existed as any more than an abstraction. Adrenaline, blood loss, general disgust in my fellow human beings all came together in a rush. My stomach heaved and I pulled over and jumped out and threw up on the side of the road. Some wag honked his horn and cheered me on as he sped by. Oh, the humanity.

I took the first exit, onto Kuehner, and turned into a pull out to survey the damage.

To myself and to my car.

The rain was pelting down. A diluted red stream ran down the right side of my body. I don't think I was shot, but I'd never been shot before, so I had no frame of reference. I had a couple of towels in the back of the car and one draped over the passenger seat from the trips to the beach. One of the towels, on the passenger side, was covered in broken glass and was soaking wet. I took it out and gently shook the glass shards to the ground and placed it to one side.

I dragged the second one out and held it in the rain for a few seconds. It didn't take long until it was dripping wet. Water was running down my face like I was in a waterfall. The stream down my right side was still running red. I gingerly touched the side of my head and neck until I found the source. There was a flap of skin hanging loose just behind my ear. It hurt a little bit, but was producing an awful lot of blood. I balled the towel and pressed it against the side of my head.

As I lifted my right arm to hold the towel in place I saw a cut on the inside of my arm, a fairly deep one on that pasty white part of the arm that never tans, an inch or so away from my the inside of my elbow on my forearm. I was going to have to tie this up somehow and wait for the bleeding to slow before I drove or I'd probably end up bleeding to death. Maybe. I wasn't a first aid expert, but it didn't look good.

I removed the towel from my head and grabbed the one draped across the back of the passenger seat. It was stiff and crusty from the salt water. I folded it lengthwise twice so it was a long, thin belt. Wrapping it around my lower arm and tying it, without assistance, taxed all of my mediocre coordination skills. I finally got it double wrapped and tied it off using my left hand and my teeth. Mobility was restricted, but there was constant pressure on the wound and from what I remember from a first aid class I took, pressure was a good thing on open wounds.

I took the towel—the one remaining towel that had suspected glass shards through it—and draped it over the broken window. I managed to put it lengthwise across, wrapping the edges around the door frame and forcing the door shut to hold it in place. It wasn't waterproof, but it would have to do for now.

It was still coming down in buckets. Gusts blew the rain hard enough I'm sure I could surf it if I had the board with me. I sat inside the car. I had to keep my arm elevated for a little while until the bleeding slowed or I'd pass out while I was driving and I didn't think that would be a good idea. I could use a breather anyway. I didn't like stress. I was in a secluded place, a little off the road cubbyhole that offered a bit of safety. I was leaking blood out multiple places on my body and ached in places I never thought I could ache. And I had no recollection of doing anything that would justify the muscle pain. The rain was beating a tattoo on the roof of the car and the windows were fogging up. There was little chance of Sweeney bumping into me in this little corner. I tipped my seat back and pulled my iPhone to listen to music.

Forgetting it was dead.

I'd have to listen to whatever music Joel had on his phone. I slid the headphones into his phone and pressed the play button.

Joel's voice filled my head.

"What is this, Day 88? Yes. Eighty-fucking-eight."

The last thing I had listened to on his phone was his audio diary. It was picking up where I left off.

"Friday. I'm fucking beat. It's been a week of ups and downs and on balance I'd say it was a positive. This diary is brought to you by the nude Joel. Please do not listen if you are under the age of eighteen or are easily offended by unfit, pasty-white bodies. I am in the tub. Hot as hell water, Epsom salts and a bit of a bubble. Dad would shit himself, but it feels fan-fucking-tastic."

My breath caught in my throat and I started quietly crying. This was recorded on Friday, the day he died. I needed to be near a beach. It was a primal thing. I started my car and cranked the heater. I was soaking wet and freezing. The ocean would be awesome tonight, but the beach probably wouldn't be safe in this weather. I headed for Santa Monica Pier.

Joel continued talking in my ears.

"Tonight off, big show tomorrow. My agent is a genius. His call this morning is going to put me on the map. Note to self: call him back and confirm the date. Things have been shifted and I'm going on the show. And that, my friends, is fucking awesome."

I heard someone knocking on the door in the background of the audio. I turned the volume up as high as it would go.

"Hang on a second, dear listeners, there's been a disturbance in the force."

I heard a clunk as the phone was put down. The recording continued. He had forgotten to stop it. Splashing noises were followed by Joel's voice in the distant background. He was welcoming someone. The voices got louder as I headed back down Topanga Canyon toward the Pacific. The road was treacherous. I had to divide my attention between the recording and the switchbacks on the road once I got south of the freeway. After a few minutes the conversation became intelligible again.

"What are you doing here Bart? I'm trying to chill. You're supposed to give a day's notice before you come over here."

I heard the water splashing as, I assumed, Joel got back in the bathtub. Bart's voice came through loud and clear.

"Joel, my friend, I'm not here as your landlord. I'm here on a social visit. I want to try and rekindle that thing we had three or four months ago. That was nice. I enjoyed it. I think you enjoyed it."

"Not a chance, Bart. I like you, sure, but I'm on a purification kick right now and it's working for me. No booze, no weed and no sex. I'm on the top of my game. Don't want to jinx it. But I'm flattered, man. Really, I am."

Bart and Joel had a thing? How in the hell did I miss that? I pulled a hard left by the L.A. Shakespearean theater. I had good memories of that place, even If they were small roles. I navigated the switchback and double-checked the iPhone after I came out of the turn. The volume was up, but there was silence. I assumed the recording had stopped by that point and was about to stop listening when Bart's voice came back, loud and strong.

"So can I get you something to drink while you're stewing in there? A beer? Rum and Coke? A nice glass of Pinot Noir"

"I told you man, I'm clean. There's some grapefruit juice in the fridge, if you're still offering."

"That'll have to do, I guess."

"What do you mean by that, Bart? Have to do?"

"Exactly what I said. If I can't get you adult beverages, grapefruit juice will have to do. I'll get one for you."

I heard the footsteps recede and Joel hum along to some show tunes. How like him. A minute or so later, as I was turning left on the Pacific Coast Highway and getting hammered by the torrential rain, I heard Bart return to the bathroom.

"Your juice. Don't know how you drink this stuff. I have the smallest sip and my face turns inside out. You must take an hour to get through this glass."

"Nah. I'm used to it. I can take this glass in one swallow. Watch."

I heard some swallowing and a clink as the glass was put down.

"That tasted funny. Did you get the juice from the fridge?"

"I did, my young friend. Added some of my own ingredients to it. You are mere minutes away from being voted 'the one most willing to comply', although I'm be lying if I said I roofied juices on a regular basis. I prefer the fruity alcohol drinks. They mask the flavor better. You downed that pretty fast, big guy. You feeling the effect yet?"

"Wha-? Whaddafuck you put in that?"

"The almighty equalizer. Rohypnol. Don't worry young fella. We're going to have a fabulous time tonight and you're not going to remember a single thing."

"Bastard. Ahhh. Ah, fuck, what izzat?"

Joel's words were more and more incomprehensible. I could hear him gasping for breath, then nothing. I pulled over to a small parking area on the side of the PCH and cried as I listened. I was hearing him die. I so wished I could un-hear this. I wiped my eyes and pulled out, continuing on to Santa Monica. Shit. I had the evidence I needed to nail Sweeney to the cross.

I reached to pull out the ear bud when I heard Sweeney talk.

"Joel. Joel?" Slap, slap. "Joel, buddy, what the fuck? Oh my God. Holy shit the fucker is dead. Jesus, Jesus, what can I do here? People don't roofie

themselves. Not normally. This will come back to me. Can't come back to me. No. Think, think, think. Need to use some misdirection. Yes. Make them think "B" when it was actually "A". Jesus, what can I do? I can't get him out of the tub. Autoerotic asphyxiation isn't an option." Fingers snapped. *"Drug overdose. Not tablets, needs to be injected. Wait, wait, wait, do I still have some shit left?"*

There was a scuffle of shoes then silence. I pulled into the visitor's center at the Santa Monica Pier and got out of the car. The bleeding had stopped on my scalp, but the rain was still pounding down and it was a good bet the rain on my head would start it up again. I took the towel I had pressed up against my head and fashioned a simple turban, tying it around my scalp just above my ears. It would do.

I still had the headphones plugged into my head. There was a considerable length of silence, but I kept listening. I walked over the pedestrian bridge to the pier. It was almost completely void of people. The wind and rain were pummeling the coast with a ferocity rarely seen, if the weather wags were to be believed. This is exactly what I needed. It cleansed my soul. I put my hands in my pockets and leaned into the wind. It was raw, primal mother earth energy, and I wanted - no, needed - to tap in to it.

It was close to 5:00. The sun hadn't set yet, but the storm had darkened the sky as if it were a permanent twilight. I walked out to the end of the pier, deep in my own thoughts about Joel and what he had meant to me and how much I was missing him now. When Bart's voice popped into my head through the ear buds I almost wet myself.

"Okay, so let's see. It's been awhile since I've done this. Shit, I'm just going to pump the whole lot of it into his arm. Won't matter if it's seen as suicide or accident, it takes the focus off me."

There were some rustling noises I couldn't identify then Bart spoke again.

"Okay that should do it. Full syringe injected, prints sorted, leave the stuff here. Easy come, easy go."

The asshole chuckled and I heard his footsteps leave the guesthouse and the recording went silent. I lifted the phone out of my pocket. The battery was dead.

I stood at the end of the pier, bloody, wet and alone, buffeted by the gusts. The wind lashed the ocean into furious caps of green foam, angry at the world. I could sympathize. Except my world, right now, was one person.

And if it killed me, he was going to pay.

28

It took Bart longer than he expected to extract his car from the rapidly growing quagmire. "This must have been what it was like trying to get out of Iraq; every step I take, it makes the mess worse." By the time the dashboard clock read 6:03pm he was finally on his way, half of the surrounding thicket trashed and stuffed in the mud hole for traction and half of that mud all over him. He stood in the pounding rain for a few minutes, arms extended, looking for all the world like a soggy, muddy Messiah.

The celestial shower removed most of the grime. Bart stripped to his underwear and wrung out the clothes, dropping them in the front seat. Shivering, he climbed back in the car, cranked the heat to full and navigated the slippery mud track up the hill and back on to Maya Drive.

He pulled on to Topanga and his mobile phone rang. He looked at the display. It was a number he didn't recognize. "Maybe the house in Malibu." He thumbed the pick-up button on the steering wheel.

"Sweeney speaking. And who would this be?"

"I've got enough evidence to put you away for Joel's death."

Sweeney's heart skipped a beat. "Ellie. So you're still alive. Disappointing. What was that you were saying?"

"Evidence, Sweeney. I've got enough to put you away for years."

"So why are you calling me, you stupid bitch? Take it to the police." He chuckled. "You're bluffing, aren't you? You have nothing that would hold up. My word against your word." He was about ten minutes from his house, a warm shower and dry clothes. "So pack up your shit and leave my country."

"Your word against mine? No, I don't think so. Your word against yours."

Bart slowed and pulled over. "What do you mean by that, missy?"

"Joel recorded you killing him. I have that recording."

"Oh, horseshit. Pull another fucking leg."

"What, you want me to prove it? How much roofie did you put in his grapefruit juice?"

Bart slumped in his seat. "Fuck."

"Right? You are fucked. I'm taking this to Perkins tomorrow morning. You've got until then to turn yourself in. This recording is pretty damning. Right up to where you shot him up. Very clear audio. Perkins will have no choice but to believe me after he hears this"

Bart punched the dash. "Wait, no, Ellie. Let's talk about this. It was an accident. Let me meet with you and explain what happen. It was an accident. Hey, I'm making this huge movie. Meeting the backers tonight. I'd love to tell them I've found the female lead."

"Oh, get fucked. What kind of person do you think I am?"

"Come on, Ellie, I told you, an accident. Give me a chance to explain.

"You pumped him full of shit to make it look like a suicide. Do the right thing."

He cursed. "Where in the hell are you?"

There was no answer. She had hung up.

He clenched his fist. "So fucking close." He checked the time. Five hours to the meeting. He couldn't let her take the recording to the police. He couldn't let her ruin his day. His life. "Fuck that fucking mother-fucking bitch" He punched the dash again. "Where in the hell is she?"

He called the last placed he knew her to be. "Bernie, where's Ellie?"

"Sweeney, I really don't want to talk to you, man. Sorry I ever met you."

"Any way to talk to your friend? Look, I need to talk to Ellie. I want to apologize to her. I was a bit hard on her."

"Too late, man. She split already. You were pretty clear."

"So let me talk to your girlfriend. They're close."

"Like I said, too late. She split right after Ellie did. She's not returning my calls. Thanks a lot, buddy. You've totally screwed up my life. Don't call me again." Bernie hung up.

Bart looked at the phone in his hand.

"Where in the hell were you when you called, Bourke?" And then he smiled to himself, scrolled though the phone's menu, found the number she called from and dialed it.

"Thank you for calling Mariasol Restaurant on the Santa Monica Pier. This is Pete. How may I help you?"

"Pete? Sorry, what was the name of the place again?"

"This is the Mariasol Cocina Mexicana Restaurant on the Santa Monica Pier. Are you calling to make a reservation?"

"No, but thank you very much, Pete. I think I may have called the wrong number. You're right on the pier, right?"

"That's right."

"I'll have to check it out some time." Bart thought for a second. "So, Pete, you guys must be pretty quiet tonight with this fantastic storm we're having."

"Yeah, it's pretty much dead. It was a little busier earlier, but they all cleared out. All that's left are a couple who I think made the reservation months ago and some poor girl who was in a car accident or something, and she's just waiting for a ride. It would be easy to get you a table sir, if you like great Mexican food."

"Thanks buddy, but I called the wrong number. Thanks for your time."

He hung up and put the car in gear. His time window was narrowing. Getting to Santa Monica, back home to change and then to Malibu would use every minute he had.

He had a couple of calls to make before he got there.

"Bobby, thank God you answered the phone."

"Who's this?"

"Bart. I would have thought my number was programmed into your phone. So, you're at home, right?"

"Of course I am. Have you looked outside? It's fucking crazy out there. Is this dinner still on?"

"Why wouldn't it be? Neither sleet, rain, hail, you know all that stuff."

"That's for postal deliveries. What in the hell are you talking about?

"Never mind that. It's not important. Yes, the dinner is still on, and I need you to do something incredibly important for me."

"Yeah, pass. Nothing ever good comes from that kind of intro. Find some other patsy."

"Wait, don't hang up. I'm not talking about hiding a body or anything. This isn't *Pulp Fiction*, for God's sake. I just need you to give me an alibi for the afternoon. I was at your place from about 1:00 until 8:00 when I left to get ready to go to the dinner, okay?"

"What the hell is up, Sweeney?"

"Nothing bad, pal. Just hiding some activities from a paramour."

"What the fuck?"

"Big words scare you. Embrace them. Face the fear. I don't want a special someone - a paramour - to know what I was up to today. Purely innocent. Just a guy covering the ass of another guy."

Bowens grumbled for a few minutes before acquiescing. "Fine. We were working on the screenplay, right?"

"Now what are you talking about?"

Bowen sighed. "The alibi. If anyone asks, you are at my place and we're looking at the screenplay."

"Right. Exactly. Good man. Appreciate this. See you tonight."

He accelerated onto the onramp of the Ventura Freeway. "Freeway to 405 to Santa Monica Freeway. Shit, that's going to take me almost forty-five minutes. Let's hope there's no traffic tonight."

He hit the freeway doing 75, checked the time and called Marty.

"Pal, Sweeney here. So, this dinner, it's hard locked to 10:30?"

"I told you before, we can't do it any earlier."

"Not earlier. I'm talking about a bit later."

"What, 10:30 isn't late enough? These people have lives, Sweeney. No. It's 10:30 or it's next week sometime. Why? What's going on?"

"No, no, no. 10:30 is fine. It's just that I had this thing with a guy and there's a slim possibility that I was going to be running late, but I'll make sure that doesn't happen." He swung into the left lane and punched it, the speedometer hitting 85. "Don't worry pal, I'll be there."

"Good. We're excited about this project, Bart. Don't fuck it up, okay?" Marty hung up.

Bart smiled at that. "Excited. The Hanks are excited about my project. Fuckin'-A." He looked up from the phone and saw was where he was.

"Shit." He cut across five lanes and just made the off ramp to the 405. "Thank Christ there's no traffic. Making good time here."

He hit speed-dial and made one last call. "George, Bart here. You excited about this meeting tonight?"

"Well, yeah, I guess. A little long in the tooth to actually say 'excited', but yes, Bart, I'm looking forward to it."

"I just got off the phone with Marty, and Marty says they are excited. And if they're excited, I'm excited."

"Good for you. I'm optimistically and realistically positive about the outcome. That's as close as I get."

"Yeah, you're a fucking drag, Listen, I called for a reason, not just to chat."

"Of course you did. What do you want now?"

"Just a small favor. You're going to be at the place in Malibu on time tonight?"

"Well, they're 'excited', I guess I better be. What's up?"

"I'm stuck with this thing I've got to get done. Not related to this project, but, you know how it is, it absolutely has to get done today. I'll probably be okay, but in the off chance that I run a bit late can you make sure they start without me? Be my proxy, as it were. I'll definitely be there, but I might be a couple of minutes late. But only maybe. Could be that I'm on time. Just covering all the bases."

"What's this mysterious thing that just has to get done today?"

Bart shook his head. Like he'd share this. Maybe later. Over a drink from a $15,000 dollar bottle of scotch. "Maybe someday I'll let you in on it, but it's a personal thing. Kinda funny, actually, in the grand scheme of things. One of those stories over a drink someday. So can you do it?"

"Do it? Do what? Start the meeting on time whether you're there or not? Pretty fucking sure I can. No problem."

Bart was nodding. These were a great bunch of people he was tied up with. "Fantastic, George. You're a pal."

"Yeah, sure. See you tonight."

Bart, on autopilot, hung up the phone and took the Santa Monica Boulevard exit. He was through the third intersection before he hit the first red light and he realized he took one exit too early. "Shit. Wrong exit. Shit, shit, shit." He sat through the red light, debating whether he should head back to the 405 and hit the Santa Monica Freeway or continue in the direction he was heading. The truck behind him laid on the horn when the light turned green, making the decision for him. "Ah, crap." He accelerated into traffic, wipers beating away the rain not quite fast enough. "Where in the hell are all of you people going in this weather? You should be inside." He slapped the steering wheel and laid on the horn. "Get the hell out of my way."

He pulled around a car in front of him and floored it, reaching sixty-five on the city street. He ran the light at the next intersection and immediately saw red and blue lights flashing in his rear-view mirror. "Oh, sweet Jesus, what now?" He pulled over to the curb and put his hands on the steering wheel.

A cop approached the car and rapped on the window. "Lower it please. And show me your driver's license and registration."

Bart looked at the glove box. The registration was sitting under the revolver. "Okay, just a second." He unbuckled his seatbelt and retrieved his wallet, took out the driver's license and handed it to the officer. "Pretty lousy weather to be out working, isn't it?"

"Do you know why I pulled you over Mr. Sweeney?"

"Probably that red light I ran. I'm in a bit of a rush. Picking up a friend at the pier and want to get back home before this gets even worse."

"Can I see your registration please?"

Bart swallowed. "Hang on a sec. It's in the glove box." He leaned forward and turned his body, blocking the cop's view of the glove box. He popped it open and pushed the revolver out of the way and grabbed his registration. He slammed the compartment shut and turned back to the cop, who now had his hand on the butt of his gun. "Whoa, relax. Here you go."

The officer looked at the registration. "Mr. Sweeney, I'm going to write you a ticket for running that red light back there. The radar wasn't on, so I can't give you a ticket for speeding, although I know you were." He handed the license, registration and the ticket to Bart. "Driving conditions are not optimal Mr. Sweeney. Take it easy until you get home."

"Thanks officer. I'll be careful." The fake smile plastered on his face didn't fool either of them. He waited until the police car pulled away before he continued. "Fuckity-fuck. Another fifteen minutes down the drain."

He hit almost every red light on the rest of Santa Monica Boulevard. By the time he reached the Pier parking lot it was 7:30 and his frustration had reached epic levels. He spotted her Beetle in the parking lot. He parked beside it and took the revolver from the glove box and got out of his car into the pounding weather. The smell of the ocean was strong. He licked his instantly drenched lips and could taste the salt. He made a mental note to have his car washed tomorrow. The corrosion would be terrible. He took a quick look at her car. The back window was broken and covered with a towel and there was a bullet hole in the back just above the engine compartment. He smiled and danced a little jig. He still had it.

The weather didn't show any sign of easing. Lightning strikes off the coast snapped through the sky like fireworks. Onshore wind drove the rain almost horizontally into his face as he walked down the pier. She was here somewhere.

He ran up the stairs to the front door of the restaurant, stuck his head in and took a quick look. Only a couple at one of the tables near the back and a skeleton wait staff hanging out until closing time. He nodded and smiled at the guy at the door. Probably Pete.

He leaned into the wind and rain and ran back down the stairs muttering to himself. "You couldn't have passed me, bitch. Where in the hell are you?" He stopped and looked off to his right. At the corner at the end of the pier a figure stood, back straight, defiantly staring out to the ocean. The rain ebbed a bit and Bart recognized Ellie. He set his jaw and strode down the pier. "You're not getting off here alive."

29

I stood at the corner of the pier, holding the railing for support. The wind whipped the hair back off my head and the rain stung my face. I was cold, but I've been colder. Surfing at Bronte in July in the rain was certainly colder than this. A lot more fun, too. The cut on the inside of my arm was no longer bleeding, but it owned a dull throb, and the slice on my scalp was starting to itch.

I missed living by the water. Maybe I'd find a place near here. I needed to find some work first. As soon as I dropped the phone and recordings off with Perkins I was going to hit this town like they've never been hit.

The wind stopped for a second and I felt a slight tremor in the planks on the deck. Someone was coming up behind me. The way my day was going it could only be one person. "How'd you find me, Bart?" I turned, my back to the wind and tried to hold the hair from my face. I could barely hear him as he yelled against the wind.

"The restaurant's phone number. Caller ID. Technology's a wonderful thing."

Ah, shit. I hadn't thought of that. And I wouldn't have thought Bart to be smart enough to figure it out. "It probably took you an hour to figure that out, didn't it?"

"Where's this recording you were talking about? Are you telling me your buddy was a super secret spy dude who could hide a recording device in plain sight?" He stepped closer, encroaching on my personal space, but on the plus side it made it easier to hear him.

I looked up at the roof of the restaurant and then back at him as he continued talking. "You're full of crap, Ellie. How did you find out about the grapefruit juice? Let me guess: you saw the empty jug and jumped to conclusions." He shook his head. "I'm going to throw you off the pier and be done with you. Not even an Australian could survive in that surf."

I took a step backwards, my ass hitting the cold railing. "Go for it. There are security cameras across the top of the restaurant. Even with this poor visibility, your pasty white head would be recognizable. Plus, you called here, so your phone records tie you to the place. You probably parked in the Pier parking lot where there are a ton of security cameras." I was guessing on that one. "I don't consider myself a martyr, but if that's the only way to get your overfed ass in jail, I'll take it. So bring it on, dick-wad, throw me over if you can. Maybe those cameras are off. Maybe today is your lucky day."

Bart looked over his shoulder, and then turned fully to look at the restaurant, peering through the rain. He definitely saw the three cameras mounted on the roof of the restaurant, all of them covering the end of the pier. I took advantage of his lapse in attention and slid along the railing, trying to get out of his reach.

He skipped ahead of me. "Nuh-uh. Where do you think you're going? We're not finished." He looked at me, at my hands, stuffed in my pockets. "What are you holding on to there? Do you actually have a recording of me?" He grabbed my left arm and tried to pull my hand from my pocket. He was stronger than he looked. "What do we have here?"

"Let go of me, you freak. I'll scream."

"Right. The scream that can overcome this wind has never left a human throat. Do your best. I can barely hear you and I can smell your breath." He wrenched my hand from my pocket. It was the wrong one. It came up empty, but I was going to have a hell of a bruise. "Not there, eh?" He reached for the other one and I scrambled, kicking out at him and trying to run. He grabbed me by the other arm, pulling Joel's phone out of my pocket. It clattered across the pier. We both dove for it, ending up on our knees, in the rain, fighting over an iPhone. Steve Jobs would have been proud.

"Jesus Christ, girl. You're strong. Are you expecting me to believe he was recording something on this when I came in?"

The bastard was winning. I grunted and dug my nails into the back of his hand. "Fuck off and let go, asshole."

Bart swung an elbow and caught me on the jaw. I saw stars. I felt something in my head go and was knocked on my back, driving my tailbone into my spine. He grabbed the phone and stood looking down at me while I tried to gather my shattered wits. Rain pelted down on my face, a deluge almost as strong as a bucket of water. I was close to drowning in the rain.

"Not that tough now, are you?" He poked me in the ribs with his toe. "Hey. Talk to me, bitch. Is this it?" He held up the phone. "Is this your precious evidence?"

I grabbed the railing and pulled myself to my feet, holding my jaw and wiping the water off my face. "What a big man, hitting a woman." I didn't give a shit any more. I lunged for the phone and knocked Bart over. He outweighed me by at least a hundred pounds, so I had to assume he slipped on the soaking wet deck. Still, I took advantage of my position and kneed him in the groin as I fell on top of him. The phone dropped to the deck as he curled up in pain. I grabbed it and struggled to my feet in the wind. "Yes, this is my precious evidence. Not for you, I'm afraid. This is going to Perkins first thing in the morning and then I'm finding an apartment near the beach and killing this town. So fuck you and your fucking fat ass." I kicked him in the ribs. "Get the hell out of here before I add assault charges." I stood over Bart and resisted the urge to spit on him. The wind eased a bit and the rain was abating. "Get lost, Sweeney. You fucked up one time too many."

He looked up at me and smiled. "Surprise." He laughed at the confused look on my face and swept both of my legs out from under me. The phone fell to the deck again and I landed on my ass, the wind knocked out of me. "Dammit, I think you bruised my coccyx. Dick." I rolled over on my side and blinked away tears. Son of a bitch that hurt.

Sweeney rolled on to his knees, took a few deep breaths and retrieved the phone and stood. "Not too fucking bright, bitch." He leaned against the railing, half doubled over. "You've hit me in the nuts so many times in the past few days I think I should get a free shot at your ovaries." He coughed and spat a bunch of phlegm at my feet. What a disgusting pig. "Oh how I'd dearly love to drown you right now. You've caused me more problems than I thought one girl could possibly cause. If those cameras weren't there -" He let the sentence hang.

I lifted myself by the railings, again. "What? What about if those camera's weren't there? What about it big guy? You think you could actually take me? I fought off surfers tougher than you on a regular basis. You're not getting off this pier with that phone, if I have to break every bone in your body." I was getting tired. The exposure to the wind and rain was draining me of energy. But adrenaline is an awesome thing. If I had to, I could get take him out. I was certain of it.

Bart laughed. "I just dropped you on your ass."

"Lucky shot. I wasn't expecting it. Now give me the phone."

He really wasn't very smart. He leaned in close, smiled at me and told me to do something I'm pretty sure was physically impossible and biologically unsound. Didn't matter. He was in range. I showed him what an elbow to the jaw felt like and followed up with a punch to the face. My hands are pretty small and therefore very boney. I caught him in the eye. It hurt my hand, but not as much as it hurt his face. This reminded me of a school dance I went to when I was eighteen and I had to break up a fight. Okay, I was fighting as much as they were, but they started it.

Did I mention he outweighed my by a hundred pounds? The elbow and fist, while emotionally satisfying to deliver, only served to antagonize him more. He snarled and grabbed me by the throat and pushed me up against a light standard. "Jesus, you're thick. You really think you'll work here again?"

My vision blurred, filled with a red haze. Someone ran down the stairs yelling. I could make out "What the hell is going on here?" as I faded. Then Bart let go of my throat and I slumped to the deck. I sucked air into my lungs. Air mixed with the heavy spray from the ocean. I choked, rolled over on to my stomach and coughed until I could breathe again. I rolled on to my back and squinted against the pounding rain. A guy in a waiter's uniform was confronting Bart.

"What the hell is going on?" The waiter flipped up his collar against the weather, a futile effort if I ever saw one.

"Back off kid. None of your business."

"Someone choking a young lady near the doors of my restaurant will always be my business. I'm calling the cops."

I looked up at the two of them. The kid was the one who let me use the phone. Pete, I think. Poor kid. Didn't know what he was getting into.

Bart lifted his shirt. Shit. The maniac had his gun.

The kid saw the grip and backed up a couple of steps, his hands up. "Hey, dude. Uncool. I don't know who you are, but that is seriously uncool."

"Put your hands down, you idiot. You see what I've got. I will use it. On both of you if you don't get the hell out of my face and back into your restaurant. You call the cops and I'll come back looking for you." He lunged at the kid who turned and ran back up the steps.

"Punk." Bart smiled down at me. "Where were we?" He nudged me with his toe. "Hello? Are you listening? I've got thing with some very important guys that I've got to get to. Running a bit late, thanks to you. So," he held up Joel's phone, "this is the evidence that will put me behind bars, is it?" He smiled and shook his head. "Anything else? Is this it? All of your case rests on my words inside this here old, cheap-assed iPhone? Not even one of the new ones?"

I dragged myself back to my feet. If I could have killed him at that moment I would have. Well, seriously maimed him. I don't think I could kill anyone, but he was pushing it. "Give it up Bart. There are enough witnesses to your assault on me. If you turn yourself in to the police and explain to them it was an accident with Joel, maybe they'll cut you a break."

He pinched Joel's phone between his thumb and middle finger. "Did you hit your head? Are you fucking nuts? Why would I turn myself in when the only thing that would even remotely give me any trouble is in this here electronic piece of shit?" He flipped the phone in his hand. "So, problem solved the easy way." He leaned back and threw the phone as far as he could into the Pacific. "Suck on that. There goes your fucking evidence."

The bastard. I launched myself at him again. That phone was all I had. I swung a punch at his head and missed and hit his neck. Thank God. If had connected with his skull I would have broken my hand. His fatty flesh though, it had give.

He stumbled and grabbed at his neck. "What the hell? Get over it. You lost. You are a loser. You can't even act well. Now fuck off and let me get the hell out of here. I've got shit I've got to do."

He strode up the pier, wind on his back, rubbing the spot on his neck where I punched him.

I slumped against the railing and screamed at the sky. Jesus Christ, what kind of shit is this? I had him cold. I had the motherfucker pinned to the virtual wall. And then this. I was bloody, sore, on the receiving end of a personal vendetta that just wasn't fair.

And the only thing I had that could right the horrible mistake was sinking to the bottom of the ocean.

Sinking.

I wiped the rain off my face and ran up the stairs to the restaurant. Pete was inside talking to his co-workers and came running over when he saw me come in. "Are you okay?"

"I'm fine, thanks. Look, it's Pete, isn't it?" He nodded. "Does anyone here have a car charger for an iPhone I can buy off them? I can't find mine. This is an emergency. I'll pay." I pulled my wallet out of my back pocket.

"Yeah, yeah, I've got one. I'll give it to you. Free of charge. Seriously, are you okay? I can call the police."

"I'll be calling them myself. Thanks. If you can get that charger for me I'll give you a fifty for it."

"It's in my car. Come on, it's just around back." He pulled a windbreaker over his wet clothes and led me out to the employee car park.

"Thanks. Why are you guys still open?"

"To rescue damsels in distress, maybe?"

I laughed. The first laugh I had all day. "Thanks. Rescue me with that charger, okay? I've got to get that asshole back."

"Whatever I can do to help. I'm going to call the police. I don't care what that guy said." He opened his car and grabbed the charger. "Take it. No money." He shielded his face from the rain with his hand and leaned in a little closer. "I'm really sorry, Miss. I feel bad about not helping you but he had a gun."

I shook my head. "He's insane. Thanks for trying, but he would have killed you if pushed any harder. Don't worry about it. And don't call the cops. He will come back if you do. Leave him to me. I'm going to make sure his fat ass gets stuck in jail."

The kid shrugged. "Thanks, but it doesn't make me feel any better. You take care of yourself and when all this gets sorted for you, come back and dinner's on the house, okay? Not hitting on you. I'm married, but you really deserve a break."

"Thanks Pete. I'll take you up on that." I kissed him on the cheek. "Now, if you'll excuse me, I've got a thing with a guy."

30

Bart, satisfied and a little bit sore, left a heel print in the driver's door of Ellie's car as he passed it, then got in his car, cranked the heat and made his way to the Santa Monica Freeway. "No bloody traffic lights this time." He chuckled to himself. "That was close. If she didn't have such a big mouth I'd be up shit creek. Now she's just a blip on the radar. Below the radar."

Bart felt no guilt. He had no concept why he should even feel guilt. There were little problems impeding his progress, and he dealt with them. That's what producers do. That's what professionals do. That's what people who controlled their destiny did. He was on the threshold of the big leagues, and dammit, as far as he was concerned, that's where he belonged.

He looked at the clock on the dashboard and blinked. "Damn. It's going to be tight. Not impossible and barring a catastrophe on the freeway system, doable, but there is no time for dallying. Or dillying for that matter." Bart giggled. He drummed his fingers on the wheel to a tune he recognized but couldn't remember. It didn't matter. It was perfect times.

He looped onto the 405 North and shortly thereafter looped again onto the Ventura Freeway West. Traffic was as smooth as a baby's bottom. "Let's all raise a glass to babies bottoms." The heavy downpour kept travelers inside, in their cozy homes, playing their cozy games.

He giggled again. "This is better than drugs, which reminds me," He reached over and popped open the glove box. "A little bit of this to keep me up and a little bit of that to keep me smooth." He dry swallowed a couple of pills. "That'll do me."

He took a deep breath and closed his eyes. Three hours. Three hours and his new life would be starting. A horn blared and he snapped his eyes open and swerved to avoid hitting the center median. "Shit. Can't do that." He peeled off a few minutes later north on Topanga Boulevard. Fifteen minutes later he pulled into his driveway. He checked his watch. "This is going to be the fastest shave and shower in the history of mankind."

The only difference between the rain outside and the shower inside was the temperature. He ran it hotter than usual, shaving in the shower to save time. He dried his hair, ran his fingers through it and dressed quickly. He grabbed a handful of bath towels and dashed back to his car, threw them over his wet, dirty seat and hopped in, on top of the world. He checked the address from the message on his phone and entered it into his navigation system. The digital bitch told him it would take fifty-five minutes and it was 9:30. "Damn, how could my life be any better? Jesus, I'm lucky. And as my pappy told me, it's better to be lucky than good."

He took the onramp from Topanga to Ventura West. The weather was starting to ease. The rain was still pounding, the but the wind had dropped considerably. The wipers were still struggling to beat the rain off the windshield, but the rain was coming straight down now, instead of the almost horizontal it was an hour ago. He took it easy with the speed. There was no need to get stopped for another ticket. That might make him late. "And this isn't something I should be late for." He did push it a little bit on the Ventura Freeway, though. There was still no traffic, including the police. The road was disturbingly empty.

He slowed, exited and turned south down Lost Hills, Las Virgenes and finally Malibu Canyon Road. The time he gained on the freeway, he quickly lost in the canyon. He wasn't willing to push it in the hazardous conditions created by the heavy run-off. His frustration was kept in check by the second pill he had taken, but it didn't completely squash it. He finally reached the bottom and accelerated into the right-hand corner on to the Pacific Coast Highway fishtailing as he tried to make up for time lost on the switchbacks. Digital bitch informed him he was ten minutes away, and it was 10:20. "Life is good."

The navigation system directed him through the hills of Malibu to the address specified near the end of a secluded cul-de-sac . He rolled down the driver's window and pressed the gate intercom button. The light turned green and as he said, "Bart Sweeney for—"

The gates swung open.

"Huh." He raised an eyebrow and rolled slowly up the long drive. He hadn't been here before, yet the place looked vaguely familiar. Half a dozen cars were parked in the covered area by the front door. He recognized some of them. Steve, George and Bobby were there. It was 10:30. He had arrived just in time.

He parked, turned off the ignition and took a deep breath. This was it. Mount Everest or Death Valley.

Mount Everest.

He approached the front door, raised his hand to knock and Tom Hanks opened the door. "My God, man, what the hell happened to your face? Marty, there's some guy here, for this here meeting I'm assuming, who looks like he was on the receiving of a serious mugging. Come in, come in." Bart, stunned, followed him into the house. He had a flash. This house was in a schlocky movie in the 80s. Lair of the baddies. He'd have to do some research later. Tom touched him on his sleeve to get his attention. "Can I get you a drink? Marty's paying."

Bernie paced. He'd been an idiot. Again. And it was quite possible he'd seen Cathy for the last time, and that wasn't something he thought he could bear. The wind was backing off, and the rain was slowing. He would have left already to prowl the streets looking for Cathy, but he didn't know where to start. Her parents were in Reno, but her work was here. She wouldn't leave her work. There were too many motels in the greater L.A. area to call. He continued to pace in the living room, weather channel muted on the TV. He glanced at it now and then. The wind had dropped off, mudslides were forecast. "Shit-hole of a city."

He dropped into his sofa and laid his head on the back. "I'm an idiot."

"Yes. You are."

He spun in his seat. "Cath. When did you come in?" He moved toward her then stopped, not sure of the reception. "You came back."

"Not for you. I'm still pissed at you. You sent Ellie out into this mess. You need to help me find her."

Bernie wiped the corners of his mouth and tried to avoid her direct gaze. "Yes. Absolutely. Have you called her?"

She shook her head. "What the hell do you think? Of course I did. It's going straight to voice mail. I'm worried. It's hell out there. She's got nowhere to stay."

"She's probably in a motel while she looks for a new place. I wouldn't stress so much. Where were you staying?"

"Were staying? Still am staying. I'm not here to move back with you, I'm here to get you off your lazy ass to help me look for her. I'm afraid she may have gone to Zuma. If she tried swimming in this she'd drown."

"She's not stupid."

"She's under a lot of pressure. You know it. First her roommate commits suicide, then it looks like he was actually killed and the icing on the cake? She gets booted out on her ass by the people she thought were friends."

Bernie shoved his hands into his pockets. "Let's go. I'll drive."

"I don't think so. I'm going to drive. One more screw-up and I'm leaving you wherever we happen to be at that moment." She led him out of the house and into her car, destination Zuma Beach.

Marty took his guests out to the pool deck to watch the storm die out over the Pacific. George cornered Bart away from the rest of the gathering. "What the hell, man? Looks like you went a couple of rounds with Mickey Rourke."

"What? Why is everybody looking at me like I've got a third eye?"

George grabbed him by the arm and dragged him to a hallway mirror. "Look at yourself."

Bart looked at the face of a man who had been elbowed to the jaw and punched in the eye and neck.

"And what the fuck is with your hand?"

Bart looked at the scratch marks. "Shit. I haven't had a chance to look in a mirror today." He turned away. "Jesus. They must think I'm some sort of thug. Fuck."

"So, pal, what happened? You kill anybody?"

Bart stared into George's eyes, looking for an indication of whether he really knew or not. "Hell no. I was, uh, mugged this afternoon."

"Really? A mugger who scratched the back of your hand? I was serious. Did you kill someone this afternoon?"

Bart turned away and looked in the mirror again. "Jesus, George. I'm not going to dignify that with an answer." He turned back, pulling his gaze away from his reflection. "I was mugged at the pier by a couple of teen girls. They're vicious. I managed to fight them off, but," he looked in the mirror again, "I didn't realize she was so strong."

"She? One girl did this?"

"They. I meant they. There were three of them."

"You said couple of girls. You might want to get your story straight."

"What the fuck are you, a cop? Three street girls, tough street girls jumped me on an almost abandoned Santa Monica Pier and while I managed to fight them off and keep my money and car keys, they got a few licks in." He smiled. "I'm getting slow and old. What can I say?"

George looked at him and nodded. "Stick with that story for now. Have you called the cops or seen a doctor?"

Bart shook his head "Who has time? It was all I could do to get home and shower and shave for this thing. Which better kick off soon."

"Not often you get a storm like this off the coast. Lucky for you, actually. Only a few people have seen you so far. How'd you shave without noticing that bruise on your neck? Or the black eye? Or feel the bruise on your jaw?"

"Shaved in the shower. Running out of time. I already told you that. I got here on the stroke of 10:30, so it's all good." Bart smiled. It was all good. It was better than good. "I say you halt the interrogation for now, officer, and we join our hosts and his other guests. Is this Tom or Colin's place?"

"Marty's. The agent business does well when you've got some high end clients."

"It's nice. It was in a movie I saw once, right? Can't remember which one. Would kill to live here, though. It's fantastic. Nothing I've ever worked on has been in this tax bracket."

"Two tips for you, Bart. First, never admit that you're overawed by your surroundings. As far as you are concerned, this is like your summer place in Venice. Second, don't let on that this place is familiar to you. You haven't been here before."

"But, I—"

"No," interrupted George, "you haven't. The house was used in a Schwarzenegger movie. Not one of his best. Marty bought it a few years after the movie came out and he still gets busloads of tourists at the front gate asking for Tony Vivaldi and yelling into the intercom "180, you stupid, spaghetti-slurping cretin - *180!*". Marty's over it. Best not acknowledge it."

"Oh. That movie. I liked the premise."

"Yeah, well, don't bring it up. Not worth it."

Bart gently pushed George toward the pool deck. "Yeah, yeah. Thanks for the heads up. Let's go mingle."

Cathy had turned on to the Ventura Freeway before Bernie realized he forgot his phone. "Shit Cath, you've got to go back."

"What in the hell for?"

"Left my phone on the sofa. You need to go back so I can get my phone."

"What are you, some sort of idiot? Screw your phone. No time."

"I'm expecting a call for a job. Come on."

"Get a grip. Nobody is going to call you at this time of night for a gaffer job. You can survive until we get back." Cathy took the Topanga Canyon Blvd South exit and floored it.

"Hey, hey. This road sucks when it's dry. It's been pouring and it's dark out. Take it easy."

"I'm angry."

"Keep it up and you'll be dead and angry."

Cathy eased off on the accelerator a bit. "Try her again."

"My phone? Remember?"

She tossed her handbag at him, saying nothing, for which he was very grateful. He found her phone and called Ellie's number. It rang four times then went to her voice mail. "Ellie, Bernie here. Really sorry for the eviction. I take it back. Come back. We love you. Cathy wants you to come back, too."

Cathy yelled from the drivers seat, "Cathy never wanted you to leave. Only spineless, gonad-less asshole here did. Call me and we'll set up a place together."

Bernie cocked an eyebrow and terminated the call. "Harsh. I apologized."

"You should never had done something you had to apologize for. Voicemail again. This isn't good."

"Yeah. Four rings then voicemail."

Cathy looked at Bernie, "Really? It rang? That means her phone is on and in coverage. It was going straight to mail before. Dammit, why didn't she answer? She better not be swimming in this."

"So, as much as I loathe violence against women, as my pappy used to say, never hit a lady, but if she hits you first, she's no lady." Bart looked at the men assembled on the back deck. The silence was uncomfortable. "Really, I just pushed them away. None of them were hurt. Not as bruised as I am. My apologies if my appearance may have taken you aback."

George broke the silence. "Nonsense. Who doesn't love a good story? Hell, all of our careers depend on good stories, right? Shall we talk about the script for Red Thunder and see where it takes us?"

Tom jumped at the opening, welcome for the change of subject. "Look, guys, Colin and I read the script. Could be tightened, I think, and the title is god-awful. I'm tempted to put my hand up for the scientist role myself, but I think I'm a generation too old. Would be good to play a bad guy for a change, though. Too much hero in my resume."

"Maybe the scientist's boss, Tom. What about that?" Bart was willing to sell his soul to get this off the ground. Tossing a secondary character as a bone was well within his moral scope.

Colin was shaking his head. "It would take people out of the movie if they saw me as the bad-guy turned hero then in Act 2 my real life father showed up as an antagonist. No, I love working with the old guy, but I think it has to be right. Right pop?"

"What he said. I'm warming to this, guys. I'm in like Flynn if we get the right female lead. Any ideas on that? Steve? You're the casting director in the room. You must have some ideas for that part." Tom looked at the assembled guests. "You've talked about this already, right? This isn't a new train of thought for you?"

Steve smiled, glanced at Bart and spoke up. "We certainly have. There's an Australian actress who I've been bumping into a lot lately. She's very capable, and she's tall so she can go head to head with your son. I've heard she's pretty physical, so some of her stunts can be done full face." He glanced at Bart, and winked. "A girl named Ellie Bourke. I don't know if you've seen her. She was in one of Bart's movies, *Beast of Bondi*, an Aussie horror flick. Did some commercials and some guest spots, but other than that she's a bit below the radar."

Bart croaked. He wiped sweat off his lip with a trembling hand.

Tom looked at him. "So you've approached her to do this project?"

"Um, not really. She's going through a bit of a hard time. Her roommate just committed suicide. Heroin overdose. She's spinning out of control right now. If we were putting this together a month ago, or maybe six months from now, I'd be agreeing with Steve. Excellent choice." Bart swallowed. "Right now, though, I don't know. I think she would be too much risk for the picture."

Tom frowned and shook his head. "I trust Steve. One of the best on this crazy business. If he likes her, I'd like to meet her. Make an assessment myself. Can you set that up in the next couple of days? I'll make time. Should only need fifteen minutes."

Steve smiled. "No problem. I'll call her first thing in the morning." He noticed Bart's expression. "You okay Bart?"

He smiled and swallowed. "Sure. Yeah. No problem." Just fucking lovely. Bart thought. I should have thrown her off the pier when I had the chance.

31

Pete saved my life. I would be back at the place buying him a hell of a meal if I made it through all of this.

But first I had to hit Bart where it hurt him the most.

He threw the phone overboard, but it was synched with Joel's laptop. Maybe. I remembered plugging the phone in to charge it and I was pretty sure his synch profile included the recordings. I didn't have the laptop, though, and I wasn't sure when Jacob was heading back to Boise with it.

I got back to my car, now with a heel shaped dent in the driver's door. Bart must have parked near me. I didn't care much about the way my car looked. It gave it character. This car would stay with me forever. I vowed then and there that even if I made it big, I'd keep this car to remind myself of the crap I had to go through to get there.

I started my car, plugged the charging cord in the ciggie lighter and plugged in my phone. I leaned my head back against the headrest and let the inefficient heater warm me. I closed my eyes and must have dropped off.

I woke with a start. The clock on my phone said 10:10. I had slept for almost an hour. It didn't help. I still hurt, I was still tired, and I still had nowhere to sleep. If cats really had catnaps it's no wonder they were aloof and evil all the time. If they felt like I feel, they felt like shit and didn't want to be bothered with anything.

I rubbed my eyes and checked my phone. I had a couple of missed calls from Cathy. Poor Cathy. The house was in Bernie's name and she was just living there. It was fully his call to kick me out. I was thoroughly disgusted with him.

And felt I should tell him. I called his number. It rang through to voicemail.

"Bernie, Ellie here. Too chicken shit to answer your phone when I call? You need to grow a pair, man. Sweeney is going down hard, and I'm the one taking him down. When you get the courage to call me back and apologize maybe you can come along and help. Until then, get stuffed."

That was that. I couldn't stand people who wouldn't stand up for themselves. I really thought Bernie was better than that. Lots of talk, but he couldn't back it up.

I pulled on to the PCH and headed north. Or west. Depends on how you read a map. I was happy to be moving under my own steam. Zuma was in this general direction and it was a comfortable place for me. If the rain tapered off much more I might take a midnight swim. The wind was gone. The weather system had almost cleared off. My cuts weren't hurting as much and the salt water would do them good.

I wracked my memory trying to remember when Jacob was heading back to Boise and came up blank. I couldn't even remember where he said he was staying. If he even did. I dialed his number, hoping that wherever he was, it wasn't too late.

Voicemail.

"Ellie here, Jacob. Urgent I reach you while you're still in L.A. Can you call me back please? And don't erase anything on Joel's laptop, okay?

Not that I think you would, but just in case. I'll explain more when you call back. Thanks."

I needed to find someplace to crash for the night. I was cold, wet and really wanted a hot shower and a soft bed to sleep in.

Without spending too much money.

Motel 8 or Days Inn or something like it. First one I saw would be it. I was north of Topanga and had decided to head back into the Valley when I saw a car come screaming off Malibu Canyon and turn right, accelerating north on PCH, just missing me. It was covered in mud. I recognized the car. It was Bart. I had to follow him. This time I was pretty sure he wasn't leading me to a trap.

Wherever he was heading, he was moving fast. I had to push my little Beetle to keep up, wipers beating the crap out of the rain. I was wide-awake now.

Pushing my car along PCH was actually fun. The rain was letting up and was moving offshore. Lightning still flashed off the coast, but the wind was gone and at this rate it would be a beautiful morning.

But I still had tonight to get through.

I lost Bart on a corner then picked him up again about a mile down the road as he slowed to turn left off PCH into the Malibu neighborhood with some of the amazing cliff-side houses. This must be that "thing with a guy" Bart was talking about. To crash or not to crash that particular party, that was the question.

My phone rang, interrupting my mulling. It was Cathy.

"Hey Cath. Missed your call. Sorry for not calling you back. What's up?"

"Uh, it's me, Cath. Bernie."

"Ass-hat. Did you get my message?" I went from relief at talking to a friend to being furious in one heartbeat.

"I didn't, no. I left my phone at home. Anything important?"

"Put Cathy on. I'm tired of listening to you."

"She's driving right now. Can't talk."

"Put it on hands-free. Like I have. Do we have to tell you everything? What are you doing driving around at this hour?"

"Looking for you Ellie. We were concerned about you - hang on a sec." I heard some talking in the background then the distinctive audio of a speakerphone.

"Ellie, Cath here. Really sorry for what Bernie did. It won't happen again. Where in the bloody hell are you? We were worried."

"I'm fine. About to torpedo Sweeney out of the water. Wish me luck." I tracked behind Bart, one corner behind him all the way through the neighborhood.

"Jesus, Elle. You're going to get yourself killed. He's a nut case."

"He hasn't succeeded so far, though God knows he's tried. Relax, Cathy. I've got to get a couple of things together and then I'll take it to the cops. Tomorrow morning, hopefully. We'll see."

"So what are you doing now?"

"Following him. He called me Nancy Drew in a derisive fashion not long ago. I guess that's what I'm doing now. Nancy Drewing it."

"Ellie, it's late and the weather is still crap. You should shut it down for the night. You can come and stay at my house."

Bernie sounded contrite, but I wasn't having any of it. "Get stuffed, Bern. I can handle myself."

Cathy sighed. Loud enough I could hear it over the rain on my roof and over the crappy line. "Ellie, I'm going to text you where I'm staying.

When you're finished with all of this shit tonight, come by and we'll split a pizza, okay? Be careful."

"You're not at Bernie's?"

"Hell no. Call me later, okay?" She hung up. I appreciated her support, and was very surprised she left Bernie. They'd been together for five years. And she left him because he bent to Sweeney's threat and tossed me out on my boney ass.

I was a little bit humbled to know I had a friend like that.

Bart, on the other hand, had no friends I was aware of. Some symbiotic parasites and a couple of ass-kissers, but nobody who could be called a friend. Unfortunate for him that he killed one of mine. He was driving slowly now, probably getting close to his destination and trying to read street numbers. I turned off my headlights and followed closer, not really sure what I was going to do.

He slowed and pulled into a drive, rolling down his window and pressing the intercom button. I parked on the side of the road, turned off the engine and got out of my car. I ran the twenty or thirty steps to the front gate and squeezed in behind him as it closed. I was running blind now. I had no idea what I was up to or what I would do. I certainly couldn't confront him until I had my hands on the evidence, but I couldn't just let him get away with murder. And by the looks of it he was going to profit, if not as a result of murder, in spite of it.

I almost gave myself away after I got through the gate. The property was massive. The driveway split into two at the gate, one lane up the left side of a garden and one up the right, both sides well lit. In and out, I guess. Bart's taillights disappeared up the right hand side.

I stood there like a deer in the floodlights for a good five seconds before I ran to the hedge along the left side. I tried to stay in the shadows as

I crept up the drive. If there were ground security I was screwed. I figured the heavy rain would keep any dogs off my back, and might have caused enough problems with motion sensors that they would be turned off. Had no idea, really. I truly was winging it. At this point I had nothing to lose.

My progress along the side of the property was slow. The bushes were thick enough that if I rushed it I would make a lot of noise. It was possible that the storm would drown out any noise, but it was just as possible that a gust of wind would carry it to the house.

After thirty minutes I was at the back corner of the house, not far from the cliff. A large bay window projected out on to the pool deck giving me a bit of cover from the rest of the property. I heard voices discussing something about a movie with aliens and vampires. It sounded like typical Sweeney horseshit. I couldn't imagine how he'd got people with the kind of money who could afford this house interested in anything he came up with. I sidled along the convex extension to the massive house. The voices got clearer and at the farthest point from the house the bay window extension ceased to be a hiding place.

The attention of the crowd of middle-aged men was on the storm. They stood shoulder-to-shoulder, drinks in their hands, some of them smoking cigars as they watched the lightning off the coast. They were all back against the doors to the deck, under cover from the rain. It seemed silly to call it a deck. There were more square feet around the pool than any apartment I've ever rented.

The lights cast deep shadows. The area they were standing in was well lit and the shadow I was in was pitch black. They couldn't see me. I've done enough work in theater to realize I was invisible to them. But I could see and hear them just fine.

Bart was there, along with Steve Bond, George, Bobby, and a few other people I didn't know. The door opened and holy shit but didn't Colin and Tom Hanks come out from inside to join the discussion. Maybe Bart really did have something going on.

Tom Hanks then said something that almost made me step out of the shadows: "No, Bart, I'm serious. Get this Ellie Bourke in front of me in the next couple of days and let me talk to her. I know what you're saying, fragile and all that, but Steve here is one of the best casting directors in the business. If he thinks she's the right person for the role, then I'm willing to go out on a limb for her."

Damn. Sweeney didn't mention any of this to me except to say he had the power to remove deals from me. Maybe this is what he was talking about. Oh, how I wanted to jump out and make a fuss. But the primary objective was to get Bart behinds bars and I couldn't do that sharing the spotlight with him.

But I could fuck with his head.

I stayed in the shadows and slipped down a set of stairs to a lower terraced area. I hopped over the low railing onto the grass that was at a lower level again. I made my way to an area directly in front of where the men were standing. The marble railing around the deck allowed me to see the eight of them without them noticing me. I was patient. Only a few opportunities, if that, would come my way.

The first happened when the crowd all looked to the north at a cluster of lightning. Bart was running a bit slow - probably some self-medication. His turn lagged the rest. I jumped up and waved my arms. He started, halting his turn and looked right at me. I flipped him the bird with both hands and dropped back out of sight.

I watched his reaction through the spindles of the marble railing. He didn't seem to know what to do. He motioned to George and then waved him off. Then plucked at his sleeve, and again waved him off. This was too special.

The second time was when they all turned from storm watching to head back inside. This time Bart lagged intentionally, it seemed. I popped up and gave him the finger and the ever-popular fist up the ass move. He was apoplectic. I dropped down again and ran to the far side of the deck, where I initially came out. I made my point with him. He could always be found. I'm sure I'll pay for it somehow, but I was living in the moment.

At that moment my priority was to get clear without getting caught.

I backtracked along the side of the house, moving even slower than I did coming in. The storm was pretty much completely gone. I didn't want any unnecessary noises triggering alarms or worse, dogs. The trek that took me ten minutes on the way in took twenty-five on the way out. I ended up in the shadows by the gate looking for something that would trigger it to open. There was no intercom button to push, it had to be done automatically, and if the automatic didn't work, there needed to be a local override.

It took me five long, slow, careful minutes of looking for it before I found a switch near the base of one of the two columns on either side of the driveway. I flicked it and the gates started to slowly open. I didn't wait for them to open all the way. Somebody would be noticing them. I sprinted to my car and beat it the hell out of there before I was tagged.

I'm not sure what I accomplished with that stunt. I felt in control, that's for sure. And I spooked the rat-bastard, so all in all it was a positive. Maybe I spooked him enough that he'd make a mistake, a slip of the tongue in front of the wrong person.

I got lost in the winding roads, driving aimlessly for about fifteen minutes until all of a sudden I was on the PCH. I headed back toward Zuma. I had nowhere to stay for the night. It was close to midnight and I didn't want to bother Cathy. Sleeping in my car on the beach was better than nothing. I'd done it before, and I'll probably do it again.

The rain stopped and the sky started to clear. The moon broke through the clouds, promising a beautiful morning. I pulled into the Zuma Beach public parking lot at 11:45. It had been a helluva long day. I turned off the engine and was closing my eyes to get some sleep when my phone rang.

I looked at the caller ID. Sweeney.

"You're dead," he said as I answered it.

"Get fucked," I replied, and hung up.

The perfect end to a perfect night.

32

"Bart," George pulled him aside. "What's wrong man? Even your bruises are pale. You look like you've seen a ghost."

"If only." Bart slid his phone back into his pocket.

"What?"

"Nothing. My meds are wearing off. I need another." Bart winced and rubbed his jaw.

"I'm sure Marty has some pain pills in this place."

"Not pain pills, Einstein. My meds. They're in my car. I can't really pop out to get them now. Scotch will have to do."

"A bit pissed that you showed up to this meeting, of all the meetings you've ever had, fucked up."

Bart looked at him and pointed to the bruises on his face.

George nodded. "Okay, point taken. We better rejoin the crowd. This is turning out quite well, I think. You should be pleased."

"You'd think, right? Yet…" He let the sentence trail off. Somehow Ellie managed to screw even this up for him. Unless he had been hallucinating. Not that remote a possibility, given the circumstances of the past few days.

Tom addressed his audience. "It's getting late gentlemen, and I've got an early tennis game with Favreau. He slaughters me when I'm at my best. And tomorrow I won't be at my best, I'm sure. The only thing left to talk about, now that the financing has been sorted, is some names. I know you've all been thinking about this and you all have your own ideas and we'll certainly consider them, but I want the weight of these decisions on Steve's shoulders." He pointed at the casting director. "This is the guy who cast Wilson, after all, possibly the single most successful and inspired casting decision since that duck got the Aflac commercials."

They laughed then started with the casting suggestions.

Tom waved them quiet. "The female lead, we're going with this Ellie Bourke, right? I still want to meet her in the next day or two at the latest. Steve, you set that up, okay?"

"I still think we should have a backup in mind. Just in case she's still too overwrought to do the part." Bart swallowed. He didn't want her anywhere near this project.

"Overwrought? There are still people who are overwrought in this world? I thought that went out with the steam engine and coal fires." Tom smiled. "I'm confident she'll be fine. You're going to set that up, right Steve?

He nodded. "Sure. I'll give Marty a call in the morning to set the time. I think she's free." He scratched his chin. "I'm telling you though, I'm still struggling with the scientist, the good guy who is actually a bad guy at the end. Need to cast against type, which will actually look like typecasting until the midway point."

Colin nodded. "Has to be my match, physically and intellectually, or it won't be believable, doesn't matter which way the seesaw is tipping. Thoughts?"

There was silence around the room. Bart settled back in his chair. He didn't care who was selected for that role. He wanted NPH, but that was patently absurd. No way they'd get him for this.

Steve spoke first. "What about the Texan kid on that show, the Asperger kid."

George chuckled. "Prady assured me he's nowhere on the autism scale, just quirks."

"Whatever, you know who I'm talking about. Think he can do serious, bearing in mind there's a big satirical side to this project?"

Mutters around the room. Energy levels were flagging as it pushed midnight. Bobby offered a suggestion. "What about Neil Patrick? He'd be great. Lean a bit on his Dr. Horrible persona. He would bring in male and females. He's smart, or at least he comes across as smart. We could put him in a weight program for a couple of months and beef him up some, if we felt we had to."

Bart groaned.

Tom leaned in. "You don't think so Bart? I think it's inspired. I think Mr. Bowens here may have missed his calling. Steve, you better be looking over your shoulder. This guy is going to take your job."

"No, that's not it." Bart looked at the faces interrogating him. "It's nothing. Great idea, if we can get him.

"We can get him. Don't worry about that." Steve sat back and crossed his legs. "An idea, Marty, Tom. Why don't I get NPH to come by when I bring Ellie? Make sure there's chemistry."

"If you can do that, I'll come by too. We're the love triangle, right? We all need to get along."

"I don't think the triangle goes all the way, Colin." Tom smiled. "Anyway, I think we can leave the rest to Steve. We've got the core. I don't need sign off on anything else casting-wise." He looked around the group sitting in his agent's living room. "Gentlemen, we've got a project to make. Meetings will start next week with storyboards and a first-cut scene by scene budget." He looked at the moneyman. "Can we meet with your people tomorrow first thing and set up some accounts? My accountant will create the shell production company tomorrow."

The small man with piles of money nodded. "Of course." He handed him a card. "Have your accountant call me and we'll meet where and whenever is convenient."

Tom stood. "Excellent, gentlemen. Let's keep a lid on this for a couple of weeks until there's some dirt under the wheels, okay? Don't want a premature notification of a non-event."

A man in a security uniform approached Marty and whispered in his ear.

"Really? Are you positive?" Marty listened, nodded a couple of times, thanked him and stood. "Security tells me the property was breached this evening. The wind and rain necessitated the turning off the motion detectors and apparently someone snuck through the gates in behind one of you in when you came in." He held up his hands. "No blame here but my own. This is my property and I should have been more careful. I just ask you to check your vehicles carefully for damage before you leave. I will, of course, make good on any repairs."

Bart blanched. It wasn't a hallucination. "You sure she's left?"

"She? We can be certain the person who broke in left. The gate was triggered manually about twenty minutes ago. Security footage shows a shadow slipping out, briefly in lights. I didn't say it was a "she". How did you know?"

Bart closed his eyes. He was tired and making stupid mistakes. "Fifty-fifty chance of being right, right?"

Marty stared at him. "I bet if you asked a hundred people the gender of the person they expected to break into a property like this, ninety-nine of them would say male, if not all of them. Not fifty-fifty." He cleared his throat. "Bart, if you know who this is, I need to know in case there is any damage. I'll want to recover any costs from her." He emphasized the last word.

"No, I don't know. Just really tired. Thinking about a break-in at my place years ago by a woman. My only break-in experience, you see. Scarred me a bit." He willed Marty to believe him. The discussion of Ellie did not need to come up in front of the Hanks.

"Okay. It *was* a girl, by the way, or a very, very sexy looking dude. Sometimes hard to tell in this town." He clapped his hands. "Security has turned on all of the floodlights outside, doubling my electric bill for the month. Check and double-check your cars, okay? I'm sure they'll be okay, but better safe than sorry."

The guests, excluding the Hanks, thanked Marty and the Hanks for their hospitality and made their way out to the parking area in front of the house. The sky was clearing, the moon breaking through the clouds.

George walked beside Bart, and slowed him down. "So, what was that all about?"

"What about?"

"The "has she left" scream for help. You get someone pregnant? Give them a nasty STD? What's this paranoia borne of?"

Bart scrubbed his fingers through his hair, wincing as he found another bruise he hadn't been aware of. "It's late, George. Let's play interrogation tomorrow, okay? Are you going to show up for the Ellie / Hanks meeting?"

"Don't change the subject. There was a definite look of fear in your eyes when you thought whoever broke in was still here. Does she scare you that much?"

"Who? I was serious, I was thinking about a break-in years ago. Biker chick forced her way in and made me take cash out of my accounts at ATMs around the city."

"Made you?"

"She had a Bowie knife to my throat."

George shook his head. "Horse hockey. That was immediate fear in your eyes. Ellie's got you crapping yourself, doesn't she?"

"Why in the hell was she even brought up in the conversation? No way I can work with her after all the attempts she's made to discredit my name. And after everything I've done for her."

"You better talk to Steve about that. Hanks wants her and is basing that on Steve's recommendation. I think he's the only one who can make it stop at this point. And then we're down to further delays looking for a younger Jenna Elfman or Sharon Stone." He clapped Bart on the shoulder and pulled away as the director winced. "Shit, sorry man. You okay?"

Bart seethed with frustration. He couldn't tell anyone that the bashes to his body were from a twenty-something year old girl who cleaned his clock. Especially when everyone in the world want him to direct her in this new project. "Son of a bitch." He let out a guttural yell. "Why the fuck is she doing this to me?"

George took a step back. "Pal, you are losing it. Are you talking about Ellie? What's she doing to you?"

Bart grabbed him by the lapels. "That bitch is doing her level best to completely ruin me, just because I spurned her advances. She knew I was gay. She just wanted to get the rent lowered."

George removed Bart's hands from his coat and pushed him slowly against his car. "Bart, old boy, you are in serious danger of losing your part in this gig, and it's one of the biggest gigs you'll ever get. Quite possibly the biggest gig you'll ever have the fortune to see. Now calm the fuck down."

Marty walked over in the middle of the discussion. "Bart, is this too much for you? You really shouldn't have come here after being mugged. Would have been better for you to get medical help. You look like a sack of shit. Let's pretend your extremely erratic behavior didn't happen, okay? My gift to you." He lightly slapped Bart's face. "Now go home and get some sleep. Lots and lots of sleep. We can talk more tomorrow."

Bart winced at the slap but Marty either didn't notice, or didn't care. He turned to George and clapped him on the shoulder. "A month from now your names are going to be in Variety, on E! and half a dozen other outlets as the brains behind this fantastic new blockbuster the average public won't see for another two years." He looked between their faces. "What I'm trying to say is that putting a piece together as complex as this doesn't happen over night. It's a long haul, one day at a time project. What happens tonight will be recorded as nothing more than a meeting of the backers. Muggings, stealthy possibly female interlopers and the rest will be washed down the rain gutters of time."

Bart cocked an eyebrow. "Very poetic, man. Thanks for the advice. You're absolutely correct. I need a bag and a half load of sleep. Thanks for your hospitality and we'll talk tomorrow." He nodded at George and climbed into his car. George and Marty were looking through the windshield at the mud on the floor and console and the towels covering the seat. "Rough night. Catch you later."

He pulled out of the drive, security standing at the gate to ensure there were no surprise entrants or departures. The floodlights were so bright that when he finally got to the street the black was intensely black. He flipped on his high beams and called George's cell.

"Bart? We just talked. What's up?"

"We weren't finished talking before the agent showed up. If there's any way you can think of to keep Bourke off this project, I'm begging you as a friend now to use it. I can't direct her and I can't be around her. Can you axe her? Maybe make sure she has so much other work going on that she's got no time for this."

"Sounds more like Steve's role, and he's 200% behind her. No odds that you'll get him to tank her."

"What the fuck is this, George? One simple request. There are thousands of actresses in this city. Why the big deal about replacing her?"

George turned out of the drive on to the street. "She's perfect for the role. I know it, Steve knows it and you, you motherfucker, you know it too. Just because she slapped you down gives you no right to tank her career. Get in line with this, or I foresee problems."

Bart shook his head. "Look, this is stupid. There are many people perfect for this role. What if she came down with something, like measles or Hep-C or something to keep her from working. We'd have to find someone else. All I'm asking is we start looking for someone right now. Just in case."

"Jesus, Bart. Do you know how that sounds? 'Just in case'? What, are you going to make her an offer she can't refuse? I suppose we should find contingencies for Colin and Neil, too, right?"

"That's another thing." Bart pulled on to PCH and accelerated. "That was my suggestion."

"Who, NPH? I distinctly heard Bowens mention it. Nothing at all from you. You were sulking in your chair like a twelve-year-old told they couldn't go to a sleep-over."

Bart punched the dash. "I fucking thought of it. Never in a million years would I have thought they'd go for it."

George chuckled. "Snooze, lose, all that shit. Don't be so shy next time. You're a soggy mess. Go home, have a double scotch and crawl into bed. You should return to the land of the living by noon and I will stake my non-existent medical degree on the fact that you will feel fan-fucking-tastic. Bart, take two or three steps back, okay? Everything you've dreamed about since you started working in this industry is about to come true. You have a big - huge - budget project with financing secured. You've got Tom and Colin Hanks involvement. You've been told NPH himself is likely to be attached. Jesus, man, what else could you ask for? This is perfect storm material. Loosen your sphincter a bit and enjoy."

33

It was a stereotypically sunny Southern California day at Zuma Beach. The only evidence of the weather last night were the piles of palm fronds on the windward side of everything that was bolted down, including my car. It gave the old girl a thatched hut look, like I was stranded on some desert isle. Something I think I could handle for a week or two.

I swam for almost an hour from sunrise at 6:30, the cold water numbing the bruises and the hard work clearing my mind. I still wasn't sure if I had what I needed to submarine Sweeney, but based on his reactions last night, I certainly had him on the ropes. He'd be doing something stupid soon. And I wanted to be there when it happened.

The salt stung the cuts at first, but the cold water staunched the flow and ended up numbing them too. It was the first time I'd been swimming since all of this crap started and the cleansing it gave me reinforced my plan to find a place on the beach.

I walked out of the water, t-shirt and shorts dripping water on the beach. I really needed to do some shopping. I was wearing all the clothes I had. Well, all the clothes I could currently get my hands on.

I reached in through the towel covered broken window and unlocked the front passenger-side door and slid, damp, into the front. I took my phone out of the glove box. Not a whole lot of security, but good enough for the beach. I had two missed calls. I returned the first one.

"Jacob Sampson speaking."

I sighed with relief. "Jacob, Ellie here. Are you still in L.A.?"

"I am for another few days. Until the autopsy is complete."

"Autopsy? You mean Joel wasn't cremated?"

"You convinced me something was rank. I called off the cremation and insisted Perkins reopen the case and do a proper autopsy."

I closed my eyes. "Awesome. You have Joel's laptop, right?"

"In a box with all of his stuff. Do you want it?"

"Yes. No. Not to keep. I need a file on it. I'm pretty sure there's an audio file proving Bart Sweeney killed your brother. When can I meet you? I can copy the file to a thumb drive or something."

"I'm doing nothing all day." He gave me the address of the hotel he was staying at in Sepulveda. "Just call me a bit ahead of time so you don't catch me in the pool when you get here, okay? I'm pasty white. It's embarrassing."

I laughed and signed off. The second call was from Steve. Maybe good news.

"Steve, Ellie here. You called this morning?"

"How are you feeling Elle? Okay? Stable? Ready to work?"

I knew what he was talking about, but I had to play it coy. "I'm always ready to work, Steve. Are you my agent now? What's on? Modern Family come through?"

"You've got a call back for Modern, but that's not why I called. You should have received a call from your soon to be ex-agent about that by now. No, I called about something potentially bigger, but you need to put your best foot forward. Are you free at 11:00?"

"This morning? Maybe. When's the Modern Family thing?"

"Tomorrow afternoon, as I understand it. Different topic, though. If you can be in Malibu at 11:00, I'd like you to meet a couple of people. If the chemistry is right, I think you may have a very good movie role."

"No tits, I hope. I'm over doing those kinds of movies."

"I've read the script, and this version has no tits." Steve laughed. "I doubt tits will be added, but I can assure you if they are it will be in a non-exploitive manner, okay?"

I grinned. Have yet to see non-exploitive tits in a movie. "We'll see. Do I need to call my agent, or will he be there?"

Steve chuckled again. "Call him, get the details on Modern Family and fire him. You don't want him on your coattails. He should have told you about Modern Family yesterday. He's a liability. I've got an agent who will work his ass off for you. If you feel bad about firing him, buy him a nice Christmas present. Trust me he didn't find Modern Family for you, and he didn't find the one I'm setting you up with today. I did. I know what talent you've got, and I know an agent who would be a perfect fit."

"Are you trying to get into my pants?" This sounded like one of those too good to be true stories.

"As delightful as that sounds, Ellie, my wife would kill me if I tried. Although it is tempting. No, I hate to see talent go to waste. You've got talent."

"You're making me blush. What's the job?" I wanted him to say it.

"I'd rather you found out there, okay? Just dress nice, look respectable and be on time. I'll see you there."

"You'll be there, but my agent isn't. That doesn't sound kosher."

"If you call up your agent and fire him, you new agent will be there. It's his house."

"I know the neighborhood, Steve. That's an agent's house?"

"He's good. Will I see you there?"

I looked at the time. I needed to get to Jacob's, get the recording and take it to Perkins, shower and change in three hours. "Nope. Not by 11:00. There is something I need to do this morning that absolutely can't wait."

"What can possibly be more important than an invite to an audition for what could be the biggest role of your career?"

"Something I've got to do for Joel. I can't explain, but it takes priority over everything else. I can do 1:00 or anytime after, but 11:00 is too soon."

Steve sighed and I could hear him tapping his fingers on something. "Okay, I'm going to make a few calls. Keep your phone on and charged. If I can change it, I will, but I can't make any guarantees."

"Understood. I'm young. If this once-in-a-lifetime opportunity passes me by, there'll be others."

"Right. I wish more people around here were as stable as you. Stay close to the phone. I'll get back to you."

I thanked him and hung up. Even with no traffic it was impossible to get from Zuma to Sepulveda to Devonshire to Malibu in three hours. Not even with a jet pack. Five would be difficult enough. The Hanks would have to wait.

I stopped at a Wal-Mart and got some cheap but respectable clothes and two thumb drives. I called Jacob on the way and told him I would be there in twenty minutes and that he should cover up the pasty white torso before he blinded the locals. I was there in eighteen.

He met me in the front lobby. "Jesus, Ellie, you look like a hobo."

"Thanks a ton. Just what a girl wants to hear. I had a bit of a run in with an asshole last night. I'm fine though. Is it okay if I use your shower while I'm here? I've got a supposedly important meeting at 1:00 I need to be decent for."

"Sure, sure. No problem."

He led me to his room where Joel's laptop was open and the file manager file was launched. I put my bag down and did a quick look for the synched audio files and found the one I thought I was looking for. I double clicked it and heard Joel's voice through the speakers. I turned it up so Jacob could hear:

"What is this, Day 88? Yes. Eighty-fucking-eight."

"Friday. I'm fucking beat. It's been a week of ups and downs and on balance I'd say it was a positive. This diary is brought to you by the nude Joel. Please do not listen if you are under the age of thirteen or are easily offended by unfit, pasty-white bodies. I am in the tub. Hot as hell water, Epsom salts and a bit of a bubble. Dad would shit himself, but it feels fan-fucking-tastic."

I stopped the recording and glanced at Jacob. He looked shattered. "This is Day 88. He had recorded an entry every day for almost three months. The end of this recording has Bart Sweeney giving your brother too much rohypnol in a glass of juice, killing him by mistake, then injecting him with a bunch of heroin in an attempt to cover it up. I'm really sorry Jacob. I need to make a copy of this and take it to Constable Perkins."

"I've had evidence my brother was murdered right here on this laptop all this time and I didn't know about it?"

I nodded. What else could I say? "Don't worry about it. If you want to listen to the rest of it, I can shower and give you some privacy."

"Thanks. At least he maintained the family image, white and pasty to the end."

I smiled, gave him a hug and took my bag to the bathroom. I needed a thorough scrub and a shave. My legs were getting out of control. I took my time, giving Jacob plenty of space to do what he needed to do.

I showered, luxuriating in the hot pounding water. It had been a wild couple of days. The cut on my scalp opened a little bit, stinging, but the one on the inside of my arm was healing over. I gingerly felt around the cut on my head, snipping away the hair in the immediate area. When I had a spot about an inch on either side of the cut chopped short I used shaving foam and the razor I used on my legs and shaved my scalp around the cut. It stung like a son of a bitch, but it was preferable to having blood dribble down my neck in a meeting with Steve and some of his important people.

When I finished toweling off, feeling clean for the first time in days, I placed a bandage on my arm, and with the help of a couple of mirrors, stuck one on my scalp. Hopefully it would hold. I pulled my hair into a ponytail. The bandage wasn't visible.

A quick teeth brush and some deodorant and I stepped out to the rest of the hotel room in my new, inexpensive but respectable enough for now clothes.

Jacob whistled. "Mucho improved." He was smiling, but his eyes were red. "I listened to all of it. I'm going with you to see Perkins. There's no way Sweeney's going to be on the streets any longer than it takes for me to find him."

"No argument from me." I opened the twin pack of thumb drives. "One with Day 88 for Perkins and co, and one with all of the days, for me. Is that okay with you?"

"Absolutely." He took the drives from me and dragged the files to them. He ejected the complete list and gave it to me. "For you." He took the single. "For Perkins."

I collected my old clothes and personal hygiene stuff and put it back in the Wal-Mart bag. "Jacob, I've got to go straight to a meeting in Malibu after the police station. We're going to have to use different cars, okay?"

"That's fine. I need to go to the morgue after and find out what's going on with Joel's autopsy. They should have finished it by now."

"Meet you there in forty-five minutes?" I was going to grab a quick bite, didn't want to buy his and didn't want him to buy mine.

We agreed to meet there at 11:30.

I left, thumb drive in my pocket, and headed further into the Valley. I put my phone on speaker and called Davie Hanson, my ineffective agent.

"Ellie, is that you? What a coincidence."

"Let me guess. You were just about to call me to let me know about a call back at Modern Family. I already know. Thanks for nothing. You are clear on the concept of being an agent, right? The more money I make, the more money you make. Fifteen percent of everything I make goes to you. I would expect a much higher level of commitment from someone who makes money on commission."

There was a pause on the line. I could imagine his confused face. "Wait a sec. How did you know about Modern Family?"

"Are you kidding? Strangers on the street are stopping me and congratulating me."

"I'm serious."

"I apparently have more contacts in this town than you do, making you an expensive - or potentially expensive - waste of space. Ironically, if you really were expensive, I'd be happy with your efforts. But since you're my agent and I'm hardly giving you any money, you're fired. I'll make sure my accountant," ha! "apportions your share from that gig, even though I know Steve Bond fed it to you. Buh-bye Davie. Don't call me back, okay?" I hung up and pulled into a fast food joint that had the best flame grilled meat in town with absolutely no nutritional value. I sat in the parking lot, stuffing my face when my phone rang. I chewed and checked the caller ID. It was Sweeney.

I swallowed my food and answered. "Hi there, Bart. Have a good meeting last night?"

"I'm just calling you up to give you one last warning. You're going to be offered a part in a movie today. Turn it down or I will make sure you don't work in this town again."

"Did you get that line from an online scriptwriting course? It's pretty bad. How are you going to stop me? Are you going to visit each and every casting director, agent, director, producer and personally tell each of them one-on-one what a bad girl I've been?"

"You can't make any casting calls if you're six feet under."

"Threats? You're resorting to threats? Three times now you tried to kill me and I'm still right here, pissing you off."

"Don't get so cocky. You've been lucky. You won't be that lucky tonight when you sleep on the beach, exposed."

I was tired of this. I wiped my mouth and took a final drink of my juice. "Adios Bart. You're not going to kill me. Too many people know what you've already done. You'll be the prime suspect. I've made it very well known that I don't commit suicide. Murder points right between your eyes. I know you're stupid, but you're not that stupid."

Silence echoed down the line.

"Bart? You still there? Bart?"

I was reaching for the "hang up call" button when he answered, very deep and honestly ominous voice. "You're not going to live beyond tonight."

I laughed. "Excellent. A definitive time frame. Then I shall wake up tomorrow, bright, refreshed and secure in the knowledge that you failed once again, just like you always do. Now Bart, be a dear and go fuck yourself. I've got things I need to do today."

I hung up and headed for the Devonshire station. A couple of things in that call intrigued me. Mainly that he knew I slept on the beach last night. Could be a lucky guess, but I don't think so. And he seemed supremely confident I wouldn't make the night. I'd have to make sure I slept somewhere he didn't expect me to sleep.

I pulled into the visitor's parking lot of the Devonshire station just in front of Jacob. He came over and gave me a big hug. "You ready to do this Elle?"

I nodded. "Let's take the asshole down."

34

Bart leaned back in his chair. "Damn her. She sounds too confident. I need to cut her legs out from under her." He scrolled through his contacts until he hit Steve's number. He tapped his foot while it rang.

"Bond."

"Steve, we need to meet."

"It's like we're dating, Bart, all the times we're going out. What's up?"

"Not just you. Bobby and George too. We need a recap of last night." Bart took a deep breath and continued. "I'm a bit hazy on some of it. Those, ah, pain pills have an amnesiac affect. I want to make sure everything I think I remember actually happened."

"I don't know if I can make it. I've got a full schedule. But it really happened. Too bad you couldn't be all there."

"You've got to, man. Call the other two for me, will you? Same place. I'm buying."

"Of course you are. What don't you remember?"

"How would I know that? Listen, honestly, this is more about Ellie than anything else. I need an agreement from you guys about her."

"Bart, you're beating a dead horse here."

Bart clenched his jaw. "Save it until lunch. We talk as a group. Be there at 11. I'll call ahead." Bart hung up and scrubbed his face with his hands. He didn't trust his memories. He still felt shaggy and had thought half of what had happened was a dream and then Ellie made that crack about the meeting. That part had to be real. He wasn't sure which other parts were so they needed to have a round table to sort out which parts in his brain were real and which were phantoms.

He arrived at the restaurant a couple of minutes late to find the other three at the back table.

"Bart, you still look like you've been on the wrong end of a shit kicking. How's the head?" George chuckled.

"Just fine, fuck you very much. We need to talk, guys."

They waited until the food was served, with obligatory scotch for Bart and George, soda water for Bobby and Steve.

Bart opened the discussion. "Thanks guys. I know you all have busy days so I appreciate you taking the time. I just want to review everything that happened last night. It seems to good to be true, and I want to make sure it wasn't all a dream." Bart laughed, but in reality most of what he said was true. He really couldn't separate reality from the dreams.

Steve finished sending a message from his phone and knocked on the table. "We need to make this fast guys. I've got a get together with Marty and interested parties at 1 so I have to leave in forty-five at the very latest."

Bart scrubbed his face. "Ellie, too?"

"Of course."

Bart shook his head. "I'm telling you, she threatened to track me down and stick a steak knife in my neck. She's a major liability. I can't direct a movie she's in."

"What are you saying, Bart," asked George. "Are you backing out of this?"

He sucked air between his teeth. "I don't want to play hardball, guys. But it is my story and I can't have her on the set. Her presence will destabilize the entire movie. There are so many things I could tell you about her, but the bottom line is she's toxic."

Steve looked at George and Bobby. Then back to Bart. "Let me get this straight. You'll walk away from this sweetheart of a deal, one which will launch the careers of everybody at this table to heights none of us have ever imagined, just because Ellie's in it?"

Bart fiddled with his cutlery. "I don't just walk away from it; I take the story with me. It's mine. I brought you in. I leave and it's over. You need to shit-can Ellie if you want this to proceed."

He sat back and looked at the menu. Surely these guys could understand one person shouldn't be able to bring down a project like this. "This is huge for all of us, gentlemen. Make the right decision."

Steve took a deep breath. "Okay, look, I'm taking Ellie to meet with the Marty and the Hanks, and I just need to put some questions in their minds about stability, okay? Chemistry. They've got to have chemistry. I'll try and screw up the chemistry. I'll let you know how it goes after the meeting, okay? What else is on the table?"

Bart smiled, satisfied for now. He wasn't bluffing and he thought they understood. "Am I to understand all of our financing is sorted?"

George nodded. "I received a call this morning from our backers. The accounts will be set up by the end of the week at the latest. The bank will let us draw against it until then. I'll send an email out this afternoon with the instructions, the process we need to follow. Okay? It's all good, though.

Approvals for more money than I've seen in ten of any of my movies put together."

"Excellent. Have we agreed on what our stars are going to cost?"

Bobby frowned. "Were you even at the meeting last night? We discussed all this. It's all sorted and agreed. I kinda thought you were wasted. Didn't realize you were that wasted. Yes. Terms were agreed. Look, you're the director. You not a producer and you're not a money guy. Let them worry about that and you just direct. And write."

"I have producer credit."

George interrupted. "In name only. You've had no experience in production before that I'm aware of, and this isn't the kind of project you start on. I'm willing to take you under my wing, but you won't be making any production decisions."

"Excuse me? Who the fuck brought this project to the table? Who invited all of you into my game? Jesus Christ, what do I have to do -"

Steve knocked on the table. "Chill, Bart. This is stupid. We're all in this, and we need to stay in this together or it isn't going to work. So let's all calm down." He looked at the other two. "Now come on, guys. Think about this. On the fucking precipice. On. The fucking. Precipice. This can tip either way. We all keep our shit together, put in the work and stop acting like assholes and we come out the other end with a pretty good movie and buckets of green." He paused and looked at each of them in the eyes again. "We keep on being dickheads, at each other's throats fighting over stupid things and generally fucking things up, this project ends up in the shit hole like 90 percent of everything that starts in this city. Let's keep it together because I don't know about you, but I'm really excited about having buckets of green."

He took a deep breath. "And that's it. That's why we're here. We're the four musketeers. We need to make hard decisions, but we make them together. Okay?" He received nods from around the table, including one, surprisingly, from Bart. "Now I want to throw something out there. For discussion, but no decision until after my meeting." He licked his lips. "I know how you feel about Ellie, Bart. Don't completely understand why, but here it is. I'm taking Ellie to see Tom Hanks. Colin and I think Neil Patrick Harris will be there, too. I know Ellie. She's very down to earth and with the exception of Sweeney here, gets along with everybody. It's extremely conceivable everybody there will end up the best of friends. When I try to pull her from the project I will get resistance from both leads, the Executive Producer and one of the star agents in this city. It will tank this project, and the buckets of green which will come with it." There was murmuring around the table, loudest from Bart. He held up is hands. "No decision at this point. We need to think about this and know how we're going to proceed. I'm suggesting we get together again tonight at 5. My place. I'll have beer and pizza. There's an MLS mid-week game on. Be good to get our heads out of this once and awhile." He looked at Bart. "You okay with that?"

"If she's in it -"

"Just park it for now, Bart. Jesus. I don't what the hell's going on between you two, but it's a bit over the top. Dial it back a bit and stop acting like a fucking child." He threw his napkin on the table. "I've got to go. Don't fuck this up for me."

Bart watched him leave. "I better go too. One of you guys get this. Follow whatever fucking process you have to follow to claim it against the project." He pushed his chair back, heaved himself up and slowly walked out.

George shook his head. "Any idea what's going on with him, Bobby?"

"He looks like shit."

"That mugging." George rubbed his chin "You think he was mugged?"

"He said he was mugged by three girls. Why would any guy admit he was mugged by girls if he wasn't? Especially a misogynist like Bart?" Bobby shook his head. "If he said he was mugged, I think it's a pretty good bet he was mugged."

"And he didn't go to the cops? He looks like hell, too. He should have at least gone to his doctor and gotten checked out."

"Nah, and for the same reason. Can you imagine him going in to his doctor and saying, 'Hey, could you check these bruises some little chicks laid on me'? No fracking way." He picked at the remains of the salad on his plate. "Goddamn rabbit food. I need a steak." He pushed his chair back. "You know the processes. You pay, okay?" He smiled. "I'll get the next one."

George sat back in his chair, sipping his scotch, watching brown Bobby walk out of the steakhouse. "That's okay," he said to nobody in particular. "I've got it."

Bart regretted leaving. He was still hungry and it was, essentially, free food. He walked back to his Glendale office in deep thought.

He realized he was being backed into a corner. A $200 million dollar movie which would gross, world wide, at least three or four times that was a powerful weapon, but it cut both ways. If they called his bluff - and he didn't consider it a bluff - he was out of the gravy train too, and his career irreparably damaged. His only option was to permanently get rid of Ellie before shooting started. He sighed. It would require an apparent about-face on his part. A magnanimous reversal of his objections. Shooting wouldn't happen for at least a month, most likely longer. That would be sufficient time to get back in her good graces, and when she least suspected it, bam. Lights out. He smiled to himself. There was nothing that could get in his way. Nothing and nobody. He pulled out his phone and called Steve.

"What's up Bart?"

"You sound a little tense there, Stevie. Relax. I've given it a lot of thought."

"In the ten minutes since we last talked? That much? Wow."

Bart exited the elevator into his office. "Hear me out. This is good. You were very eloquent. I know when I'm barking up the wrong tree. You were completely correct in your assessment. There are buckets of green waiting for all of us, as long as we all push in the same direction. If the leads and Hanks' like Ellie, she's in. No objection from me. I'll deal with our little personality issue myself. It'll make us both stronger."

"You better not be bullshitting me, Bart. I'm going out on a very thin limb here with these guys. I don't want you coming back after the fact, after I've sold this talented unknown and kicking up a stink."

"Relax Steve. I'm not going to kick it up. I'll be there with you to make sure everything goes well and to convince all parties concerned I'm 100% on board."

Steve thought about that. "I don't know. It's not in the original plan."

Bart sat at his desk and put his feet up. "I'm the director, right? I should be at these types of meetings also. You can't disagree with that."

And Steve couldn't. "Fine. Marty's at 1:00 pm. I'll see you there. Just promise me you don't change your mind and ambush us."

Bart laughed. "Wouldn't think of it. See you there." He hung up the call and smiled. "No, there'll be no ambush at the meeting. That will be in a canyon in a couple of weeks. Or maybe off a boat." He stopped at his secretary's desk on the way out. "I'm going to Marty's place for a meeting. Should be back by 4:00, if I come back. And if I don't, see you tomorrow."

"Marty?"

"Marty. The agent. You know, the guy on Cliffside in Malibu."

"Oh. Marty. Okay then, see you tomorrow." She returned to her tabloid extolling the virtues of the latest cleansing diet.

Bart shook his head and left. It would be a tight drive. He debated calling Ellie in advance of the meeting to let her know he was coming, then decided against it. It would be worth it to see the look on her face. Priceless.

He did call Bernie, though. Time to start sowing the contrition seeds.

"Bernard, this is Bart. I'm calling to apologize."

"Sweeney? Why in the hell should I talk to you?"

Bart bit his tongue. "I'm in a meeting with Ellie in a little over half an hour. I've buried the hatchet with her. It was a silly argument anyway. My old man stubbornness and her youthful exuberance collided. We've sorted it out. We're best of buddies now. I truly regret putting you through that awkward mess of kicking her out. I've got no problem with her now. If you want her to move back there, no problem."

"The damage is done, Bart. Get screwed."

Bart took a deep breath and fought to keep from saying what he wanted to say. "Bernie, you're not thinking this through. You have a perfect opportunity to win your way back in. Instead of me saying it's okay for her to live there, you can just as easily say you stood up to me and I caved in. You win the girl, everything's cool and you look like the hero."

"Really? You'd do that for me?"

"Bernie, buddy, we've worked together. I made a terrible mistake pulling that shit on you before. My humblest apologies. Truly. We're going to need crew on this movie we've got going and I'd love it if you were part of it."

Bernie was babbling now. "Look, Bart, if you're seeing Ellie, tell her that, okay? That I stood my ground and faced you down? She'll tell Cathy and I won't look like I'm chasing her too hard."

"You're an idiot, Bernie. If you love her you're supposed to chase her. But I will, yes. Whatever misguided way you want to play it." He hung up.

Bernie was going to have a similar accident to Ellies, if he could figure out how to swing it.

35

I dropped the thumb drive on Perkins desk. "Like I told you the last time, this wasn't a suicide."

Jacob tapped the desk. "I've heard it on the original machine and will be willing to sign an affidavit to that effect. There is no question, in my expert opinion, that Sweeney killed my brother and covered it up by injecting him with heroin to make it look like a suicide, or accidental overdose. If the autopsy hasn't been done already I'd suggest looking at the site of the injection. You'll find a large amount of the drug there, and very little in the rest of his system."

Perkins picked up his notebook and then put it down again. "I'll listen to this and I'll confer with the coroner. I can't promise any more than that."

I was about to say something when Jacob rested his hand on my arm. "Thanks, Constable. Ellie and I can see our way out. If it's okay with you, I'm going to talk to the medical examiner, just to ask some questions, okay? I'm not trying to step on anyone's toes. Ellie here needs to get to Malibu, and unless I'm mistaken, she needs to get her bum in gear. Thank you again for your time"

He didn't wait for a response and I'm not sure if there even was one. We pivoted and were out of there in record time. "So what do you think, Jacob? Will that be enough?"

"It would be in Boise. I don't see why it wouldn't be here. You run to what you have to run to and I'll have a chat with the good doctor. Call me when you're finished and let me know how it goes. Good luck."

I thanked him and raced down to my car. I'd have to hit every light to get there in time. And I didn't have GPS, so I'd be creeping though Malibu to find this place. I knew where I was going, but I didn't know how to get there. I followed Bart last night so I wasn't paying attention to the street signs on the way in.

At 12:55 I pulled on to Cliffside Drive. "Damn." I chuckled. This time I'd be here legitimately. I pressed the buzzer at the Gate. "Ellie Bourke here? I'm meeting Steve Bond?" I don't know why I said that like it I was asking questions. I get that way when I'm nervous.

The gate slowly swung open. I pulled into the very large yard and parked beside cars which were worth at least ten times my Beetle. Maybe a hundred times. I loved it.

The front door opened as I walked up the steps. Steve Bond stood there with a smile on his tanned face, pearly whites blinding me. "Really great you could show, Ellie. Come on in."

"Thanks for adjusting the time. I really appreciate it." The inside of the house was incredible. I can honestly say not only had I never seen anything like it, I'd never imagined anything that grandiose. "This is spectacular, Steve. It's out of this world."

Steve laughed. "Come on out to the pool. There are some people I want you to meet. One of them you already know."

"Who's that?"

"Bart Sweeney. He asked to come along. He's directing this project and while he initially had reservations about you being in the picture, he's come around. For the greater good, as it were."

I stopped and shook my head. "No way. Count me out. I don't care if it's the next Citizen Kane, if he's in it, I'm not."

Steve, to give him credit, didn't force the issue. He frowned, a concerned frown. "What's going on between you two? He was pretty much the same way."

I shook my head. "Some other time. I'll let you know privately, not around whoever else is out on that patio. Doesn't really matter who it is."

Steve rubbed his forehead and thought for a minute. "Look, Ellie, I'm going to ask you for a huge favor, okay?" He pointed out to the pool deck. "Colin Hanks, Tom Hanks, an agent for the stars and some assorted lawyers are out there. Forget about Bart. I'm kind of in agreement with you. I can understand if you've got hesitations working with him. Not sure why you do, but you no doubt you have good reason." He took a deep breath. "But be honest with yourself: a meeting with the Hanks and their agent doesn't come by every day. Take advantage of this opportunity. Plus, I'll look like a complete idiot if I went back there without you. If you can't do it for yourself, at least do it for me." He held out his arms. "Give me a hug. You look tense. Platonic-type, not the creepy uncle type, okay?"

I smiled and took his hug and gave him one back. I took a deep breath and shook my head at the situations I seemed to get myself into. "Look, I'll go out there for you, but I'm not talking to Bart and I'm not going to pretend I like him. We're clear with that, right?"

"Right-o. Let's go do this."

I was a bit freaked. I loved Colin Hanks in everything I'd seen him in, since *That Thing You Do*. And his dad was legend. I didn't belong in this company, but like they said, fake it until you make it. What was it Melon-Head said? 'You only succeed in this business when you know, absolutely know in your heart, you will succeed.' Well, I was trying to believe. I really was. I followed Steve to the pool deck and shook hands with the father and son, the super agent Marty and the two lawyers, whose names I didn't remember. Bart stood and held out his hand and I ignored him. I didn't care if he felt uncomfortable.

Marty spoke first. "Has Steve told you anything about this project?"

I shook my head. "He's been pretty mum about it all. Kind of mysterious."

Marty looked at Bart, at me and then at Steve. "Steve, you run through the plot for Ellie. Isn't NPH supposed to be here too? We want to make sure the chemistry is right."

Steve smiled. "He's tied up with his kids. Might be by later. He's in though. Loves the idea."

"NPH? NP-Dr. Horrible-H? He's in this?" I could handle that. Steve explained the story line, which sounded absurd at first, then, slowly, it gelled. It was an interesting environmental twist. I looked at Tom and Colin. "So what parts do you two play?"

The father put up his hands. "Oh, I'm strictly behind the scenes on this one. I've got a dozen things in production, pre-production, development. You know how it is. Want to ride this wave as long as I can."

The son snorted. "More like two dozen. You're greedy, old man." He turned to me. "I'm playing the alien vampire. You know, that sounds funny when I say it out loud." He shook his head. "The scientist will be owned by NPH. Really looking forward to working across from him. Love what he does."

"Cool. Sounds like it's going to be a fun movie. Not sure what I'm here for, though. Is there a part in it for me? Usually my sack of shit agent calls me almost too late for an audition and I go through the cattle call like everyone else. What's different here?"

Steve rested his hand on my arm. "Okay, first, did you fire him? Your agent?"

"Yeah, like you said." I'm pretty slow some days. Oblivious is more like it. It still wasn't clicking with me.

"Marty, what do you think?"

He shrugged. "I think it's pretty clear. Colin?"

"Definitely. Pops?"

"Up to you, son. If my opinion counted for anything, mind you, I'd say yes."

I put my hand up, like in grade school. "Excuse me, guys, can you clear something up for me? What in the hell are you talking about?"

Tom laughed. "You really haven't told her anything, have you?" He leaned forward and put his arms on his knees. "The third in the love triangle. You." He pointed a finger at me. "We wanted an unknown." He waggled his hand. "Relatively unknown. You come with great recommendations. Steve here tells us you're very physical."

"I'm a klutz."

"Be that as it may. You're young, strong, tall, beautiful. Everything we're looking for."

"You haven't seen me act." I looked at Bart when I said that. He looked away just as I caught his eye. There was a loathing there that unsettled me.

"We've dug up your library of work."

"I've got a library?"

Steve put his hand on my knee, to shut me up, I think. "Ellie, we're offering you a role in a movie opposite Colin Hanks and Neil Patrick Harris. The budget is a couple hundred million dollars. Tom is backing this and you're asking silly questions? The part is yours if you want it." He grimaced. "Actually, we really want you to take the part."

I looked at Bart. "Is he directing?"

Bart cleared his throat. "Director and writer. Let's bury the hatchet, Ellie. The past is the past. This is a phenomenal opportunity for you."

"I don't care. I can't work with you." I couldn't believe this. What kind of luck was I having? I stood. "Steve, can you show me out? I really appreciate the offer guys, and I'm sure you're going to make a fantastic movie, but there's no way in hell I'm going to work with this guy attached to it." I jabbed a finger in Bart's direction. "And if you knew what this guy did, well, you wouldn't work with him either." I waited for Steve to show me the way to the front door because, frankly, I was lost. I could find my way around outside, but I didn't think it would be a good idea to let them know.

Marty and the father/son team were conferring about something, then Marty came and joined us on the walk out. "What is it Ellie? You're taking a pretty strong stand. Did Bart try to cop a feel? Shit like that happens."

I shook my head. "I wish that's all it was. I'd tell you, but he'd deny it, and we'd get into a he said/she said thing which would probably get me sued for slander or defamation. I can never keep the two straight."

"Between us. Out of earshot of him. In confidence. What did he do?"

I took a deep breath. This was probably a big mistake, but it would feel good to get this off my chest to his peers. "Okay, Bart killed my roommate by giving him too much rohypnol, then tried to cover it up by shooting him full of heroin. I've been getting threatening calls from him for the last three days. Just this morning he told me you guys would be offering a part and told me I'd be dead if I took it."

Marty looked at Steve. "Is she serious? Are you freaking serious?" He stopped. "Can you come back and tell the rest of the people that? It has bearing, I think, on what we're trying to do. Just a bit, I think."

I shook my head. "It won't end up good. I appreciate the offer you guys made, but I think I'll stay below the radar for a little while."

I turned to head back to the door when a security guy jogged up. "Marty, the cops are here with an arrest warrant."

"For me? What the hell?"

"No, it's for one of your guests. Should I let them in?"

"Hell yes. They're big, and they have guns. Send them back to the pool deck." Marty smiled. "Ellie. Hang around, okay?"

He strode with purpose back to the cliff side of the house. I almost had to jog to keep up. "Gentlemen, I think we've found a solution to our problem." He swiveled to Sweeney. "You've signed your contract, right?"

He nodded. "Yesterday. Very generous. Thank you."

Marty turned to one of the lawyers. "Sven, can you read the morals clause of his contract?"

A short, extremely blond lawyer flipped to a section in the contract and cleared his throat. "It says: *This contract will become null and void, and the intellectual property will remain with the licensee in the event that a) the licensor, Mr. Sweeney, is charged with an intentional violation of any law, including any serious violation which may result in the licensee being found partially or wholly liable for Mr. Sweeney's actions, b) the licensor acts in a way which is prejudicial to the interests of the licensee, c) the licensor -*"

Marty held up his hand. "That's good enough, Sven. Point B covers it, and A fills any potential gaps." He looked at Sweeney. "Right Bart?"

"What did she tell you? It's all bullshit." He turned on Steve. "I warned you she was unstable. I fucking warned you."

Tom had one of those sardonic grins on his face as he stood. "Marty, you always throw the best parties. Can you tell me, the executive producer of this here flick, what in the hell is going on?"

Before Marty had a chance to answer the security guy walked on to the deck with four policemen, including Deputy Dawg himself, Constable Perkins. He looked at me with raised eyebrows and I pointed at Bart. What a day this was turning out to be.

Perkins approached Bart. "Mr. Sweeney? I'm arresting you for the murder of Joel Sampson. You have the right to remain silent. Anything you say may be used against you in a court of law."

Sweeney sputtered like my car did on cold mornings. He finally got words out after he was Mirandized. "You've got no proof. It's her word against mine. Who'd believe her over me?" Both father and son's hands went up in unison. "It was a fucking accident. It wasn't supposed to happen. Who ever heard of someone dying from roofies?"

Perkin's removed his handcuffs from his belt. "Mr. Sweeney, I said you have the right to remain silent. I suggest you take advantage of that right."

"I'm serious. It was - "

Perkins interrupted him. "Rohypnol mixed with grapefruit juice is particularly toxic. The juice magnifies the effect."

Sweeny licked his lips. "You've got nothing. I threw the recording in the ocean."

"I had a copy, ass-hat. I hope you rot in hell." God, this felt better than I thought it would.

Sweeney lunged across the patio and tried to grab me by the throat. Again. I backpedalled as Steve and Colin Hanks jumped in and grabbed him before Perkins could react.

Perkins and two of his colleagues bundled the foaming, frantic Sweeney out the front of the house. Marty took me gently by the arm. "Could you reconsider our offer, Miss Bourke?"

I was strumming like a power line in a high wind. "Did what happened just happen?"

Steve nodded. "Sweeney is out of the picture. Did he really kill Joel? I liked that kid. He made me laugh."

I was two sides of the same coin. I was sad for my loss. Joel was the best friend and ally I ever had and that pompous fat ass killed him. On the other hand, I was getting the opportunity of a lifetime. And Bart was finished. I took a deep breath. "If I understood the morals clause, if he fucks up you get to fire him and keep the story, right?"

Sven nodded. "That about sums it up."

"So who's going to direct?" I looked at the father. "You? I liked *That Thing You Do*. I know you can direct."

"Remember? A dozen projects lined up? I'd love to, but I'm kind of busy."

"Two-dozen, dad. Quit hiding it under a bushel." The son thought for a second. "Marty, what's Favreau doing? This is the kind of thing he likes. Or is he doing another Marvel project?"

"I'll check with him. And if it's not him there are a dozen good directors around the track who we can use. So, Ellie, speak now or forever regret your decision."

I nodded. Smiled and nodded so hard I thought I was going to get whiplash. "Hell, yeah. Where do I sign?"

36

"G'day L.A., unless you're listening to this live, then G'day Sydney. Another week behind us. A week of many, many changes for our guest, Ellie Bourke. You'll remember she was here just last weekend. That hellacious storm we had a couple of nights ago wasn't the only thing changing the landscape around here. If you follow the movie business closely, really, really closely, you'd have heard about the arrest of the once not so great Bartholomew Sweeney, he of *Beast of Bondi* and a dozen other forgettable horror flicks fame. He killed, allegedly, the young and talented comic Joel Sampson and tried to cover it up. Our guest not only was a close friend and roommate of that young man, but she was instrumental in the arrest. A regular Nancy Drew. I've known Ellie for a few years now, and it doesn't surprise me in the slightest. In addition to being a part-time detective this week she has had, I'm led to believe, a couple of career moves which will guarantee her face will be one of the best known faces in this little town within the next six months."

Ross Melon took a breath and smiled at Ellie. "We'll have a good long chat with the young lady from my home town right after this new rockabilly duet from Kanye West and Taylor Swift." He pointed at the producer and pulled off his headphones. "You good? Ready for the big time?" He laughed at Ellie's blush. "Make no mistake, Miss Bourke. This movie you're in will either be the biggest hit or the biggest flop this decade. Either way, your name will be known. You're private life of obscurity is over."

"I can't talk about the movie yet Ross. At least not specifics. I can talk generalities, but no names, okay? You push too hard and I'll spill. I get verbal diarrhea."

"Yeah, sure. We'll keep it nice and vague. I can do that. You have to come back later and tell the whole story."

"I'll give you an exclusive. Promise."

Mellon scratched his ear. "The song's over in a minute. Are you comfortable talking about Joel and Sweeney or do you want to stick to the generalities about the TV and movie work you've been getting?"

"Let's start with Joel and Sweeney, but if I give you the cut the throat motion, switch topics, okay? It'll mean I'm about to cry and I don't want to do that on the radio."

"You got it." He waited until the last verse started then dropped the audio and walked on the song. "Sounds like Kanye and Taylor have kissed and made up. I'm sure they'll make beautiful babies." He let the song roll for a beat. "So we've got Ellie Bourke here and I have to tell you, she's had one of the most incredible weeks I've ever heard of. You were here a week ago and you were telling us you were ready to pack it in, and your roommate had committed suicide. Am I right?"

"Yeah. And then I found out he was killed, that our landlord killed him and tried to cover it up by pumping him full of heroin, was shot at, slept in my car two separate nights and got offered a recurring spot in a very popular TV show and the female lead in a huge sci-fi movie. It's been a hell of a week. Oops. Can I say that?"

"We're live in Australia right now, so yes. When we rebroadcast it to American listeners we'll beep that offending bit out for the prudes. But back to your litany. I'm exhausted just listening. I don't know where to start."

"You've never been short on words before."

"I've never been in the presence of someone who could accomplish what you have in a week."

"I had some help."

"Nah. As I understand it, it was all you, all the way. Lucky for me I've got a call on the line for you. They can ask the questions while I sit here in stupefied awe. Caller, you're on the air."

"Ellie?"

"Yeah, that's our guest today pal, try and keep up."

"Ellie, this is Jacob. I - listen, Melon head, or whatever your name is, this lady pretty much single-handedly brought my brother's killer to justice. I know that sounds corny, but that's what she did. If it wasn't for her, Joel's killer would be directing the next big blockbuster, making a bucket load of money and walking around free. She stood up for her principles, and turned in a killer."

"That's really nice of you Jacob, but you helped me a lot. I don't know if I could have done it without you."

"Not true. Look, Ellie, I'm about to board a flight back to Boise. I'm going to be coming back. I like it here. I like you. I'm going to see about getting on the L.A.P.D. Dog Squad. Can I call you when I get back in the city?"

"You heard it here first, folks, our own little Ellie Bourke getting propositioned on the phone by a Midwestern cop."

"You going to let me answer Melon-Head?" Ellie arched an eyebrow. "Yeah, Jacob. Call me. I'll buy you dinner. It'll be nice."

Ross laughed. "Hang on the line for a minute, if you can Jacob. We've got another break in a few minutes, but before we get there, tell me, Ellie, what's the TV show, and what's the movie?"

"I really can't name any names yet, but the TV show is a huge hit, and my personal favorite, and really it's just a guest spot. Maybe just a few shows, but I've got my fingers crossed. The movie, well that's going to be something special. I can't wait until I can tell you about it. It's a great story, a fantastic cast and we start rehearsals in a couple of weeks. And that's all I can tell you right now." Ellie laughed. The first real laugh she had in a long time.

It was a phenomenal end to a phenomenal day

ABOUT THE AUTHOR

Tony McFadden is a Canadian now happily living in Australia, a land with very little snow, writing near the beach whenever possible.

You can find him on the interwebs at www.TonyMcFadden.net,

Also by Tony McFadden

Matt's War
Daly Battles: The Fall of PyongYang
Target: Australia

G'Day USA

Book 'Em
Family Matters
Unprotected Sax
(with Charles McFadden)

Have Wormhole, Will Travel
Killing Time

Mac D: Private Investigator
A Step Too Far (A Mac-D Mystery)
Hunter / Prey

.

The Murder of Jeremy Brookes
Number Fifteen

Batteries Not Included
Broken
Dead Tomorrow
Under the Shadows

www.ingramcontent.com/pod-product-compliance
Lightning Source LLC
Chambersburg PA
CBHW011030190726
48290CB00011B/2773